The Gulistan of Sadi

THE ROSE GARDEN

The Gulistan of Sadi

THE ROSE GARDEN

OF

SHEKH MUSLIHU'D-DIN SADI OF SHIRAZ

Translated by

EDWARD B. EASTWICK, C.B., M.A., F.R.S., M.R.A.S.

With a preface, and a life of the author,
from the Atish Kadah

INTRODUCTION BY IDRIES SHAH

The Octagon Press
London

ISBN: 0 863040 69 1

Published for The Sufi Trust by
The Octagon Press

First Impression in this edition 1996

INTRODUCTION

WAS Sadi born in 1194, and did he die in 1291? Or are his dates c1200 to c1290? Perhaps, instead, he was born in 1184? Which countries did he visit, and why? Was he a real Sufi, since he wore the blue mantle of the dervish? Or was he merely using the Sufis as a community which would give him cheap board and lodging?

If these matters—and many others of a similar kind—rivet your attention, you properly belong to the numerous and not undistinguished people of scholarship (the academics and orientalists) who are not really concerned with the meaning and intention of Sadi's work. Curiously, however, some of them imagine themselves to be Sufis.

Equally, if you are excited by the assertion that putting Sadi's works under your pillow will confer loquacity and literary ability without labour; or if you find thrilling possibilities in the belief that reciting passages from the *Gulistan* alone will give you higher consciousness, you are likely to be one of the cultists who form another portion of the Sheikh's readership. Like them, however, you could probably find such fuel for an overheated imagination anywhere.

This is the second category of people who have found Sufi literature of such interest, but who have not been able to unlock its value and have hence effectively debarred themselves from finding, in the Sufi phrase, "in it what is in it."

The third group of people are those who take

extracts,. not necessarily esoteric ones, and excite themselves with them. Among them we may even include many of today's scientists, who almost jump for joy (or annoyance) when it is pointed out that Sadi mentions the blood travelling through the veins, four centuries before the discovery of its circulation by Harvey, or roughly three hundred years before Caesalpinus. They join those who wonder at Ghazzali, another major Sufi, talking about the magic lantern in the 12th century, or at Rumi's speaking of evolution seven hundred years before Darwin—not to mention Sadi's mention of hot-air balloons five hundred years antecedent to Montgolfier.

These three categories—scholars, cultists and selective thinkers—should be distinguished from the fourth category, the Sufis and real would-be Sufis. For the last named, Sufi literature is valuable primarily for what it can teach and what effect it can have: not only for the collecting of information or the administration of an emotional stimulus.

Like all Sufi materials, Sadi's *Rose Garden* contains information, and is formulated, to gain acceptance in the culture in which it is projected—and is an instrument of enlightenment and experience. It is not for nothing that people say "*Har lafz-i-Sadi, Haftad-o-do maani*" ("Each word of Sadi has seventy-two meanings").

The reading of Sadi, among Sufis, undoubtedly produces insights. In Sufi school usage, first the exterior meaning is absorbed, then the secondary meaning. This tension between the two levels, can lead to the ability to see further ranges of significance, until the stage may be reached when we find understanding beyond verbalisation. And this is a stage, be it remarked, very different from the confused non-verbalisation of emotionality or anti-verbalism which are such currently popular fads.

I shall give a single example of perspective change, which occurs in the very first chapter of this book, on page 23 of this edition:

The key is in the proverb given here as: "Well-intentioned falsehood is better than mischief-exciting truth."

The actual Persian text says: *Dorogh-i-maslihat-amiz bih zi rasti-i fitna-angiz.* Its true translation is: "The untruth admixed with policy is better than the mischief-provoking truth."

This is a cosmological reference, only partly reflected in the social situation being dealt with in the overt text. According to the Sufic doctrine, Truth is present on earth, but is mixed with secondary (and therefore relatively false) elements in order to operate in this sphere. Hence the first phrase of the couplet: Truth may even appear as untruth. The second phrase stresses that truth is not truth at all if it is used to cause trouble, since such an employment of it pollutes it.

Many other passages in this translation can yield understanding, without a knowledge of Persian.

Since I alluded to this special usage of literature in *The Sufis* (1964) many people have said that they have immersed themselves in Sufi literature, but have succeeded only in extracting highly imaginative or confused 'meanings'. Some have concluded from that that I should either have kept quiet about the whole thing and allowed the knowledge of this factor to continue to be operated only in concealed Sufi schools; or else that I should have published "complete interpreted texts".

For those who still think such things, it should be mentioned that giving out "complete interpretations" would be like publishing the answers to problems for people who have to work through the problems themselves. It would simply lead to people studying the answers instead of doing the work: this was discovered many centuries before my time. As for concealing the material and making it available only to "initiates", this ignores the fact that there are a large number of people who *can* actually profit from the literature plus the hint as to how it can be used. At the very worst, some of these can get a fair inkling of the meanings, and may then be regarded as candidates for further teaching under a suitable teacher.

We are just as concerned with the hundreds who do understand relatively easily as with the thousands who do not. There is a place in Sufi studies for both types, and for all shades in between.

But for those who are still impressed by credentials (and they will always exist, and this foible should not be allowed to exclude them from our field until they have overcome it) Sadi can display the most impeccable background, in Middle Eastern terms.

Descended from the Prophet, author of some of the greatest classics of the East, contemporary of Jalaluddin Rumi, educated at the elite Nizamiyya College, of Baghdad, where he was a Fellow, companion of the great Sufi Sheikh Suhrawardi, disciple of the very great Gilani, tireless fighter against hypocrisy and self-deception, he was included in the great biographical collection of Jami, the poet and mystic who is honoured as a major authority on Sufi matters. His affiliation, too, was with the Naqshbandi ("Designers") School, the Path of the Masters, one of whose chief tasks is the reformulation of Sufi teachings in all cultures and at all times.

IDRIES SHAH

PREFACE.

THE Gulistān of Sâdī has attained a popularity in the East which, perhaps, has never been reached by any European work in this Western world. The school-boy lisps out his first lessons in it; the man of learning quotes it; and a vast number of its expressions have become proverbial. When we consider, indeed, the time at which it was written—the first half of the thirteenth century—a time when gross darkness brooded over Europe, at least—darkness which might have been, but, alas! was not felt—the justness of many of its sentiments, and the glorious views of the Divine attributes contained in it, are truly remarkable. Thus, in the beginning of the Preface, the Unity, the unapproachable majesty, the omnipotence, the long-suffering, and the goodness of God, are nobly set forth. The vanity of worldly pursuits, and the true vocation of man, are everywhere insisted upon:

"The world, my brother! will abide with none,
By the world's Maker let thy heart be won." (p. 24.)

In Sâdī's code of morals, mercy and charity are not restricted, as by some bigoted Muḥammadans, to true believers:

"*All Adam's race* are members of one frame;
Since all, at first, from the same essence came.
If thou feel'st not for others' misery,
A son of Adam is no name for thee." (p. 38.)

Evil, it is said, should be requited with good, thus:

"Whenever then
Thy enemy thee slanders absent, thou
To his face applaud him." (p. 57.)

and:

"Shew kindness even to thy foes." (p. 67.)

See also the story of the Khalīfah Hārūn's son (p. 67); and of the recluse (p. 76):

"The men of God's true faith, I've heard,
Grieve not the hearts e'en of their foes.
When will this station be conferred
On thee, who dost thy friends oppose?"

Sâdī not only preached the duty of contentment and resignation, but practised what he preached. In a life prolonged to nearly twice the ordinary period allotted to man, he shewed his contempt for riches, which he might easily have amassed, but which, when showered on him by the great, he devoted to pious purposes; being minded that:

"The poor man's patience better is than gold." (p. 99.)

Thus, when the Prime Minister of Hulaku Khān sent him a present of 50,000 dīnārs, he expended it in erecting a house for travellers, near Shīrāz. But it will be sufficient for those who would form a just estimate of Sâdī to peruse his works, especially the IIIrd and VIIIth books of the Gulistān, which set forth his good sense, humility, and cheerful resignation to the Supreme will, in the clearest light. Of the history of his long and useful life we, unfortunately, know but little; and that little is comprised in the notice of him which is here subjoined from the Ātish Kadah. Ross, however, with much diligence and acuteness, has drawn from his works themselves some other interesting particulars relating to him. It appears that his father's name was Åbdu'llāh, and that he was descended from Ålī, the son-in-law of Muḥammad; but that, nevertheless, his father held no higher office than some petty situation under the Dīwān. From Būstān, II. 2, it appears that he lost his father when but a child; while, from the 6th Story of the VIth Chapter of the Gulistān, we learn that his mother survived to a later period. He was educated at the Nizāmiah College at Baghdād, where he held an Idrār, or fellowship (Būstān, VII. 14), and was instructed in science by the learned Abū'l-farj-bin-Jauzī (Gulistān, II. 20), and in theology by Åbdu'l-Ḳādir Gīlānī, with whom he made his first pilgrimage to Makkah. This pilgrimage he repeated no less than fourteen times. It is to his residence at Baghdād—where Arabic, as he tells us in the IIIrd Chapter of the Gulistān, was spoken with great purity—that we, perhaps, owe the profusion of Arabic verses and sentences which are scattered through his works. He had, however, scarce reached his mid-career when that imperial city was taken and sacked by the Tartar Hulaku, with a prodigious massacre of the inhabitants; on which occasion he gave expression to his regrets in a Ḳaṣīdah, or elegy.

Sådī was twice married. Of his first nuptials, at

Aleppo, we have a most amusing account in the 31st Story of the IInd Chapter of the Gulistān. His enforced labour with a gang of Jews in the fosse of Tripolis was not likely to increase his good opinion of the Christian sect; for it appears from that story, that his taskmasters, the Crusaders, had not made him prisoner in war, but while practising religious austerities in the desert; and he, therefore, certainly deserved more lenient treatment. Whatever might, however, have been Sâdī's opinion of Christians[a]—and it certainly was not very favourable—he speaks with reverence of their Lord, as he does also of St. John the Baptist. Thus, in his Badīya, he says, "It is the breath of Jesus, for in that fresh breath and verdure the dead earth is reviving:" and, in the Gulistān, II. 10, we find Sâdī engaged in devotion at the tomb of John the Baptist, of which he says—

"The poor, the rich, alike must here adore;
The wealthier they, their need is here the more."

where it is to be remarked that his prayers were offered only to the Deity; but he knelt at the tomb, supposing, with other Muḥammadans and Roman Catholics, that it was not only allowable, but salutary, to entreat the intercession of holy men.

Sâdī married a second time at Sanāa, the capital of Yaman; and, in the Būstān, IX. 25, pours out his regrets for the loss of his only son. His notices of the female sex are, in general, not very laudatory, and his

[a] *Vide* Chapter III. Story 21:

"A Christian's well may not be pure, 'tis true,
'Twill do to wash the carcase of a Jew."

opinions on this head seem to have strengthened as he grew in years. Ross mentions Europe, Barbary, Abyssinia, Egypt, Syria, Palestine, Armenia, Asia Minor, Arabia, Persia, Tartary, Afghānistān, and India, as the countries in which he travelled; and Kæmpfer, who visited Shīrāz A.D. 1686, tells us that he had been in Egypt and Italy; and that, to his knowledge of Oriental tongues, he had even superadded an acquaintance with Latin, and, in particular, had diligently studied Seneca. Sâdī himself informs us that he was at Dihlī during the reign of Uglamish, who died A.H. 653 = A.D. 1255, and there exist some verses in the Urdū dialect which he is said, but perhaps without much reason, to have composed. Jāmī supposes that the beautiful youth whom Sâdī encountered at Kashgaṛh, and who is mentioned in the 17th story of the Vth chapter of the Gulistān,[b] was the famous poet of Dihlī, Amīr Khusrau; and it is certain that it was owing to the eulogies of Khusrau that Sâdī was invited by Sulṭān Muḥammad to Multān, where that prince offered to found a monastery for him.

Sâdī seems to have spent the latter part of his life in retirement. He died on the evening of Friday, in the month of Shawwāl, A.H. 690 = A.D. 1291, says Daulat Shāh, and was buried near Shīrāz. Kæmpfer, in 1686, and Colonel Franklin, in 1787, visited his tomb, and the latter mentions it as being "just in the state it was in when Sâdī was buried." In person, Sâdī was, as Ross conjectures, of a mean appearance, low of stature, spare and slim. In the picture which Colonel Franklin saw of him, near his tomb, he is represented as wearing the

[b] Ross's Translation.

khirkah, or long blue gown of the darwesh, with a staff in his hand.

The great beauty of Sâdī's style is its elegant simplicity. In wit he is not inferior to Horace, whom he also resembles in his "curiosa verborum felicitas." Of his works the Gulistān may be ranked first. The numerous translations of his writings shew that his merits have not been altogether unappreciated even in these Western regions. George Gentius has the credit of first making known to European readers the Gulistān, by his "Rosarium Politicum," published at Amsterdam, A.D. 1651, of which it is sufficient to observe that it exhibits, along with the energy, all the roughness of a pioneer. A century and a half elapsed between the appearance of this Latin translation and the English one of Gladwin, which, though deserving of much commendation, is somewhat too free;[c] as are also those of Dumoulin, published at Calcutta in 1807, and of Lee, published in London in 1827. In

[c] Thus, at p. 53, l. 11, of my edition of the Persian text, اگر مستوجبِ عقوبتم *agar mustaujib-i ůḳūbatam*, is translated by Gladwin, "Shouldst Thou doom me to punishment;" and p. 55, l. 14, اینقدر بس که روي در خلقست *īn ḳadr bas kih rūī dar khalḳast*, "This is sufficient with a mortal face," which is very incorrect. At p. 76, l. 10, he renders ز موري *za mūrī*, "to an ant," which, as well as being incorrect, destroys the sense. At p. 79, l. 18, اتفاق مي سازم *ittifāḳ mī sāzam* is rendered, "I am reflecting"! At p. 80, l. 13, از نهيبِ بردِ عجوز *az nahīb-i bard-i ůjūz*, is translated by "in the depth of winter." At p. 147, l. 10, for سودِ سرمايهٔ عمرم, *sūd-i sarmāyah-i ůmram*, we find "the chief comfort of my life." At p. 149, l. 10, he omits an entire line.

1823 Mr. James Ross, a retired civilian, published a new translation,[d] which he dedicated, by permission, to

[d] At p. 18, l. 12, of the Persian preface (my edition), Ross translates نخل بندم ولي نه در بوستان *nakhl bandam walī nah dar būstān*, "I am a gardener, but not in a garden,"—where he appears to me to lose the whole pith of the sentence, viz., the implied comparison between the flowers of an artificial flower-maker and those of nature. At p. 7, l. 16, we find نسل و تبار *nasl wa tabār* rendered, in Ross, "The tree of their wickedness,"—where he evidently mistakes the Arabic word for the Persian. At p. 12, l. 10, كه سلطان بلشكر كند سروري *kih Sulṭān ba lashkar kunad sarwarī* is rendered, "For a king with an army constitutes a principality,"—which is altogether wide of the obvious meaning that "A king rules through his troops." At l. 17, in the same page, we find پادشاهي كه طرح ظلم فكند, *pādshāhī kih ṭarḥ ẓulm fikanad*, "A king that can anyhow be accessory to tyranny,"—where the obvious meaning of طرح *ṭarḥ*, "le fondement," as Semelet rightly translates it, is overlooked, though so clearly shewn by the use of پاي *pāe* in the next line. At p. 20, l. 4, Ross strangely mistakes رعايت *riāyat* for رعيت *raīyat*, and renders در رعايتِ مملكت سستي كردي *dar riāyat-i mamlakat sustī kardī*, "was easy with the yeomanry in collecting revenue"! In the same line both he and Semelet wrongly translate پيشين *pīshīn*, "ancient," whereas it is evident from the sequel of the story that the king was cotemporary with Sâdī, who knew one of his soldiers, and the word should, therefore, be rendered "former." At p. 23, l. 19, Ross gives a new sense to حرامي *ḥarāmī*, "revenue-embezzler." At p. 25, l. 16, Ross translates مُشار اليه بالبنان و معتمد عليه عند الاعيان *mushārun ilaihi b'ilbanān wa mūtamad alaihi āndu'l-āiyān*, "Towards whom all turned for counsel, and upon whom all eyes rested their hope,"—which does not

the Chairman and Court of Directors of the East India Company, and which he especially informs us was in-

contain a single word of the original, for even اعيان *aîyān* cannot here be rendered "eyes." In the last line of the same page, Ross renders تاريكي *tārīkī*, "Chaos," completely and most gratuitously destroying the beautiful metaphor. At p. 28, l. 20, we have a tolerable instance of a free translation; حاكمرا اين سخن پسنديده آمد *ḥākim-rā īn su<u>kh</u>an pasandīdah āmad*, "When the prince heard this sentiment he subscribed to its omnipotence"! The two first lines in p. 29 are sadly mistranslated,

چو كعبه قبلهٔ حاجت شد از ديار بعيد
روند خلق بديدارش از بسي فرسنگ

Chū kâbah ḳiblah-i ḥājat shud az diyār-i baîd,
Rawand <u>kh</u>alḳ ba-dīdārash az basī farsang.

which he renders thus, "When the fane of the Cablah at Mecca became their object from a far-distant land, pilgrims would hurry on to visit it from many farsangs." The Kâbah it is needless to remark, is the Black Temple at Mecca, and the Ḳiblah is the place to which people turn in prayer. قبله *Ḳiblah,* therefore, should here be taken with *ḥājat,* with which it is connected by an *iẓāfah,* and the از ديار بعيد *az diyār-i baîd* as evidently belongs to روند *rawand,* from which it should not be separated by a stop. At p. 31, l. 7, 8, the couplet is so translated as to become quite unmeaning. At p. 32, l. 13, Ross translates ملك بر آن لشكري خشم گرفت *malik bar ān lashkarī <u>kh</u>ishm girift,* "The sovereign let loose the army of his wrath"—a mistake which it is hardly possible to imagine a mere beginner would make. Gladwin rightly translates the sentence in his curt, free manner, "the king

tended to be literal, and thereby useful to the Students of the East India College. He prefixed to it a very

being displeased;" and Semelet, who reads برو *bar-ū* for بر آن لشكري *bar ān lashkarī*, renders it "le roi se met en colère contre lui." At p. 34, l. 6, همچنان دو فكر آن بيتم كه گفت *hamchunān dar fikr-i ān baitam kih guft*, where بيتم *baitam* is for بيت هستم *bait hastam*, as Gladwin and Semelet rightly take it, whereas Ross renders it "applicable to which is that stanza of mine." At p. 38, l. 7, Ross renders بحيف *ba-ḥaif* "at a low price," instead of "by force," and he also mistakes the sense of بطرح *ba-ṭarḥ*. At p. 41, l. 10, گرچه نعمت بفر دولتِ اوست *garchih nīmat ba-far-i daulat-i ūst*, is translated, "Though it be for their benefit that his glory is exalted"—a sense which can in no way be extracted from the words. At p. 41, l. 13, Ross renders مراورا از بندگان بسياهي بخشيد *marūrā az bandagān ba-siyāhī bakhshīd*, "he *forced* her upon a negro," a strange sense of بخشيدان *bakhshīdan*. At p. 53, l. 10, Ross translates حصا *ḥaṣa*, in defiance of the dictionary and of the other translations, "the black stone," instead of "pebbles," as Gladwin rightly renders it. In the next line he translates مستوجب *mustaujib*, "doomed," for "deserving." At p. 55, l. 14, he translates روي در خلقست *rūī dar khalḳast*, "this much is sufficient that it has a threadbare hood!"—a translation so amazing that one must suppose he read the passage differently, though it stands so in Gentius, whose text he professed to follow. At p. 57, l. 16, Ross has evidently misunderstood the sentence, چيزي نكردي كه بكار آيد *chīzī na kardī kih bakār āyad*,—which he renders, "that nothing be omitted that can serve a purpose." At p. 61, l. 10, Ross gives a ridiculous version of خامانِ مجلس در جوش *khāmān-i majlis dar jūsh*, "and the rawest of the assembly bubbled in unison."

valuable essay on the works and character of Sădī; but, of his Translation, I regret to say that I cannot speak in terms of unqualified praise. In 1828, M. Semelet published the Persian text of the Gulistān in Paris, and six years afterwards, a most excellent Translation, to which the first place must undoubtedly be assigned;[e] while Gladwin's version occupies the second; that of Ross, the third; and that of Gentius, the fourth.

At p. 64, l. 7, سر و پا برهنه *sar o pā barahnah* is rendered, "naked from head to foot," instead of "with bare head and feet." At p. 64, l. 15, Ross translates ببالینش *ba-bālīnash*, "to his *bier*," instead of "pillow." At p. 69, l. 2, بدست این مطرب *ba-dast-i īn muṭrib* is rendered, "in the hand of this minstrel," instead of "by means of this musician." At p. 74, l. 7, Ross translates هبوب *hubūb*, "zephyr"! and, at p. 76, l. 3, هنيء *hani-a*, "immense;" and l. 9, گور *gūr*, "an elk." At p. 95, l. 8, Ross renders صف *ṣaff*, "group." At p. 102, l. 6, تعرض سوال *taărruẓ-i suāl*, "prostitution of begging." At p. 109, l. 18, گدائي هول *gadāī haul* is rendered, "an importunate mendicant." At p. 178, l. 14, لقمه ادرار فروشند *lukmah-i idrār farūshand* is rendered, "that they may entitle themselves to the bread of charity." At least ten times this number of inaccuracies might have been noticed, but these will be sufficient to shew how unsafe a guide Ross proves himself as a translator.

[e] I have found but very few passages in which it appears to me that M. Semelet has failed to give the sense of the original. One is in Chap. I. (p. 4, l. 13), where he renders سري *sarī*, "le premier;" and line 17 of the same page, where درشتي *durushtī*, is rendered "la masse." At p. 34, l. 7, he renders پيلبان "un gardien de chameaux." At p. 162, l. 14, فلاح *falāḥ*, is translated "le paysan." There are some other inadvertencics, which will be found referred to in the notes.

For the publication of the present Translation, the only apology that seems requisite is the fact that those of Gladwin and Ross have long been out of print. Moreover, if the Eastern saying be true that

هر لفظ سعدي *har lafẓ-i Sâdī,*
هفتاد و دو معني *haftād wa dū mânī.*

"Each word of Sâdī has seventy-two meanings," there is room for a septuagint of translators. There is, however, another ground on which the Translation now offered to the public may claim notice, that it is, I believe, the first attempt, on anything like an extensive[1] scale, to render Persian poetry into English verse. Ross, in his Introductory Essay, asserts, in the words of Cowper, that "it is impossible to give, in rhyme, a just translation of any ancient poetry of Greece or Rome, and still less (here he means "still more" impossible) of Arabic and Persian." It will be for the Oriental scholar to judge how far I have departed from the true meaning of the original in putting it into English verse. For myself, I can only say I have not knowingly allowed myself any license except on very few occasions, on each of which I have excused myself in a note. I have also endeavoured to make the metre correspond in some degree to that of the Persian, and I have uniformly

[1] Atkinson has published some spirited versions extracted from the Shāh-nāmah; but I speak here of a continuous work. I do not mention Miss Costello's "Rose Garden of Persia," which is merely a translation from the French, and exhibits about as much of the originals as Moore's "Lalla Rookh," that is, nothing but a certain Oriental tone and gilding.

done my best to preserve the play upon words which occurs so often, and which is accounted such a beauty in the East.

I have only further to add that, to mark the Arabic passages, italics have been adopted; and that where I have had occasion to insert any explanation, the words employed are enclosed in brackets.

EDWARD B. EASTWICK.

HAILEYBURY COLLEGE,
October 1st, 1852.

LIFE OF SÂDĪ.

SHEKH MUṢLIḤU'D-DĪN, surnamed Sâdī, is the most eloquent of writers, and the wittiest author of either modern or ancient times, and one of the four monarchs of eloquence and style. In the opinion of this humble individual (the author of the Ātish Kadah) no one has appeared since the first rise of Persian Poetry who can claim a superior place to Firdausī of Tūs, Niẓāmī of Ḳum, Anwarī of Abīward, and Shekh Sâdī. In short, all I could say of the qualities which adorned his mind and heart, and of his perfections, displayed and secret, would not amount to the thousandth part of the reality, or be more than a trifling indication of the whole. In accordance with this, my master, the august and felicitous Mīr Saiyid Âlī Mushtāḳ, used to call Sâdī the "Nightingale of a Thousand Songs," intending to express that in every branch of poetry he displayed the perfection of genius. In a word, I used to busy myself with reflecting, whether in the revolutions of Time there had ever been a period, when men of learning were more lightly esteemed than at present; or, with reference to the want of appreciation evinced by the generation in which we live, whether bards were ever more undervalued than now? until I saw it mentioned in a Biography that a number of Poets once questioned Muḥammad Hamkar (Praise be to God! the like of him does not exist in these days) as to the comparative excellence of Sâdī and Imāmī of Herāt. He answered them with this verse,

"Not to Imāmī's strain,
Can I or Sâdī e'er attain!"

On reading this, I returned thanks to God that this age is guiltless of such folly as this. Men of sense will be alive to the disgraceful injustice of such a sentence, though as to himself Muḥammad Hamkar pronounced rightly. It is quite true that Imāmī is a far superior poet to the author of the verse quoted above, but there is not the shadow of a pretence for comparing him with the illustrious Sâdī, nor is there a single person save the three great poets whose names are given above, who can be placed in the same rank. With relation to the preceding anecdote a stanza occurred to me as I was composing the life of Sâdī, which perhaps is not altogether devoid of point, and which I will here set down.

One said, "The palm of merit has been given
To Imām of Herāt, o'er Sâdī, by
Muḥammad Hamkar;—what think'st thou?" "Good Heaven!
How much does Hamkar[a] herein err!" said I.

Sâdī is said to have been a disciple of Shekh Shahā-

[a] There is a play on the words "*Hamkar*" and ستمکر *sitamkar*, "unjust," which cannot be preserved in English.

bu'd-dīn; and Daulat Shah[b] writes that he lived to the age of one hundred and twenty years; and that after his tenth year he spent thirty years in various countries in acquiring learning, and thirty years more in travelling and making himself practically acquainted with things, and thirty years more in the environs of Shīrāz, in a spot which for beauty equals the Garden of Paradise; where men of learning and eminence resorted to him, and where he employed himself in devotion. Here he was supplied with delicious viands by his disciples, and it was his wont after satisfying his hunger to wrap up what was left and suspend it in a basket, and the wood-cutters who used to cut bushes in the neighbourhood of Shīrāz took these fragments away. One day, a person, by way of experiment, disguised himself as a wood-cutter and went to the place where the fragments were. On reaching towards them, his arm became stiff and remained stretched out. He cried out, "O Shekh! come to my aid!" Sâdī replied, "If this be the dress of a bush-cutter, where are the scars on thy hands and feet? or if thou art a robber, where is thy strong arm and firm heart that without a wound or pain thou makest these outcries?" He then prayed for him and the man was healed.

They also relate that a devout person of Shīrāz saw in a dream that the angels in heaven were moved, and that the cherubs were singing softly the poetry of Shekh Sâdī, and said that "this couplet of Sâdī is worth the praises and hymns of angel-worship for a whole

[b] The name of the author of a celebrated Biography of Learned Men.

year." When he awoke, he went to Sâdī and found him with ecstatic fervour reciting this couplet,

> To pious minds each verdant leaf displays,
> A volume teeming with th' Almighty's praise.

The devotee related to Sâdī the vision before mentioned, and besought him to pray in his behalf.

The repartees of Sâdī are numberless; nor is it requisite to recount what is known to all. Once in his travels he arrived at Tabrīz, where he learnt on inquiry after Khwājah Hamām,[c] that he had a son of great beauty and accomplishments; and that he guarded him from acquaintance with strangers with the most scrupulous care, insomuch that he took him to the private baths. Sâdī went to the bath on the day that the Khwājah had fixed to come, and concealed himself in a corner until he arrived with his son; when laying aside his mantle, he stepped in. Khwājah was displeased when he saw him, and seating his son behind him, he asked Sâdī, whence he came? and what was his profession? Sâdī replied that he came from the fair land of Shīrāz; and that he was a poet. Khwājah said, "Holy God! in this country the men of Shīrāz are more plentiful than dogs!" "It is just the reverse in my country," replied Sâdī, "for there the men of Tabrīz are less[d] than dogs." There happened to be there a vessel of water. . Khwājah said, "It is strange,

[c] Name of a famous poet.

[d] The wit lies in the double sense of كمتر *kamtar*, which means "fewer"—answering to بيشتر *bīshtar*—"more numerous," and also "inferior."

the people of Shīrāz are bald-headed like the bottom of this vessel." "Stranger still," replied Sâdī, turning up the cup, "the heads of the people of Tabrīz are as empty as the mouth[e] of this." "Prithee," rejoined Khwājah with a discomfited look, "Do they ever quote the poems of Hamām in Shīrāz?" "Yes," answered Sâdī, and he then repeated this concluding verse of one of Hamām's odes,

"Hamām divides[f] me from my love—one day
That veil, I hope, will be removed away."

Khwājah said, "I conjecture that thou art Shekh Sâdī? for to no one else belongs such quickness." Sâdī answered in the affirmative; on which Khwājah kissed his hand, and made his son pay his respects, and took his illustrious visitor home with him, where he showed him every attention for some time—"Would that I too had been with them!"[g]

I have repeatedly perused the writings of this poet, whose whole works deserve to be transcribed here. Some extracts, however, of his elegies, odes, didactic poems and facetiæ, which appear to me to possess the most perfect beauty, are all that I am able to extract; and I shall quote this one passage from his prose writings,

[e] I have changed this repartee a little, at the risk of losing somewhat of its point.

[f] Hamām was sitting between his son and Sâdī. In the original sense, a Ṣūfīistic one, a veil is said to be between Hamām and his beloved one, *i.e.* God.

[g] This is an exclamation of the author, and is to be found in the Ḳur'ān.

though I have not admitted any other prose extract from any writer into this book:

"They asked a philosopher, 'Who should be called fortunate, and who unfortunate?' He replied, 'He is to be called fortunate, who sowed and reaped; and he must be reckoned unfortunate, who died and left [what he possessed without enjoying it.]'"

The rest of his sayings, full of wisdom as they are, must be sought in the Gulistān, to which the reader is referred.

Sâdī flourished in the reign of Sâd Atābak, whence his name of Sâdī, and he died in Shīrāz, in the year 691 A.H. (This is the date according to D'Herbelot, but according to Daulat Sháh, 690, see p. xi.)

A LIST OF THE WRITINGS OF SÅDĪ.

AS ENUMERATED BY ROSS.

---

1 to 6.—Risālah; or Treatise.
7.—Gulistān.
8.—Būstān.
9.—Arabian Ḳasāids.
10.—Persian Ḳasāids.
11.—Marāṣī; or Dirges.
12.—Mixed Poems, Persian and Arabic.
13.—Poems, with recurring lines.
14.—Plain G͟hazals.
15.—Rhetorical Ghazals.
16.—Works written in later life.
17.—Writings in earlier life.
18.—Poems addressed to Shamsu'd-dīn.
19—Fragments.
20.—Facetiæ.
21.—Tetrastichs.
22.—Distichs.

I BOAST not the stock of my own excellence;
But hold forth my hand, like a beggar, for pence.
I have heard in the day of hope and of fear,[a]
God's mercy the good and the sinner will spare:
If thou, too, herein seest faults, be it thine
Like thy Maker to act; like Him be benign.

Būstān of Sādī.

---

[a] That is, in the day of resurrection.

PREFACE.

IN THE NAME OF GOD, THE MERCIFUL, THE COMPASSIONATE!

Praise be to God! (May he be honoured and glorified!) whose worship is the means of drawing closer to Him, and in giving thanks to whom is involved an increase of benefits. Every breath which is inhaled prolongs life, and when respired exhilarates the frame. In every breath therefore two blessings are contained, and for every blessing a separate thanksgiving is due.

COUPLETS.

Whose hands suffice? whose voices may
The tribute of His praises pay?
O! ye of David's line! His praises sing,[1]
For few are grateful found to him [their King.]

STANZA.

Best for the slave his fault to own,
And seek for pardon at God's throne:
For none can hope to pay aright
A homage worthy of his might.
  The raindrops of his mercy, shed
  On all, descend unlimited,
  His bounteous store for all is spread.
Dark though their sins may be, He does not rend
  The veil that clokes His creatures' shame;
Nor stays His bounty, though they oft offend,
  [But aye continueth the same.]

[1] This is a quotation from the Ḳur'ān; Chap. xxxiv., v. 12.

STANZA.

All-Gracious One! who, from Thy hidden store,
On Guebre[2] dost, and Pagan, alms bestow!
When will Thy mercies crown Thy friends no more?
Thou, who with love regardest e'en Thy foe!

He biddeth His chamberlain, the morning breeze, spread out the emerald carpet [of the earth,] and commandeth His nurses, the vernal clouds, to foster in earth's cradle the tender herbage, [*lit.*, "the daughters of the grass"] and clotheth the trees with a garment of green leaves, and at the approach of spring crowneth the young branches with wreaths of blossoms; and by His power the juice of the cane becometh exquisite honey, and the date-seed, by His nurture, a lofty tree.

STANZA.

Cloud and wind, and sun and sky,
Labour all harmoniously,
That while they thee with food supply,
Thou mayst not eat unthankfully.[3]
Since all are busied and intent for thee,
Justice forbids that thou a rebel be.

It is a tradition of the Chief of Created Beings, and the Most Glorious of Existences, the Mercy[4] of the Universe, the Purest of Mankind, and the Complement of Time's Circle, Muḥammad Muṣṭafa (On whom be blessing and peace!)

COUPLET.

Gracious Prophet! intercessor! worthy of obedience, thou!
Beautiful, of mien majestic, comely, and of smiling brow.

[2] Byron has Anglicised the word "Guebre," and it seems more euphonious than گبر *Gabar*, or Moore's "Gheber."

[3] بغفلت نخوری *ba-ghaflat na-kh'urī*, "thou shouldst not eat carelessly," or according to Gladwin, "in neglect." This must mean "carelessly with reference to God," *i.e.* "unthankfully."

[4] That is, "means of obtaining mercy from God for all creatures."

COUPLET.

To the wall of the faithful what sorrow, when pillared [securely] on thee?
What terror where Nūḥ[5] is the pilot, though rages the storm-driven sea?

VERSE.

All perfect he, and therefore won
His lofty place, and [like a sun]
His beauty lighted up the night.
Fair are his virtues all, and bright.
Let peace and benediction be
On him and his posterity!

[The tradition is] that whenever one of his sinful servants in affliction lifteth up the hands of penitence in the court of the glorious and Most High God, in the hope of being heard; the Most High God regardeth him not; again he supplicateth Him, again God turneth from him; again humbly and piteously he beseecheth Him; [then] God Most High (Praise be to Him!) saith, "*O my angels, verily I am ashamed by reason of my servant, and he hath no God but myself; therefore of a surety I pardon him,*"[6] that is to say, "I have answered his prayer and accomplished his desire, since I am ashamed because of his much entreaty and supplication."

COUPLET.

God's condescension and his mercy see!
His servant sinneth, and ashamed is He!

The devout dwellers at the temple of His glory confess the faultiness of their worship saying, "*We have not worshipped Thee as Thou oughtest to be worshipped!*" and those who would describe the appearance of His beauty are amazed and say, "*We have not known Thee as Thou oughtest to be known.*"

[5] Nuḥ is the Oriental form of the name of the Prophet Noah.

[6] These words being in Arabic, an explanation of them is afterwards given in Persian, introduced by "that is to say."

STANZA.

If one His praise of me would learn,
What of the traceless can the tongueless tell?
Lovers[7] are killed by those they love so well;
No voices from the slain return.

STORY.

A devout personage had bowed his head on the breast of contemplation, and was immersed in the ocean of the divine presence. When he came back to himself from that state, one of his companions sportively asked him—"From that flower-garden where thou wast, what miraculous gift hast thou brought for us?" He replied, "I intended to fill my lap as soon as I should reach the rose-trees, and bring presents for my companions. When I arrived there the fragrance of the roses so intoxicated me that the skirt of my robe slipped from my hands."

VERSE.

O bird of morn![8] love of the moth be taught;
Consumed it dies nor utters e'en a cry!
Pretended searchers! of this true love nought
Know ye,—who know tell not their mystery.
O loftier than all thought,
Conception, fancy, or surmise!

[7] The soul and the Deity are often, by Oriental writers, imaged by the lover and his beloved one.

[8] The nightingale is so called as singing in the morning twilight. Gladwin reads اي مرغِ صحر *ai murgh-i ṣaḥr*, and translates, "O bird of the desert!" and in my edition of the Text I unfortunately retained this reading, which, however, I now think incorrect, and prefer reading with M. Semelet, اي مرغِ سحر *ai murgh-i saḥar*, "O bird of the morning!" The comparison is this, that as the nightingale, for all its warblings, is not so true a lover as the moth, which perishes in the brilliance it adores without a sigh; so the truly devout are not those who speak of their devotion, but those who are wrapt into silent ecstacy.

All vainly Thou art sought,
[Too high for feeble man's emprise.]
Past is our festive day,[9]
And reached at length life's latest span;
Thy dues are yet to pay,
The firstlings of Thy praise by man.

RECITAL OF THE GLORIOUS QUALITIES OF THE MONARCH OF THE TRUE FAITH (MAY GOD MAKE CLEAR ITS DEMONSTRATION[10]) ABŪ-BAKR-BIN-SÂD-BIN-ZANGĪ.[11]

The fair report of Sâdī, which is celebrated by the general[12] voice; and the fame of his sayings, which has travelled the whole surface[13] of the earth; and the loved reed,[14] which imparts his discourse, and which they devour like honey; and the manner in which men carry off the scraps of his writing, as though they were gold leaf[15]—are not to be ascribed to the perfection of his own excellence or eloquence, but [to this, that] the Lord of

[9] Life is finely compared by Oriental writers to an entertainment which is succeeded by the darkness and silence of night.

[10] Gladwin has a different reading, where the benediction refers to the king, "may God perpetuate his reign!"

[11] بن *Bin* signifies "son of."

[12] Literally, "which has fallen into the mouths of the common people." So the Latin "volitare per ora virûm."

[13] Richardson's Dictionary makes بسيط *basīṭ* an adjective only, but in this passage it is evidently a substantive.

[14] The Oriental قلم *kalam* (calamus) or pen is, as every one knows, a reed. This leads to various poetical fantasies. Thus Maulavī Rūmī,

"Hear the reed's complaining wail!
Hear it tell its mournful tale!
Torn from the spot it loved so well,
Its grief, its sighs our tears compel."

[15] This expression may also mean "bills of exchange." Gladwin so translates it. Others think it means a diploma of honour, amongst whom is M. Semelet.

the Earth, the Axis of the Revolution of Time, the Successor of Sulaimān, the Defender of the People of the True Faith, the Puissant King of Kings, the Great Atābak[16] Muẕaffaru'd-dīn Abū-bakr-bin-Sâd-bin-Zangī, God's shadow on earth *(O God! approve him and his desires!)* has regarded him with extreme condescension and bestowed on him lavish commendation, and evinced a sincere regard for him. Of a verity, from attachment to him, all people, both high and low, have become favourably inclined towards me, *since men adopt the sentiments of their kings.*[17]

QUATRAIN.

Since to my lowliness thou didst with favour turn,
My track is clearer than the sun's bright beam.
Though in thy servant all might every fault discern;
When kings approve, e'en vices virtues seem.

VERSE.

'Twas in the bath, a piece of perfumed clay
Came from my loved one's hands to mine, one day.
"Art thou then musk or ambergris?" I said;
"That by thy scent my soul is ravished?"
"Not so," it answered, "worthless earth was I,
But long I kept the rose's company;
Thus near, its perfect fragrance to me came,
Else I'm but earth, the worthless and the same."[18]

16 اتابک *Atābak* is a Turkish word signifying "father of the prince." It was originally applied to a prime minister or great noble of state. It afterwards became the title of a dynasty of Persian kings, originally Turkumāns, who reigned from 1148 to 1264 A.D. To the sixth of these, Sâd-bin-Zangī, Sâdī dedicates his "Gulistān." He reigned thirty-five years, and died A.D. 1259.

17 A quotation from the Ḳur'ān.

18 By this simile, which in the original is of exquisite beauty, Sâdī would express his own unworthiness, and the estimation imparted to him by the King's favour.

Lord! for the Faithful's sake his life renew,
Double the guerdon to his virtues due,
Exalt his friends', his nobles' dignity,
And those destroy, who hate him or defy;
As in the Ḳur'ān's verse, Thy will be done,
Protect, O God! his kingdom and his son.

VERSE.

Happy in truth the world through him—may he
Be happy! and may Heaven-sent victory,
Like a proud banner, him o'ercanopy!
He is the root, then may the tree be blest! [19]
Fairest are aye the plants whose seed is best.

May the most High and Holy God preserve to the day of resurrection the fair territory of Shīrāz in the security of peace through the awe inspired by its just rulers, and the magnanimous spirit of its sagacious superintendents!

VERSE.

Knowest thou not in distant lands,
Why I made a long delay?
I, through fear of Turkish bands,
Left my home and fled away.
Earth was ravelled by those bands
Like an Æthiop's hair; and they,
Slaughter-seeking, stretched their hands,
Human wolves, towards the prey.
Men like angels dwelt within,[20]
Lion-warriors roamed around.
Back I came, how changed the scene!
Nought but peacefulness I found:
Tigers though they late had been,
Changed their fierceness, fettered, bound.

[19] The State is here compared to a tree, of which the King is the root.

[20] "Within," *i.e.*, in the city of Shīrāz, then one of the most populous on earth. The surrounding districts were suffering from an irruption of savage Turks.

Thus in former times I saw,
 Filled with tumult, trouble, pain,
Earth uncurbed by rule or law.
 But strife owned our monarch's reign,
Heard Atābak's name with awe,
 Heard, and all was peace again.[21]

VERSE.

The clime of Fārs[22] dreads not Time's baneful hand,
While one like thee, God's Shadow, rules the land.
None at this day can shew on earth's wide breast,
A haven, like thy gate, of peace and rest.
'Tis thine to guard the poor: a grateful sense
Is due from us—from God thy recompense.
Lord! shield the land of Fārs from faction's storm,
Long as winds blow, or earth retains its form.

CAUSE OF WRITING THE "GULISTĀN."

One night I was reflecting on times gone by and regretting my wasted life; and I pierced the stony mansion of my heart with the diamond of my tears, and recited these couplets applicable to my state.

DISTICHS.

One breath of life each moment flies,
A small remainder meets my eyes.
Sleeper! whose fifty years are gone,
Be these five[23] days at least thy own.
Shame on the dull, departed dead,
Whose task is left unfinished;

[21] I have been obliged to render these last three lines very freely. There is in them, however, nothing to delay the student.

[22] Fārs is that province of Persia of which Shīrāz is the capital.

[23] This is an indefinite number, used to express any short period.

In vain for them the drum was beat,
Which warns us of man's last retreat.
Sweet sleep upon the parting-day[24]
Holds back the traveller from the way.
Each comer a new house erects,
Departs,—the house its lord rejects.
The next one forms the same conceit;
This mansion none shall ere complete.
Hold not as friend this comrade light,
With one so false no friendship plight.
Since good and bad alike must fall,
He's blest who bears away the ball.[25]
Send to thy tomb an ample store;[26]
None will it bring—then send before.
  Like snow is life in July's sun,
  Little remains; and is there one
  To boast himself and vaunt thereon?[27]
With empty hand thou hast sought the mart;
I fear thou wilt with thy turban part.[28]
Who eat their corn while yet 'tis green,
At the true harvest can but glean.
To Sâdī's counsel let thy soul give heed,
This is the way—be manful and proceed.

[24] These verses may seem unconnected, but they are not more so than in the original; the rendering is most close.

[25] This is an allusion to the game of *chaugān*, which is a sort of tennis played on horseback. He who bears off the ball is the winner.

[26] Of good deeds—which are here compared to the provisions for a journey.

[27] This is somewhat freely translated. Gladwin reads عرة هنوز *ghirah hanūz*, and translates, "Art thou yet slothful?" I prefer reading و خواجه غرّة هنوز *wa khw'ājah gharrah hanūz*;—literally "and my gentleman is still boastful."

[28] "Thou hast" and "thou wilt" must be here read, for the sake of the metre, as one syllable. It is frequently impossible to avoid stiffness and other faults in the versification, that the literal translation may be preserved.

After deliberating on this subject I thought it advisable that I should take my seat in retirement and gather under me my robe, withdrawing from society, and wash the tablet of my memory from vain words, nor speak idly in future.

COUPLET.

Better who sits in nooks, deaf, speechless, idle,
Than he who knows not his own tongue to bridle.

At length one of my friends who was my comrade in the camel-litter[29] and my closet-companion[30] entered my door according to old custom. Notwithstanding all the cheerfulness and hilarity which he displayed, and his spreading out the carpet of affection, I returned him no answer, nor lifted up my head from the knee of devotion. He was pained, and looking towards me said,

STANZA.

Now that the power of utterance is thine,
  Speak, O my brother! kindly, happily,
To-morrow's message bids thee life resign,
  Then art thou silent of necessity.

One of those attached to me [*i.e.*, a kinsman *or* a servant] informed him regarding this circumstance, saying, "Such an one [*i.e.*, Sâdī] has made a resolution and fixed determination to pass the rest of his life in the world as a devotee, and embrace silence. If thou canst, take thy way, and choose the path of retreat.[31]

[29] The كجاوه *kajāwah* is nothing more than two panniers slung one on each side a camel, and each containing a traveller; who of course would prefer a friend as his *vis-à-vis* in such a situation. The expression then means simply a comrade in travel.

[30] As we should say "a bosom-friend."

[31] Gladwin understands this as an exhortation to adopt a similar abnegation of the world. I cannot agree with this opinion, and think that the speaker simply desired Sâdī's friend to withdraw if he could make up his mind to leave him (اگر تواني *agar tawānī* "if thou art able").

He replied, "By the glory of the Highest, and by our ancient friendship! I will not breathe nor stir a step until he hath spoken according to his wonted custom, and in his usual manner: for to distress friends is folly, but the expiation of an oath is easy.[32] It is contrary to rational procedure and opposed to the opinion of sages, that the Ẕū'l-faḳār[33] of Âlī should remain in its scabbard, or the tongue of Sâdī [silent] in his mouth.

STANZA.

What is the tongue in mouth of mortals?—say!
'Tis but the key that opens wisdom's door:
While that is closed who may conjecture,—pray?
If thou sell'st jewels or the pedlar's store?

STANZA.

Silence is mannerly, so deem the wise,
But in the fitting time use language free;
Blindness of judgment just in two things lies,
To speak unwished, not speak unseasonably.

In brief, I had not the power to refrain from conversing with him, and I thought it uncourteous to avert my face from conference with him, for he was an agreeable companion and a sincere friend.

COUPLET.

When thou contendest, choose an enemy[34]
Whom thou mayst vanquish or whom thou canst fly.

[32] The non-observance of a rash oath is expiated by fasting three days, or by feeding and clothing ten poor persons, or by setting one captive free.

[33] Ẕū'l-faḳār was the name of a two-edged sword which Muḥammad pretended to have received from the Angel Gabriel; and which he bequeathed to his son-in-law Âlī. The author of the Ḳāmūs says that it was the sword of Âṣ-bin-Munabbih, an unbeliever, who was slain at the battle of Badr.

[34] In these lines lie some difficulties well descanted on by M. Semelet, but which require but a word here. The words در ستیز *dar sitīz* may be translated "in strife," in which case

By the mandate of necessity I spoke, and we went out for recreation, it being the season of spring, when the asperity of winter was mitigated, and the time of the roses' rich display had arrived.

COUPLET.

Vestments green upon the trees
  Like the [costly] garments seeming,
Which at Îd's festivities
  Rich men wear [all gaily gleaming.]

STANZA.

'Twas Urdabihisht's first day, the Jalālian[35] month of spring,
From the pulpits of the branches slight we heard the bulbuls[36] sing
The red red branches were be-gemmed with pearls of glistening dew,
Like moisture on an angry beauty's cheek, a cheek of rosy hue.

[So time passed] till one night[37] it happened that I was walking at a late hour in a flower-garden with one of my friends.[37] The spot was blithe and pleasing, and

supply ببين *babīn* before the next line; or spite of the dictionaries, those words may perhaps mean "try for one," "choose," in which case there is no ellipse. گزير *guzīr* can hardly mean "aid," here—the "du secours" of M. de Sacy; but rather "a means of success," the چارة *chārah* of Castell.

[35] Jalālu'd-dīn, King of Persia, began to reign A.H. 475=1082 A.D. His æra dates from that year. Urdabihisht is the second month of the Jalālian year, and corresponds with our April.

[36] The bulbul, it is almost unnecessary to say, is the nightingale.

[37] I must confess that I think the sense would be greatly improved if we could get rid of با يكي از دوستان *bā yakī az dūstān*, and read شب‌را *shab-rā* for تا شبي *tā shabī*, in which case it would be the same friend who persuaded Sâdī to give up his

the trees intertwined there charmingly. You would have said that fragments of enamel were sprinkled on the ground, and that the necklace of the Pleiades was suspended from the vines that grew there.

STANZA.

A garden where the murmuring rill was heard;
While from the trees sang each melodious bird;
That, with the many-coloured tulip bright,
These, with their various fruits the eye delight.
The whispering breeze beneath the branches' shade,
Of bending flowers a motley carpet made.

In the morning, when the inclination to return prevailed over our wish to stay,[38] I saw that he had gathered his lap full of roses, and fragrant herbs, and hyacinths, and sweet basil, [with which] he was setting out for the city. I said, "To the rose of the flower-garden there is, as you know, no continuance; nor is there faith in the promise[39] of the rose garden: and the sages have said that we should not fix our affections on that which has no endurance." He said, "What then is my course?" I replied, "For the recreation of the beholders and the gratification of those who are present, I am able to compose a book, 'the Garden of Roses,' whose leaves the rude hand of the blast of autumn cannot affect; and the blitheness of whose spring the revolution of time cannot change into the disorder of the waning year.

taciturnity, that walked with him at night, and received the promise of the "Gulistān."

[38] Every line of Sâdī is said to have هفتاد و دو معني *haftād wa dū mânī*, "seventy-two meanings," and this sentence may fairly be thought to have a different meaning from the one given in the text. It may be rendered, "the desire to return, in order to repose, prevailed with us."

[39] I prefer translating عهد *âhd* thus. Gladwin translates it "continuance;" and M. Semelet renders it by "la saison."

DISTICHS.

What use to thee that flower-vase of thine?
Thou would'st have rose-leaves; take then, rather, mine.
Those roses but five days or six will bloom;
This garden ne'er will yield to winter's gloom."

As soon as I had pronounced these words, he cast the flowers from his lap, and took hold of the skirt of my garment, [saying] "*When the generous promise, they perform.*" It befel that in a few days a chapter or two were entered in my note-book, on the advantages of society,[40] and the rules of conversation,[41] in a style that may be useful to orators, and augment the eloquence of letter-writers.[42] In short, the rose of the flower-garden still continued to bloom, when the book of the "Rose Garden" was finished. It will, however, be then really perfected when it is approved and condescendingly perused[43] at the court of the King, the Asylum of the

[40] The seventh chapter, در تاثیرِ تربیت *dar tāsīr-i tarbiyat.* Ross translates معاشرة *muāsharat,* "education," which is hardly defensible. It means rather "enjoyable intercourse."

[41] The eighth chapter, در آدابِ صحبت *dar ādāb-i ṣuḥbat.*

[42] Richardson's Dictionary is silent as to this word مترسلان *mutarassilān.*

[43] A string of titles separates the latter part of this sentence, which I have somewhat freely translated, from the پسندیده آید *pasandīdah āyad,* "it is approved." The more literal rendering would be, "It will, however, be really complete when it shall have been approved at the court of the King, the Asylum of the World," etc., "and [when] he shall have condescended to peruse it with the benign glance of imperial favour." Owing to the length of the titles, the passage is rather involved, and all the translators appear to me to deal unfairly by it. Ross and Gladwin both omit to translate ابو بکر بن سعد بن زنگي *Abū-bakr-bin-Sâd-bin-Zangī;* whence it would almost seem that they overlooked the circumstance that the Sâd-bin-Atābak was the son of Abū-bakr, who was the son of a former Sâd, and who admitted the second Sâd to reign jointly with himself.

world, the Shadow of the Creator, and the Light of the Bounty of the All-provider, *the Treasury of the Age, the Retreat*[44] *of true Religion, the Aided by Heaven, the Triumphant over his Enemies, the Victorious Arm of the Empire, the Lamp of the excelling Faith, the Beauty of Mankind, the Glory of Islām, Sâd, the son of the Most Puissant King of Kings, Master of attending Nations, Lord of the Kings of Arabia and Persia, Sovereign of Land and Sea, Heir to the Throne of Sulaimān, Atābak the Great, Muẓaffaru'd-dīn Abū-bakr-bin-Sâd-bin-Zangī : (May God most High perpetuate the good fortune of both, and prosper all their righteous undertakings !)*

VERSE.

If the imperial favour should it grace,
'Twill rival China's[45] paintings, Arjang's pictured leaf.[46]
Ne'er with chagrin can it o'ercloud the face;
For the rose garden[47] is no place for grief,
And its fair preface bears, impressed by fame,
Great Sâd Abū-bakr-Sâd-bin-Zangī's name.

[44] كهف *Kahf* signifies "a cave," especially the cave in which the seven young Christians of Ephesus took refuge from the persecutions of the Emperor Decius. They are called the اصحاب كهف *aṣḥāb-i kahf*, "lords of the cave."

[45] M. Semelet quotes Gentius as to a great city on the confines of India called Sina, and possessing an edifice adorned with paintings, to which he supposes allusion is here made. I should rather suppose that Chinese paintings were meant.

[46] Richardson's Dictionary tells us that Arjang is the name of the house of the painter Manes. M. Semelet holds it to mean a book of his; and Ross translates the passage by "the picture-portfolio of Manī." Manī or Manes, the founder of the Manichæans, was a painter of wondrous skill, who lived in the reign of Shāhpur or Sapor, the son of Ardasīr Bābakān. He was burnt alive by order of Bahrām.

[47] An equivoque on the word Gulistān.

EULOGIUM OF THE MIGHTY NOBLE, FAKHRU'D-DĪN ABŪ-BAKR-BIN-ABŪ-NAṢR.

A second time the bride of my imagination, conscious of her want of beauty, lifts not up her head, nor raises the eye of despondency from the instep of bashfulness, and comes not forth adorned among the bevy of beauties, save when decked with the ornaments of the approbation of the mighty, wise, just, and divinely-supported Lord, the Victorious over his Foes, Prop of the Imperial Throne, Counsellor of State, Shelter of the Indigent, Asylum of the Poor, Patron of the Eminent, Friend of the Pure, Glory of the People of Fārs, Right-hand of the Empire, Prince of Favourites, Ornament of the State and of Religion, Succour of the True Faith and of the Faithful, Pillar of Kings and Princes; Abū-bakr-bin-Abū-naṣr (May God prolong his life, increase his dignity, cause his breast to expand with joy, and double his reward! for he is extolled by the nobles of all quarters of the globe, and is an assemblage of all laudable qualities).

COUPLET.

When his kind care, protective, one defends,
Pious his sins become, his foemen, friends.

To each one of the other servants and attendants a separate duty is assigned; such that if in the performance of it they indulge in any negligence or sloth, they assuredly incur the liability of reproof, and expose themselves to rebuke; all save this tribe of Darweshes [of whom Sâdī is one] from whom thanks are due for the benefits they receive from the great, and whom it behoves to recount the fair virtues [of their benefactors] and offer up prayers for their welfare:[48] and the per-

[48] Ross here and in several places renders خیر *khair* by "charity." I cannot think it has this meaning in this place, where, if "alms" were intended, خیرات *khairāt* would, in my opinion, be used.

formance of such duties as these is better in absence than when present, for in the latter case it borders on ostentation, and in the former it is far from outward show and allied to acceptance with God.

VERSE.

Straight grew the sky's crook'd back[49] from that fair hour,
When the great mother, Time, produced a son like thee;
Signal that act of God's wise, gracious power,
In forming one who should to all a blessing be!
Lasting his fortune, whose fair name survives;
For after him, his memory shall by fame endure;
To thee the praise of learned men nought gives:
The soul-entrancing cheek needs not the toilette's[50] lure.

AN APOLOGY FOR THE OMISSION OF SERVICE, AND THE CAUSE OF SELECTING SECLUSION.

A faultiness and neglect which takes place in the assiduity of my service at the court of my lord arises à-propos to what a body of the sages of Hind said of the excellence of Buzurchimihr.[51] At length they were unable to discover any defect in him but this, that in utterance he was slow (that is,[52] delayed long), so that his hearers were obliged to wait a long time until he could explain himself. Buzurchimihr heard this and said, "It is better to be anxious what I shall say, than to suffer remorse for what I have said."

[49] However unpalateable to European taste, I am obliged to present this strange metaphor in all its marvellous monstrosity.

[50] Metre compels me to substitute the temple for the priestess. Instead of "toilette" it should be "tire-woman."

[51] Buzurchimihr was the prime minister of Nūshīrwān, king of Persia, in whose reign Muḥammad was born.

[52] The word here rendered "slow" is, in the text, Arabic, and is there explained in Persian to mean "delayed long." In English the latter expression becomes superfluous.

DISTICHS.

The well-taught orators,[53] the men of age,
First ponder well and then their thoughts declare:
Waste not thy breath in thoughtless speech; if sage
Thy counsel, slowness will it nought impair.
Reflect, then speak; and let thy utterance cease
Ere others say, "Enough!" and bid thee "Peace!"
Men by the power of speech the brutes excel,
The brutes surpass thee if thou speakest not well.

And more especially in the presence of the Eye[54] of Royalty (glorious be his victory!), which is the rallying point for the wise, and the centre where profound sages meet; if I should display boldness in pursuing the conversation I might be guilty of presumption, and should be producing my trumpery[55] before his incomparable Excellency; and a glass-bead were not worth a barley-corn in the jewellers' mart, and a lamp gives no light in the sun, and a lofty minaret shows low at the foot of mount Alwand.[56]

[53] سخن دان پرورده پیر کهن. M. Semelet connects the پیر کهن *pīr-i kuhan* with the پرورده *parwardah*, and translates it thus, "L'homme éloquent, instruit par un vieux maître," which may well be admitted among the seventy-two meanings of each sentence of the divine Sâdī.

[54] This word (اعیان) is in the plural, but the vazīr alone is meant. The expression, "Eye of the king," is, as is well known, one of the titles of a vazīr.

[55] Here is said to be an allusion to the Ḳur'ān, c. xii. v. 88. يَا اَيُّهَا ٱلعَزِيزُ جِئْنَا بِبِضَاعَةٍ مُزْجَاةٍ *yā aiyuhā'l âzīzu ji'nā bi-bizâātin muzjātin*, "O most excellent! we have come with little money;" where the brothers of Joseph are addressing him when about to buy corn.

[56] At eight or ten leagues to the east of Tehrān is the remarkable peak of Alwand, or Alburz, as the inhabitants of Tehrān call it. It is covered with eternal snow, and, according to Olivier, sometimes emits smoke.

DISTICHS.

He who exalts his neck with pride
Is girt with foes on every side;
Sâdī lies prostrate, free from care:
None of the fallen ere make war.
Reflection first, speech last of all,
The basement must precede the wall.
True, that the art of making flowers I know;
But shall I try it where real flow'rets grow?
A beauty I—but will my cheek look fair,
When they with Canaan's glory[57] me compare?

They said to the sage Luḳmān,[58] "From whom didst thou learn wisdom?" He replied, "From the blind, who advance not their feet till they have tried the ground." *Try the egress before you enter.*

HEMISTICH.

Try first your powers, and then try a wife.

[57] These lines require a little expansion, which I have given to them. Sâdī says, that though he may have a reputation for learning, it would appear altogether contemptible at the Court of the vazīr, himself so wise, and surrounded by such a galaxy of sages; just as a maker of artificial flowers would make himself ridiculous if he practised his art amid real flowers, or as an ordinary beauty would forfeit all pretensions to loveliness if compared with Joseph, the beauty of Canaan, whose charms, according to Musalmān, were incomparable.

[58] Luḳmān, after whom the thirty-first chapter of the Ḳur'ān is called, is by some reckoned among the Prophets, and called the cousin of Job; and by others, the grand-nephew of Abraham; others say he was born in the time of David, and lived to that of Jonah; others, again, call him an Æthiopian slave, liberated by his master for his fidelity. His fables and maxims are celebrated in the East, and the Greeks probably borrowed their account of Æsop from his history.

VERSE.

Dauntless the cock in war, yet to what end
Shall he with brazen-taloned hawks contend?
Capturing the mouse the cat doth lionly;
Gauged with the leopard but a mouse is she!

Nevertheless, in reliance on the liberal disposition of the great, who conceal the faults of the humble, and use no endeavour to disclose the defects of their inferiors, I have inserted in this book, in a concise way, a few narratives of rare adventures, and traditions, and tales, and verses, and manners of ancient kings, and I have expended some portion of precious life upon it. Such was my motive for composing the Gulistān.

STANZA.

This verse instructive shall remain when I,
Scattered in dust, in several atoms lie;
In short, since in no mundane thing I see
The signs impressed of perpetuity,
This picture shall my sole memorial be;
Perhaps hereafter, for this pious task,
Some man of prayer for me too grace shall ask.

Mature consideration as to the arrangement of the Book, ordering of the chapters, and conciseness, made me[59] deem it expedient that this delicate Garden, and this densely wooded grove, should, like Paradise,[60] be divided into eight chapters, in order that it may become the less likely to fatigue.

[59] M. Semelet's reading دیدم *dīdam*, is perhaps better than the one here adopted, in which امعان نظر *imān-i naẓar* is made the nominative to دید *dīd*. I confess I should like to insert و *wa* before ایجاز *ījāz*.

[60] Here is an equivoque on the word بهشت *bihisht*, which means "Paradise," but with a little alteration becomes بهشت *ba-hasht*, "in eight." The Musalmān divide Paradise into eight regions.

LIST OF THE CHAPTERS.

DATE OF THE BOOK.

Six hundred six and fifty years had waned
From the famed Flight[61]; then when no sorrow pained
My heart, I sought these words, with truth impressed,
To say, and thus have said: to God belongs the rest.

[61] The flight of Muḥammad, the Æra by which the Musalmān reckon, took place on the 16th of July, 622. Consequently the date of the Gulistān is A.D. 1258.

CHAPTER I.

ON THE MANNERS OF KINGS.

Story I.

I have heard of a king who made a sign to put a captive to death. The hapless one, in a state of despair, began in the dialect he spoke[62] to abuse the monarch, and use opprobrious language; as they say, "Every one, who washes his hands of life, utters all he has in his heart."

COUPLET.

He that despairs, gives license to his tongue,
As cats by dogs o'erpressed rush madly on.

COUPLET.

The hand, when flight remains not, in despair
Will grasp the point[63] of the sharp scymitar.

The King asked, "What does he say?" One of the vazīrs, who was of a good disposition,[64] said, "O my Lord! he says that [*Paradise, whose breadth equalleth the heavens and the earth, is prepared for the godly*], *who bridle their anger, and forgive men; for God loveth the*

[62] Literally, "he had." So also in Gaelic, "I have no English," for "I speak no English."

[63] M. Semelet translates سر *sar*, by "la poignée," which appears less correct. Sâdī says, "In despair the naked hand will seize the point of a sword held by a foe." Ross and Gladwin render سر *sar* by "edge," which is rather ذباب *ẕubāb* or لب *lab*.

[64] Richardson's Dictionary very strangely omits this meaning of محضر *maḥẓar*.

beneficent."[65] The King had compassion upon him, and gave up the intention of [spilling] his blood. Another vazīr, who was his rival, said, "It beseems not such as we are to speak aught but truth in the august presence of kings. This person reviled the king, and spoke unbecomingly." At this speech the King frowned and said, "That untruth of his is more acceptable to me than this truth which thou hast spoken; for that inclined[66] towards a good purpose, and this to malevolence; and the sages have said, 'Well-intentioned falsehood is better than mischief-exciting truth.'"

COUPLETS.

Words which beguile thee, but thy heart make glad,
Outvalue truth which makes thy temper sad.
They by whose counsels kings are ruled, 'twere shame
If good in all they said were not their aim.

This maxim was inscribed over the vaulted entrance of Farīdūn's[67] palace.

[65] This is a quotation from the Ḳur'ān, c. iii. v. 134; and it is very essential to note this, as the vazīr can hardly be said to have told a falsehood in putting a text enjoining mercy into the mouth of the captive; at least, there is a shade of difference between this and inventing something out of his own head. This very text is said to have been quoted to Ḥasan, grandson of Muḥammad, when a slave threw something boiling hot over him. At the first sentence, Ḥasan replied, "I am not angry"; at the second, "I forgive you"; and at the conclusion, viz., "God loveth the beneficent," he added, "Since it is so I give you your liberty and four hundred pieces of silver."—*Vide* Sale's Koran, p. 47, Note D.

[66] M. Semelet seems to think that روی *rūī* is here used in an uncommon sense, but the literal translation is simply "its countenance was towards good,"—an easy metaphor.

[67] Farīdūn was the seventh king of the first dynasty of Persian kings. He overcame the tyrant Ẓaḥḥāḳ, and imprisoned him in the mountain Damāvend.

DISTICHS.

The world, my brother! will abide with none,
By the world's Maker let thy heart be won.
Rely not, nor repose on this world's gain,
For many a son like thee she has reared and slain.
What matters, when the spirit seeks to fly,
If on a throne or on bare earth we die?

Story II.

One of the kings of Khurāsān[68] beheld, in a dream, Sulṭān Maḥmūd[69] Sabuktagīn, a hundred years after his death, when all his body had dissolved and become dust, save his eyes, which, as heretofore, moved in their sockets and saw. All the sages were at a loss for the interpretation of this, except a darwesh, who made his obeisance, and said, "His eyes still retain their sight, because his kingdom is in the possession of others."

VERSE.

Full many a chief of glorious name
  Beneath the ground now buried lies,
Yet not one token of his fame
  On earth's wide surface meets our eyes.
That aged form of life bereft,
  Which to earth's keeping they commit,
The soil devours; no bone is left,
  No trace remains to tell of it.
The glorious name of Nūshīrvān
  Lives in his deeds year after year.

[68] Khurāsān, according to Richardson's Dictionary, is the ancient Bactria, lying to the north of the Oxus, but at present it is used of Afghānistān, from the Bolān to Herāt, and the frontiers of Persia.

[69] Maḥmūd succeeded his father, Sabuktagīn, on the throne of Ghaznī, A.D. 997, and died after a reign of thirty-three years, and after he had conquered great part of Hindūstān, and taken the cities of Dihlī and Kanoj.

Do good, my friend! and look upon
This life as an occasion won
For acting well, ere yet we hear
Of thee, that thy career is done.

Story III.

I have heard of a prince who was of low stature and mean appearance, while his other brothers were tall and handsome. One day, his father surveyed him with loathing and contempt. The son had penetration enough to discover [his feelings], and said, "O my father! an intelligent dwarf is superior to an ignorant giant. Not every thing that is higher in stature is more valuable: '*The sheep is clean and the elephant unclean.*'

COUPLET.

Least of earth's mountain's is Sinai, yet all
In worth and rank with God beneath it fall.

STANZA.

Hast thou heard how the lean sage wittily
A bloated fool's presumption stilled?
'The steed of Arab race, though slim he be,
Transcends a stall with asses filled.'"

His sire laughed, and the Pillars of the State approved, and his brothers were mortally offended.

VERSE.

While a man's say is yet unsaid,
His weakness, merits, none descry;
Think not each waste's untenanted:
A sleeping tiger there may lie.

I have heard, that at that time a dangerous enemy to the King shewed himself. When the two armies encountered, the first person who galloped forward on the field of battle was that young prince, exclaiming,

STANZA.

I'm not he that, on the battle-day, my back will meet
thy sight;
I'm one whose head thou'lt follow 'mid the dust and
gory fight.
He must stake carelessly his blood who joins in war's
grim strife;
Who flies in war risks carelessly his fellow-soldier's life.

He said this, and rushed on the hostile array; after overthrowing several veteran warriors he came back. As soon as he presented himself to his father, he kissed the ground of obedience[70] and said,

STANZA.

Thou who my stature didst with scorn survey,
Think not that roughness marks the bold in war;
The slender courser in the battle-day
Will the fat stall-fed ox outvalue far.

They relate that the host of the enemy was numerous, and this side fewer. A body of the latter prepared to fly; the young prince uttered a shout and said, "O men! exert yourselves, that ye may not be clothed in the dress of women." The horsemen were inspired by his words with increased ardour, and made a simultaneous charge. I have heard that on that day they obtained a victory over the enemy. The King kissed his head and his eyes and embraced him, and each day entertained a stronger regard for him until he made him his heir. His brothers envied him, and put poison in his food. His sister saw it from a window, and closed the casement sharply. The young prince, by his acuteness, understood her meaning, and drew back his hand from the food, and said, "It is impossible that men of merit should perish, and those who have none should occupy their places."

[70] This expression is a very common one. It simply means, "kissed the ground obediently."

COUPLET.

What though the phœnix from the world take flight,
'Neath the owl's shadow none will ere alight.

They acquainted the father with this circumstance. He sent for the brothers and gave them a fitting reproof. Afterwards he assigned to each a suitable portion of his dominions, so that faction subsided and discord was appeased. In relation to this[71] they have said, that "Ten darweshes may sleep under one blanket, but one country cannot contain two kings."

STANZA.

The man of God with half his loaf content,
To darweshes the remnant will present;
But though a king seven regions should subdue,
He'll still another conquest keep in view.

Story IV.

A horde of Arabian robbers had fixed themselves on the summit of a mountain, and had stopped the passage of caravans, and the inhabitants of the country were in terror of their ambuscades, and the forces of the Sulṭān were repulsed by them, because they had possessed themselves of an inaccessible retreat in the crest of the mountain, and made it their refuge and place of abode. The governors of provinces in that direction took counsel as to the means of getting rid of the annoyance they

[71] Gladwin leaves the از اینجا *az īnjā*, untranslated. M. Semelet translates it simply by "et." Ross inserts, "but the ferment was increased," as an explanation. Hence it appears to me that all the translators have missed the right meaning of the concluding passage, which I am of opinion is simply an explanation of how the discord subsided, viz.: because each brother had a separate kingdom allotted to him. To suppose, with Ross, that the discord increased, would give a singularly abrupt termination to the story.

occasioned, saying,[72] "If this band maintain themselves any time in this fashion, resistance to them will become impossible."

DISTICHS.

A single arm may now uptear
A tree if lately planted there;
But if it for a time you leave,
No engine could its roots upheave.
A spade may the young rill restrain,
Whose channel, swollen [by storms and rain]
The elephant attempts in vain.

They came to the decision[73] to depute a person to reconnoitre them: and these watched their opportunity until the robbers made a foray on a tribe and their hold was evacuated, when they despatched a small body of experienced veterans to conceal themselves in a defile of the mountain. At night, when the robbers returned, having accomplished their expedition, and brought back their spoil, they laid aside their arms and deposited their booty. The first enemy that attacked them was sleep.[74] As soon as a watch[75] of the night had passed—

COUPLET.

The solar orb sank down in night's thick gloom,
As, in the fish-maw, Jonas found a tomb.[76]

[72] I think M. Semelet has done well in supplying كه *kih* here, and should wish it to be supplied in my edition of the text.

[73] Literally, "the word was fixed on this," a Persianism which must be freely rendered.

[74] There should be a full stop at بود *būd*, and a comma at بگذشت *ba-guzasht*. M. Semelet's punctuation is preferable to that of my edition, which is copied from Gladwin's.

[75] That is, at nine o'clock, since the night is reckoned from six p.m., and each watch is of three hours' duration.

[76] This is certainly a strange comparison. It seems to me a simile with the slenderest possible thread of similarity.

The valiant men leapt forth from their ambuscade and bound the hands of all of them, one after the other, behind their backs. In the morning they brought them to the palace of the king. He gave a sign to put them all to death. It happened that among them was a stripling, the fruit of whose youthful prime was but just ripening, and the bloom of the rose-garden of whose cheek had just expanded. One of the vazīrs kissed the foot of the king's throne, and bowed the face of intercession to the ground and said, "This child has not yet tasted the fruit of the garden of life, nor reaped enjoyment from the flower of his youth. I rely on the clemency and virtues of his Majesty, that he will oblige his slave by sparing his life." The King looked displeased at these words, and his lofty understanding did not approve them, and he said,

COUPLET.

"The good in vain their rays will pour
On those whose hearts are bad at core.
T' instruct the base will fail at last,
As walnuts on a dome you cast.[77]

It is better to cut off their race and tribe, and more advisable to extirpate them root and branch;[78] since, to extinguish a fire and to leave the embers, and to kill a serpent and preserve its young, are not the acts of wise men.

STANZA.

What though life's water from the clouds descend,
Thou'lt ne'er pluck fruit from off the willow-bough;
Not on the base thy precious moments spend,
Thou'lt ne'er taste sugar from the reed, I trow."

[77] If you throw walnuts on a dome they will fall down again, and perhaps on your own head; such is the meaning of this strange, but frequently occurring simile.

[78] Literally, "root and foundation," which corresponds to our expression as used in the text.

The vazīr heard these words, and, willing or not, assented to them, and extolled the excellence of the king's judgment and said, "What my lord *(may his dominion be eternal!)* has been pleased to say is the essence of truth: for had he been reared in the bond of the society of those evil persons he would have become one of them. However, your slave is in hopes that he will receive his education in the society of good men, and will adopt the character of the wise, since he is yet but a child, and the rebellious and perverse habits of those bandits have not fixed themselves in his nature; and in the traditions of the Prophet [it is said] "*There is no person born but assuredly he is begotten* [with a natural disposition] *to the faith of Islām; then his parents make a Jew of him, or a Christian, or a Magian.*

STANZA.

Lot's wife consorted with the unjust, and she
Quenched in her race the light of prophecy.
And the cave-sleepers'[79] dog sometime remained
With good men, and the rank of man attained."

When he had thus spoken, a number of the councillors of state united with him in intercession, so that the king abstained from shedding his blood and said, "I have spared his life, though I disapprove of it."

QUATRAIN.

Knowest thou what Zāl to valiant Rustam said?
Deem not thy foeman weak, without resource;
Full many a rill, from tiny springlet fed,
Sweeps off the camel in its onward course.

In short, the vazīr took the youth to his house and reared him delicately, and appointed a learned preceptor

[79] For an account of the Seven Sleepers who fell asleep in a cave near Ephesus in the reign of the Emperor Decius A.D. 253, and awoke A.D. 408, under that of Theodosius the Younger, *vide* the Ḳur'ān, c. 18, and M. Semelet's notes on this passage of the Gulistān.

to instruct him, who taught him elegant address and quickness in repartee, and all the manners fit for the service of kings, so that he was viewed with approbation by his compeers. At length the vazīr related somewhat of his abilities and good qualities to his Majesty the king, saying, "The instruction of the wise has produced an effect upon him, and has expelled from his disposition his former ignorance." The king smiled at these words and said,

COUPLET.

"The wolf's whelp will at last a wolf become,
Though from his birth he finds with man a home."

After this, two years passed away, and a set of dissolute fellows in the quarter where he lived joined themselves to him, and formed a league with him, so that at a favourable opportunity he slew the vazīr with his two sons, and carried off an immense booty, and took the place of his father in the robber's cave, and became an avowed rebel. They acquainted the king. The king seized the hand of amazement with his teeth,[80] and said,

VERSE.

"Who can from faulty iron good swords frame?
Teaching, O Sage! lends not the worthless worth.
The rain, whose bounteous nature's still the same,
Gives flowers in gardens, thorns in salt land birth.
Salt ground will not the precious spikenard bear;
Waste not thereon the seed of thy emprise:
Who benefits on evil men confer,
Upon the good no less heap injuries."

Story V.

I saw at the gate of the palace of Ughlamish[81] the son of an officer endowed with intellect, quickness of

[80] Orientals represent surprise by biting the fore-finger.

[81] Ughlamish was the son of the celebrated Tartar conqueror, Jangīz Khān, and reigned towards the year 656 of the Hijrah.

parts, understanding and sagacity beyond description. Even from the time of his childhood the signs of greatness were found on his forehead, and the rays of luminousness visible and distinct in his countenance, and many hearts were enamoured of him.

COUPLET.

And high above his head shone lustrously
The star of wisdom and of majesty.

In short, he became a favourite of the Sulṭān, for he possessed beauty of person and perfection of mind: and the sages have said, "Wealth consists in talent, not in goods; greatness, in understanding, not in age." His compeers grew envious of him, and accused him of treason, and used fruitless endeavours to put him to death.

HEMISTICH.

While friends are true what can the foe effect?

The king asked him, "What is the cause of their hostility towards you?" He replied, "I have satisfied all who are under the shadow of the royal dominion, except the envious, who cannot be contented, except by the waning of my good fortune. May the wealth and auspicious destiny of my lord remain perpetual!"

VERSE.

This can I do—inflict distress on none;
Envy 's its own distress—what can I there?
Perish, O envious one! for thus alone
Canst thou escape from thy self-nurtured care.
The wretched long to witness the decay
Of fortune's favours to the happier few:
But, though the bat be visionless by day,
Can we for this a fault or failing view
In the sun's fount of light? 'T were better far
A thousand of such eyes no vision knew,
Than the bright radiance of the sun to mar.

Story VI.

They relate of one of the kings of Persia, that he had extended the hand of oppression upon the property of his subjects, and had entered on a course of tyranny and injustice. The people were reduced to extremity by the snares of his cruelty, and from the anguish of his tyranny took the road of exile. As the people diminished, the resources of the State were impaired, and the treasury remained empty, and enemies pressed him on every side.

STANZA.

He who in adversity would succour have,
Let him be generous while he rests secure.
Thou that reward'st him not, wilt lose thy slave,
Though wearing now thy ring.[82] Wouldst thou secure
The stranger as thy slave, be to him kind;
And by thy courtesy enslave his mind.

One day they read, in his presence, the book of the Shāh-nāmah, in the part which relates to the decline of the empire of Ẕaḥḥāḳ, and the reign of Farīdūn. The vazīr asked the king, saying, "Farīdūn possessed not treasure, territory, or troops; in what manner was the kingdom secured in his favour?" He replied, "Just as you have heard; the people rallied round him from attachment to him, and gave him their support: he gained the kingdom." The vazīr rejoined, "O king! since sovereignty is acquired by the people's resorting to one, why dost thou scatter the people from thee? unless, indeed, thou dost not purpose to be a king."

COUPLET.

Since monarchs by their troops their States control,
Cherish thy host, O king! with all thy soul.

[82] I have not translated بگوش *ba-gūsh*, "in the ear." The ring in the ear is the badge of servitude in the East.

The king asked, "What causes the soldiery and the people to rally round you?" He replied, "A king must be just, that they may resort to him, and merciful, that they may sit secure under the shadow of his greatness—and thou hast neither of these two qualities."

DISTICHS.

Kingcraft yokes not with tyranny:
The wolf cannot the shepherd be.
Tyrants who on their people fall,
Sap their own State's foundation-wall.

The counsel of the faithful vazīr suited not the king's temper. He ordered him to be bound and sent him to prison. No long time had elapsed when the sons of the king's uncle rose in revolt, and arrayed an army against him, and demanded the kingdom of their father. Numbers who had been driven to despair by his tyranny, and were dispersed, gathered round them and lent them their support, so that the kingdom passed from his hands.

STANZA.

The king who dares his subjects to oppress,
In day of need will find his friend a foe—
A mighty one. Soothe, rather, and caress
Thy people; and in war-time thou wilt know
No fear of foes; for a just potentate
The nation's self will be a host to guard the State.

Story VII.

A king was seated in a vessel with a Persian slave. The slave had never before beheld the sea, nor experienced the inconvenience of a ship.[83] He began to

[83] M. Semelet explains this as meaning of "sea-sickness;" but I think the context shews it has a more general meaning. It is evident the vessel was floating quietly along, so that when the slave was thrown in he was not swept away, but easily reached the rudder.

weep and bemoan himself, and a tremor pervaded his frame. In spite of their endeavours to soothe him, he would not be quieted. The comfort of the king was disturbed by him; but they could not devise a remedy. In the ship there was a philosopher,[84] who said, "If you command, I will silence him." The king answered, "It would be the greatest favour." The philosopher directed them to cast the slave into the sea. He underwent several submersions, and they then took him by the hair and dragged him towards the ship. He clung to the rudder of the vessel with both hands, and they then pulled him on board again. When he had come on board, he seated himself in a corner and kept quiet. The king approved, and asked, "What was the secret of this expedient?" The philosopher replied, "At first he had not tasted the agony of drowning, and knew not the value of the safety of a vessel. In the same manner a person who is overtaken by calamity learns to value a state of freedom from ill."[84]

STANZA.

Sated, thou wilt my barley-loaf repel.
  She whom I love ill-favoured seems to thee.
To Eden's Hourīs[85] Īrāf would seem hell:
  Hell's inmates ask—they'll call it heavenly

COUPLET.

Wide is the space 'twixt him who clasps his love,
And him whose eyes watch for the door to move.[86]

[84] I think Ross and Gladwin, as also M. Semelet, wrong in rendering حکیم *hakīm*, "a physician;" to tally with which the two former translate عافیت *āfiyat*, by "health." M. Semelet, on the contrary, very properly gives "*incolumitas*" as its equivalent.

[85] For the Hourīs, *vide* Sale's Koran, p. 393; and for Īrāf (or Purgatory), Sale, p. 111.

[86] In expectation of seeing his loved one come in.

Story VIII.

They said to Hurmuz Tājdār,[87] "What fault didst thou find in the vazīrs of thy father that thou didst command them to be imprisoned?" He replied, "I discovered no fault in them; but I saw that they had a boundless fear of me in their hearts, and that they had not entire confidence in my promise. I feared that through dread of injury to themselves they might attempt my destruction; wherefore I put into practice the maxim of the wise men who have said,

STANZA.

Thou who art wise, fear him who feareth thee,
Though thou like him a hundred wouldst despise:
Seest thou not, how in last extremity,
The cat will lacerate the leopard's eyes?
Hence, too, the snake the shepherd wounds; for he
Dreads the raised stone and down-crushed agonies."

Story IX.

One of the Arabian kings was sick in his old age, and the hope of surviving was cut off. Suddenly a horseman entered the portal, and brought good tidings, saying, "By the auspicious fortune of my lord we have taken such a castle, and the enemies are made prisoners, and the troops and peasantry in that quarter are entirely reduced to obedience." When the king heard this speech he heaved a cold sigh, and said, "These joyful tidings are not for me, but for my enemies; that is, the heirs of my crown."

[87] Hurmuz Tājdār, or "the crown-wearer," was so called because, wishing to dispense justice on all occasions himself, without the intervention of others between himself and his subjects, he continually wore the crown, to denote his readiness to discharge his kingly functions. He was the son of Nūshīrvān, and his tutor, Buzurchimihr, has been already mentioned in the Preface.

STANZA.

In this fond hope, dear life, alas! has waned:
That my heart's wish might not be wished in vain:
Hope, long delayed, is granted. Have I gained
Aught?—Nay. Life spent returns not back again.

STANZA.

Death's hand has struck the signal-drum;
Eyes! now obey your parting knell!
Hands, wrists, and arms, all members, come,
And bid a mutual, long farewell!
Hope's foe, Death, has me seized at last;
Once more, O friends! before me move;
In folly has my time been past:
May my regrets your warning prove!

Story X.

In a certain year I was engaged in devotion at the tomb of the Prophet Yaḥiya,[88] in the principal mosque of Damascus. It happened that one of the Arabian princes, who was notorious for his injustice, came as a pilgrim thither, performed his prayers, and asked [of God] what he stood in need of.

COUPLET.

The poor, the rich, alike must here adore:
The wealthier they, their need is here the more.

He then turned towards me and said, "On account of the generous character of darweshes, and the sincerity of their dealings, I ask you to give me the aid of your spirit, for I stand in dread of a powerful enemy." I

[88] St. John the Baptist, whose remains were said to be interred in a church at Damascus. After the conquest of Syria by the Musalmān, this church was converted into a mosque, and called the mosque of the tribe of Ummiyah.

replied, "Shew mercy[89] to thy weak subjects, that thou mayst not experience annoyance[89] from a puissant foe."

VERSE.

With the strong arm and giant grasp 'tis wrong
To crush the feeble, unresisting throng.
Who pities not the fallen, let him fear,
Lest, if he fall, no friendly hand be near.
Who sows ill actions and of blessing dreams,
Fosters vain phantasies and idly schemes.
Unstop thy ears, thy people's wants relieve,
If not, a day[90] shall come when all their rights receive.

DISTICHS.

All Adam's race are members of one frame;
Since all, at first, from the same essence came.
When by hard fortune one limb is oppressed,
The other members lose their wonted rest:
If thou feel'st not for others' misery,
A son of Adam is no name for thee.

Story XI.

A darwesh, whose prayers were accepted with God, made his appearance in Baghdād. They told this to Ḥajjāj-bin-Yūsuf,[91] who sent for him, and said, "Offer up a good prayer for me." The darwesh said, "O God! take away his life." "For God's sake!" asked he, "what prayer is this?" He replied, "It is a good prayer for thee, and for all Musalmān."

[89] There is here a rhyme in the words رحمت, *raḥmat*, and زحمت *zaḥmat*, which cannot be preserved in English.

[90] That is, the day of resurrection.

[91] Ḥajjāj-bin-Yūsuf was the Governor of Arabian Îrāķ, under the Khalīfah Âbd-ul-malik, A.H. 65. He was notorious for his oppression.

DISTICHS.

Oppressor! troubler of the poor!
How soon shall this thy mart[92] be o'er!
What good will empire be to thee?
Better thy death than tyranny.

Story XII.

An unjust king asked a religious man, "What sort of devotion is to be esteemed highest?" He replied, "For thee to sleep at noon,[93] in order that in this state thou mightest cease for an instant to oppress mankind."

STANZA.

A tyrant lay, his noontide slumber taking:
Said I—'Tis best this scourge should sleeping lie;
And he whose sleep is better than his waking,
'Tis best for such an evil one to die."

Story XIII.

I have heard of a prince who had turned night into day, and had drunk wine all night; and, in the height of his intoxication, uttered this couplet,

COUPLET.

"Of all my bright and gladsome moments the gladdest is this one;
When of good or ill I reck not, and I harbour fear of none."

A darwesh, entirely destitute of clothing, lay beneath his palace, outside, in the cold, and exclaimed,

92 The termination of life is here, as often elsewhere, compared to the closing of a market.

93 Ross renders it, "to sleep till noon." If any one prefers this rendering I have nothing to say against it, except that perhaps تا *tā* would be used in place of the *izāfat* were it correct. The noontide-sleep is customary in hot climates.

COUPLET.

"Thou with whom none may in success compare,
Grant thou art griefless; say, Have I no care?"

The king was pleased with this address. He held out from the window a purse containing a thousand dīnārs, and said, "O darwesh! hold thy lap." He replied, "Whence shall I get a lap, I who have not a garment?" The king's compassion for his wretched state increased; he added to the purse a rich robe, which he sent out to him. The darwesh, in a short time, spent and squandered that sum of money, and came back.

COUPLET.

Money abides not in the palm of those who careless live,[94]
Nor patience in the lover's heart, nor water in the sieve.

At a time when the king did not concern himself about him, they announced his state. He was displeased, and his countenance changed at this intelligence. And for this reason men of sagacity and experience have said, that it is requisite to beware of the violence and despotic temper of kings; since for the most part their high thoughts are engaged with the arduous affairs of State, and they will not endure the vulgar throng.

DISTICHS.

Let him not hope kings' favours, who omits
To watch the moment which his prayer befits.
Till thou observest the just time for speech
Do not by useless words thy cause impeach.

The king said, "Drive away this impudent and prodigal mendicant who, in so short a time, has dissipated such a treasure, and does not know that the royal treasury is to supply morsels to the poor, not feasts to the fraternity of devils."

[94] Wandering devotees, who have renounced the world and are, therefore, careless.

COUPLET.

The dolt, who in bright day sets up a camphor light,
Soon thou wilt see his lamp devoid of oil at night.

One of the vazīrs, who was a man of prudence, said, "O my lord! to such persons one ought to give an allowance, by instalments, of what is just enough for their support, that they may not become lavish in their expenses. But as to what thou commandest, namely, to treat him with violence, and to drive him away, it is not consonant with true generosity to make one expect favour and then to wound his spirit with disappointment."

COUPLET.

Ope not thyself the door of greediness;
But roughly it to close beseems thee less.

STANZA.

None see the Ḥijāz pilgrims, faint with thirst,
Crowd to the margin of the briny sea:
Where'er the fountains of sweet water burst
Their way; there men, and birds, and ants will be.

Story XIV.

One of the former kings showed remissness in protecting his dominions, and treated his army with severity. On the appearance of a powerful enemy, all turned their backs.

COUPLETS.

Soldiers, from whom the State withholds its gold,
Will from the scymitar their hands withhold.
What valour in war's ranks will he display,
Whose hand is empty on the reckoning day?

I had a friendship with one of those who had declined service. I reproached him and said, "He is base and unthankful, and vile and ungrateful, who, on a slight change of fortune, deserts his old master, and lays aside the obligations of favours received for years." He replied, "If I was to tell you [how matters stood] you would acquit me. Suppose my horse had no barley, and my saddle-cloth was in pawn; and one cannot valiantly risk one's life for a Sulṭān who is miserly to his soldiers."

COUPLET.

Give thy troops gold that for thee they may die;
Else they'll go seek a better destiny.

COUPLET.

The well-fed warrior will with ardour fight;
The starved will be as ardent in his flight.

Story XV.

One of the vazīrs had been dismissed from office, and had entered the community of darweshes, and the blessed influence of their society took effect upon him, and his peace of mind was restored to him. The king's heart became again reconciled to him, and he offered him employment. The vazīr declined it, and said, "Discharge is better than charge."

QUATRAIN.

Those who in safety's quiet nook repose
Have stopped the teeth of dogs and tongues of men;
Far from the slander and the reach of foes,
They tear their paper and destroy their pen.

The king said, "It is most certain that I have need of a man of consummate wisdom, who may be suitable for the councils of the State." He replied, "The sign of a man of consummate wisdom is not to engage in such matters."

COUPLET.

The Humā[95] is for this of birds the king:
It feeds on bones and hurts no living thing.

APOLOGUE.

They said to a lynx,[96] "How didst thou come to choose service in attending on the lion?" He replied, "Because I feed on the remains of his quarry, and pass my life in security from the malice of my enemies under the shelter of the awe which he inspires." They rejoined, "Now that thou hast come under the shadow of his protection, and avowest thy thankfulness for his favours; why dost thou not approach nearer, that he may include thee in the circle of his especial favourites, and reckon thee among his devoted adherents?" He replied, "I am not so secure from his violence."

COUPLET.

Though for a hundred years the Guebre feeds his flame,
Did he once fall therein, 'twould feed on him the same.

Sometimes it happens that the counsellor of his majesty the Sulṭān is rewarded with gold, and at another time, it may be that he loses his head; and the sages have said, "You ought to be on your guard against the changeableness of the temper of kings; for, sometimes they are displeased at a respectful salutation, and at other times they bestow dresses of honour in return for abuse:" and they have observed that, "Great facetious-

[95] The Humā is the Phœnix; or, as D'Herbelôt tells us, a sort of eagle which feeds on bones, and is therefore called by the Persians Ustukhwān Kh'ur, the Ossifrage. This bird, from its not injuring other animals, is thought of happy augury, and from its name is derived the Persian adjective همایون *humāyūn*, "auspicious."

[96] The other translators avoid rendering this word, and call it the Siyāh Gūsh. The literal meaning is, "black ear."

ness is an accomplishment in courtiers; but a fault in wise men."

COUPLET.

To keep thy place and dignity be thine ;
To courtiers wit and pleasantry resign.

Story XVI.

One of my companions came to me with complaints of his ill-fortune, saying, "I have but little means of subsistence, and a large family, and I cannot support the burthen of poverty; it has frequently entered my head that I would go to another country, in order that, live how I may, no one may know of my welfare or the reverse.

COUPLET.

Full many a starving wight has slept[97] unknown ;
Full many a spirit fled that none bemoan.

Again, I am in dread of the rejoicing of my enemies, lest they should laugh scoffingly at me behind my back, and impute my exertions in behalf of my family to a want of humanity, and say,

STANZA.

See now, that wretch devoid of shame ! for him
Fair fortune's face will smile not, nor has smiled ;
Himself he pampers in each selfish whim,
And leaves his hardships to his wife and child.

And I know something, as you are aware, of the science of accounts ; if by your interest a means [of subsistence] could be afforded me, which might put me at ease, I should not be able to express my gratitude sufficiently to the end of my life." I replied, "O my friend ! the king's service has two sides to it,—hope of a livelihood, and terror for one's life ; and it is contrary

[97] Here used for "died."

to the opinion of the wise, through such a hope to expose oneself to such a fear.

STANZA.

None in the poor man's hut demand
Tax on his garden or his land.
Be thou content with toil and woe,
Or with thy entrails feed the crow."

He replied, "These words that thou hast spoken do not apply to my case, nor hast thou returned an answer to my question. Hast thou not heard what they have said : 'that the hand of every one who chooses to act dishonestly trembles in rendering the account'?"

COUPLET.

God favours those who follow the right way,
From a straight road I ne'er saw mortal stray.

"And the sages have said, 'Four kinds of persons are in deadly fear of four others: the brigand of the Sulṭān, and the thief of the watchman, and the adulterer of the informer, and the harlot of the superintendent of police;' and what fear have those of the settling, whose accounts are clear?"

STANZA.

Wouldst thou confine thy rival's power to harm
Thee at discharge? then while thy trust remains,
Be not too free; none shall thee then alarm.
'Tis the soiled raiment which, to cleanse from stains,
Is struck on stones and asks the washer's pains.

I answered, "Applicable to thy case is the story of that fox which people saw running away in violent trepidation.[98] Some one said to him, 'What calamity has happened to cause thee so much alarm?' He replied, 'I have heard they are going to impress the camel.' They rejoined, 'O Shatter-brain! what connection has a camel with thee, and what resemblance hast thou to it?' He

[98] Literally, "falling and rising."

answered, 'Peace! for if the envious should, to serve their own ends, say, "This is a camel," and I should be taken, who would care about my release so as to inquire into my condition? and before the antidote is brought from Īrāķ, the person who is bitten by the snake may be dead.'[99] And in the same way thou possessest merit, and good faith, and piety, and uprightness; but the envious are in ambush, and the accusers are lurking in corners. If they should misrepresent thy fair qualities, and thou shouldest incur the king's displeasure and fall into disgrace, who would have power, in that situation of affairs, to speak for thee? I look upon it as thy best course to secure the kingdom of contentment, and to abandon the idea of preferment, since the wise have said,

COUPLET.

'Upon the sea 'tis true is boundless gain:
Wouldst thou be safe, upon the shore remain.'"

When my friend heard these words he was displeased, and his countenance was overcast, and he began to utter words which bore marks of his vexation, saying, "What judgment, and profit, and understanding, and knowledge is this? and the saying of the sages has turned out correct, in that they have said, 'Those are useful friends who continue so when we are in prison; for at our table all our enemies appear friends.'

STANZA.

Think not thy friend one who in fortune's hour
Boasts of his friendship and fraternity.
Him I call friend who sums up all his power
To aid thee in distress and misery."

[99] The ترياق *tiryāķ* is an antidote against poison. Some think it is treacle; and others the bezoar-stone. Others would derive it from *θήρ* "a noxious beast," and *ἀκέομαι* "to heal." This sentence is a proverb in common use.

I saw that he was troubled, and that my advice was taken in bad part. I went to the president of finance,[100] and, in accordance with our former intimacy, I told him the case; in consequence of which he appointed my friend to some trifling office. Some time passed away; they saw the amenity of his disposition, and approved his excellent judgment. His affairs prospered, and he was appointed to a superior post; and in the same manner the star of his prosperity continued to ascend until he reached the summit of his desires, and became a confidential servant of his Majesty the Sulṭān, *and the pointed-at by men's fingers, and one in whom the ministers of State placed their confidence.* I rejoiced at his secure position and said,

COUPLET.

Have no doubts because of trouble nor be thou discomfited;
For the water of life's fountain[101] springeth from a gloomy bed.

COUPLET.

Ah! ye brothers of misfortune! be not ye with grief oppressed,
Many are the secret mercies which with the All-bounteous rest.

COUPLET.

Sit not sad because that Time a fitful aspect weareth;
Patience is most bitter, yet most sweet the fruit it beareth.

[100] ديوان *dīwān* may, as M. Semelet remarks, have several meanings; but the one evidently intended here is what I have given; for Sâdī's friend, we are told, had a talent for accounts.

[101] Muḥammadans believe in a fountain of life, to taste one drop of which bestows immortality. They say that خضر *Khiẓr*, or Elias, who, they suppose, was the general of the first Alexander, discovered this fountain, and drank of it, and hence he can never die.

During this interval I happened to accompany a number of my friends on a journey to Ḥijāz.[102] When I returned from the pilgrimage to Makkah he came out two stages to meet me. I saw that his outward appearance was one of distress, and that he wore the garb of a darwesh. I said, "What is thy condition?" He replied, "Just as thou saidst: a party became envious of me, and accused me of disloyal conduct; and the king did not deign to inquire minutely into the explanation of the circumstances; and my former companions, and even my sincere friends, forbore to utter the truth, and forgot their long intimacy.

STANZA.

When one has fallen from high heaven's decree,
The banded world will trample on his head;
Then fawn and fold their hands respectfully,
When they behold his steps by fortune led.

In short, I was subjected to all kinds of tortures till within this week that the good tidings of the safety of the pilgrims[103] arrived, when they granted me release from grievous durance, with the confiscation of my hereditary estate." I said, "At that time thou wouldest not receive my suggestion, that the service of the king is like a sea-voyage, at once profitable and fraught with peril; where thou either wilt acquire a treasure, or perish amid the billows.

COUPLET.

Or with both hands the merchant shall one day embrace the gold;
Or by the waves his lifeless form shall on the strand be rolled."

I did not think it right to lacerate his mental wounds

[102] Arabia Petræa.
[103] The pilgrims to Makkah.

further, or to sprinkle them with salt. I confined myself to these two couplets and said,

STANZA.

"Knewest thou not that thou wouldst see the chains upon thy feet,
When a deaf ear thou turnedst on the counsels of the wise?
If the torture of the sting thou canst not with courage meet,
Place not thy finger in the hole where the sullen scorpion lies."

Story XVII.

Certain persons were associates of mine, whose external conduct was adorned with rectitude. A great personage entertained a strong opinion in their favour, and had settled a pension upon them. But one of them did an act which was unbecoming the character of a darwesh. The favour of that person was estranged, and their market was depreciated.[104] I wished to set my companions free as regarded their allowance, and resolved to wait on their patron. The porter would not suffer me to enter, and treated me with insolence. I excused him, in accordance with what they have said,

STANZA.

"To door of king, or minister, or peer,
Draw thou not nigh unless with patrons girt;
For if a poor man at the gate appear,
Warders his collar seize, and dogs his skirt."

As soon as the favourite attendants of that great man were informed of my condition, they brought me in with respect, and assigned me a place of distinction. However, I submissively seated myself lower, and said,

[104] That is, their supplies were cut off.

COUPLET.

"Permit me, a slave of low degree,
To sit among those who wait on thee."

He replied, "My God! my God! what room is there for this speech?"

COUPLET.

What though my head and eyelids thou shouldst press,
I'd bear thy love-airs for thy loveliness.

In short, I seated myself, and conversed on all subjects, till the circumstance of my friends' disgrace was introduced. I said,

STANZA.

"What did the Lord of past munificence
See in his servants that he deemed them vile?
God's rule is boundless, and, with love immense,
He notes our sins, but us sustains meanwhile."

These words were approved by the prince, and he ordered that they should make ready the means of maintenance for my friends, according to the former custom, and that they should make up to them the supplies which they would have received during the time their allowance was stopped. I returned thanks for this favour, and kissed the ground of obedience, and asked pardon for my boldness; and as I was departing I said these words,

STANZA.

"The Kâbah[105] is the place of answered prayer,
Therefore, from many a league the pilgrim throngs
To view its fane; from distant lands repair
The hurrying crowds. Thus, too, to thee belongs
Patience, with supplicants like me to bear;
For none cast stones at trees save fruit be there."

[105] The temple at Makkah.

Story XVIII.

A prince inherited from his father an immense treasure. He opened the hand of munificence, and did justice to his generous disposition, and lavished on his soldiers and subjects incalculable sums.

STANZA.

The aloes-tray, from which no fragrance came,
  If placed on fire, its inodorous state
Will change, more sweet than ambergris. So fame,
  Thou for thyself by generous deeds create;
  The unsown seed will never germinate.

One of his courtiers, who lacked discretion, began to admonish him, saying, "Former monarchs acquired this treasure by their exertions, and stored it up for a wise purpose. Hold back thy hand from this procedure, for emergencies are before thee and foes behind. It must not be that in time of need thou shouldst fail.

STANZA.

Expend thy treasure for thy people's sake,
  The share of each[106] would be a single grain;[107]
Rather from each a grain of silver take,
  And thou wilt thus each day a treasure gain."

The prince frowned at these words, which were not in unison with his sentiments, and said, "God (may He be honoured and glorified!) has made me sovereign of this realm, that I may gratify my own wants and be liberal to others. I am not a sentinel to keep guard over [what I have].

[106] In the original, "each father of a family."
[107] A grain of rice.

COUPLET.

Ḳārūn [108] with forty treasures was of life bereft;
But Nūshīrwān's still ruling in the fame he left."

Story XIX.

They relate that once, during a hunting expedition, they were preparing for Nūshīrwān the Just some game, as roast meat. There was no salt; and they despatched a slave to a village to bring some. Nūshīrwān said, "Pay for the salt you take, in order that it may not become a custom, and the village be ruined." They said, "What harm will this little quantity do?" He replied, "The origin of injustice in the world was at the first small, and every one that came added to it, until it reached this magnitude."

STANZA.

If but one apple from the peasant's field [109]
The king should eat, his men uproot the tree;
And does the Sulṭān but his sanction yield
T' extort five eggs—his followers will see
Cause with a thousand pullets to make free. [110]

COUPLET.

Not always will the wicked tyrant live;
The curse upon him will for aye survive.

108 Ḳārūn is said by Oriental writers to have been the first cousin and brother-in-law of Moses, whose sister he is said to have married. Moses taught him alchemy, by which he acquired vast riches; but, being called upon by Moses to pay a fortieth for religious purposes, he refused, and endeavoured to suborn false evidence against the lawgiver, who, therefore, caused him to be swallowed up by the earth.

109 In the original the word is باغ *bāgh*, "garden."

110 In the original, "put on the spit."

Story XX.

I have heard of a revenue-collector who was ruining the peasantry in order to fill the treasury of the Sulṭān, in ignorance of that saying of the wise, which they have uttered: "Whosoever afflicts the creatures of the Most High God in order to win the regard of a creature, the Most High God will raise those same creatures against him to destroy him utterly."

COUPLET.

Flames cannot with such speed wild rue consume,
As tyrants perish by the wronged heart's fume.[111]

POINTED ILLUSTRATION.

They say that among all animals the lion is chief, and the ass lowest; and yet the wise are agreed that an ass that bears burdens is better than a lion that tears men.

DISTICHS.

True, the poor ass is dull; but then
For carrying loads 'tis dear to men.
The carrier ox, the patient ass,
Man's tyrant, cruel man surpass.

Some of his misdeeds became known to the king, who tortured him on the rack, and put him to death, with a variety of torments.

STANZA.

The Sulṭān's praise thou canst not gain
Till thou canst win his people's heart:
Wouldst thou God's pardoning grace obtain?
Then to his creatures good impart.

One of those who had been oppressed by him passed near him, and looked on his agonies, and said,

[111] I have advisedly used this expression (though it makes but indifferent poetry), as it is the exact equivalent to the Persian دود دل *dūd-i dil.* Ross has a ridiculous mistake here, for which see preface to this Translation.

STANZA.

"Not every one who with strong arm bears sway,
Can boast of his extortions in the end;
To swallow the rough bone thou mayst some way
Devise; but once permit it to descend
Down to the navel, 'twill thy belly rend."

Story XXI.

They relate that an oppressor smote a pious man on the head with a stone. The darwesh had not power to retaliate; but he kept the stone carefully beside him until a season when the king was wroth with that officer,[112] and confined him in a pit. The darwesh came and smote him on the head with that stone. He said, "Who art thou? and why hast thou struck me on the head with the stone?" The darwesh replied, "I am such a one, and this stone is the same which, on such a day, thou didst cast at me." The other rejoined, "Where hast thou been this long while?" The darwesh answered, "I was awed by thy rank; now that I behold thee in this dungeon I took advantage of the opportunity: as the wise have said,

DISTICHS.

'Seest thou that fortune crowns the unworthy?—then
Choose thou submission too, with wiser men.[113]

[112] Ross makes a curious mistake here, which is adverted to in the preface to this Translation, *q.v.* M. Semelet prefers reading, instead of بر آن لشكري *bar ān lashkarī*, برو *bar ū*, but as it occurs a few lines before in the preceding story, and in a similar description, I should retain it.

[113] M. Semelet rightly observes that there is an ellipse here, which I have supplied by the words "Choose thou," and a slight modification of the sense of the second line.

Hast thou not sharp and rending claws? then yield—
For so 'tis best—to beasts, the battle-field.
He that has grappled with a hand of steel
Will, in his silver[114] arm, the anguish feel:
Wait thou till fortune shall his arm restrain;
Then, at thy will, thou mayst thy foeman brain.'"

Story XXII.

A certain king had a horrible disease, to repeat a description of which would not be agreeable. A body of Greek physicians unanimously decided that there was no remedy for the pain except the gall of a man possessed of certain qualities. The king ordered search to be made for him. They found a peasant-boy with the qualities which the physicians had mentioned. The king sent for his father and mother, and, by immense presents, made them content; and the Ḳāẓī gave his decision that it was lawful to shed the blood of one of the subjects to save the king's life. The executioner prepared to put him to death. The boy looked up to heaven and smiled. The king asked, "In this condition what place is there for laughter?" The boy replied, "Fathers and mothers are wont to caress their offspring, and complaints are carried before the Ḳāẓī, and justice is sought from kings; yet now my father and mother have, for the sake of worldly trifles, delivered me over to death, and the Ḳāẓī has given his sentence for my execution, and the Sulṭān looks for his own recovery in my destruction; save God Most High I have none to protect me.

COUPLET.

Where shall I from thy hand for succour flee?
'Gainst thine own power I'll justice seek from thee."

The king's heart was touched by these words; he wept,

114 سیمین *sīmīn*, "silvery," is often used to signify "delicate," when applied to the human form.

and said, "It is better for me to perish than to shed innocent blood." He kissed his head and eyes, embraced him, bestowed on him abundant presents, and set him free. They say, too, that the king recovered that same week.

STANZA.

Just thus that couplet I recall, as said,
On the Nile's bank, he of the elephant:
'Wouldst thou know what the ant feels 'neath thy tread?
Think if on thee my beast its foot should plant!'

Story XXIII.

One of the slaves of Amrūlais[115] had run away. Some persons went in pursuit of him, and brought him back. The vazīr bore him a grudge. He gave a sign to put him to death, that the other slaves might be deterred from acting similarly. The slave touched the ground with his head before Åmrū, and said,

COUPLET.

"Whate'er befalls me is most just, if thou think'st fit:
Command is thine; why should thy slave complain of it?

However, inasmuch as I have been reared by the bounty of thy family, I do not wish that in the resurrection thou shouldst be made to answer for my blood. If, then, thou desirest to put thy slave to death, at least do so in conformity with the law, that thou mayst not be called to account at the resurrection." The king asked, "How am I to interpret the law?" He replied, "Grant me permission to slay the vazīr, after which, in retaliation for his death, thou mayst order me to be executed." The king laughed, and said to the vazīr, "What dost thou advise?" He answered, "Sire! for the sake of the tomb of thy father, set free this rascal,

[115] The second Sulṭān of the dynasty of the Saffārides, who reigned in Fārs, A.H. 267.

that he may not plunge me also into misfortune. The fault is mine for slighting that saying of the wise, which they have thus delivered:

STANZA.

'When with a practised slinger thou wouldst fight,
Thou by thy folly thine own head wilt break:
Ere 'gainst thy foe thine arrow wings its flight,
See thou beyond his range position take.'"

Story XXIV.

A king of Zūzan [116] had a minister [117] of a beneficent disposition, and gracious presence, who was courteous to all, when in their company, and spoke well of them behind their backs. It happened that he did something which was disapproved in the sight of the king; who ordered him to be amerced and punished. The officers of the monarch were sensible of his former kindnesses, and pledged to requite them. Wherefore, while he was under their custody, they treated him with courtesy and attention, and forbore to inflict on him harshness or reproach.

STANZA.

Wouldst thou with foes have peace? whenever then
Thy enemy thee slanders absent, thou
To his face applaud him. Since evil men
Must [118] speak, and thou lov'st not their gall; fill now
Their mouths with sweets; thus them to speak allow.

[116] Ross strangely translates this "King Zūzan;" on what ground I am at a loss to conjecture. I concur with M. Semelet, Gladwin, and Gentius, in regarding زوزن *Zūzan* as the name of a city, either in Khurāsān, between Hirāt and Nishāpur, or in Khuzistān, in which case it would be the capital of the Susiana of the Greeks.

[117] We may so render خواجه *khwājah,* as is evident from the context. Perhaps, however, it may mean "eunuch."

[118] Instead of سخن آخر *sukhan-i ākhir,* I am clearly of

He acquitted himself of a portion of that which furnished matter for the king's orders[119] respecting him, and remained in prison for the rest. One of the neighbouring princes sent a secret message to him to the following effect: "The worth of such excellence [as thine] has not been appreciated by the sovereigns of those parts; nay, it has been rewarded with disgrace. If the precious mind of such a one *(may God prosper him at the last!)* should incline towards us, the utmost endeavours will be used to show him respect; for the nobles of this country will rejoice to see him; and await an answer to this letter." When the minister was acquainted with the purport of the letter, he was alarmed at his danger, lest, if it should become known, some disastrous results might take place. He immediately wrote a short answer, as he thought advisable, on the back of the letter, and sent it off. One of the king's attendants was apprised of this circumstance, and informed the king of it, saying, "Such a one, whom thou commandedst to be imprisoned, holds a correspondence with the neighbouring princes." The king was incensed, and ordered inquiry to be made into the matter. They seized the courier, and read his despatches. These were written to this effect: "The favourable opinion of your Highnesses exceeds your servant's merits, and it is impossible for him to accept the offer which you have condescended to make, inasmuch as he has been nurtured by the fostering care of this royal house; and, for a slight withdrawal of favour,

opinion that we ought to read سخن آخر *su<u>kh</u>an ā<u>kh</u>ir*, and render the words as above. Why should the "last word" be the only one that needs sweetening?

119 Several passages, among which this is one, prove that the meaning "reproof," "censure," ought to be admitted into the dictionaries under the word خطاب *<u>kh</u>iṭāb*.

he cannot act ungratefully towards his benefactor: since they have said,

COUPLET.

'He whose unceasing favours are bestowed on thee,
Excuse his life's sole act of tyranny.'"

The king was pleased with his gratitude. He bestowed on him rewards, and a dress of honour, and asked his forgiveness, saying, "I have committed a mistake, and I have made thee suffer though innocent." He replied, "Sire! your slave sees no fault in you in this matter; but the decree of God Most High was so that evil should befal this slave; wherefore it is better it should come from your hand, since you possess the claim of former benefits conferred upon him, and of innumerable kindnesses: and the sages have said,

DISTICHS.

'Art thou by creatures injured?—do not grieve;
None joy or pain from creatures e'er receive.
Know that by God both friends and foes are given
Yes! for the hearts of both are swayed by Heaven.
What though the arrows from the bowstring fly,
The wise well know the archer's agency.'"

Story XXV.

One of the Arabian kings commanded the officers of his exchequer to double the allowance of a certain person, whatever it might be, saying, "He is regular in attendance at court, and ready at command; while the other servants are all engaged in amusements, and neglect their duty." A wise person heard it, and said, "The elevation of the different ranks of creatures in the court of God (may He be honoured and glorified!) is analogous to this."

VERSE.

If for two mornings one attends the king,
Doubtless the third a favouring glance will bring:
So in God's court; who worship truly there
Hope to be not excluded in despair.

DISTICHS.

Greatness consists in bowing to God's will;
Rebellion proves thee baffled, outcast still.
Who bears impressed the tokens of the just,
Will place his head submissive in the dust.

STORY XXVI.

They relate of an oppressor that he purchased fire-wood of poor men by force and gave it to the rich gratuitously.[120] A devout person passed by him and said,

COUPLET.

"Art thou a serpent that all travellers stings?
Or owl, that where it lights, destruction brings?

STANZA.

Grant that thy violence may with us prevail,
With the all-seeing God 'twill surely fail.
Beware, lest earth's much injured sons be driven
To raise 'gainst thee their suppliant voice to heaven."

The tyrant was wroth at these words, and frowned, and heeded him not, until one night when fire spread from the kitchen to the stack of wood, and consumed all his property, and from a soft bed removed him to glowing ashes. It happened that the same devout person passed by. He heard him say to his friends, "I know not

[120] So I feel bound to render this most obscure sentence, in which I follow Gladwin. M. Semelet and Ross translate it differently, but I believe on no other authority than their own conjectures. As بي طرح *bī ṭarḥ* is "rude," so بطرح *ba ṭarḥ* may be "graciously."

whence this fire broke out in my house." He replied, "From the ṣmoke[121] of the hearts of the poor."

STANZA.

Beware of the sigh of the wounded heart,
For the secret sore you'll too late discern;
Grief, if thou canst, to no bosom impart,
For the sigh of grief will a world o'erturn,

MAXIM.

On the crown of king Kaikhusrau was written,

STANZA.

How long shall men my buried dust tread down?
Through many a lengthening year and distant day.
From hand to hand to me descends this crown,
To others so, it soon will pass away.

Story XXVII.

A person had reached perfection in the art of wrestling. He knew three hundred and sixty precious sleights in this art, and every day he wrestled with a different device. However, his heart was inclined towards the beauty of one of his pupils. He taught him three hundred and fifty-nine throws, all he knew save one, the teaching of which he deferred. The youth was perfect in skill and strength, and no one could withstand him, till he at length boasted before the Sulṭān that he allowed the superiority of his master over him only out of respect to his years, and what was due to him as an instructor, and that but for that he was not inferior in strength, and on a par with him in skill. The king was displeased at his breach of respect, and he commanded them to wrestle. A vast arena was selected. The great nobles and ministers of the king attended. The youth entered, like a furious elephant,

[121] That is, "from their sighs."

with a shock that had his adversary been a mountain of iron would have uptorn it from its base. The master perceived that the young man was his superior in strength. He fastened on him with that curious grip which he had kept concealed from him. The youth knew not how to foil it. The preceptor lifted him with both hands from the ground, and raised him above his head, and dashed him on the ground. A shout of applause arose from the multitude. The king commanded them to bestow a robe of honour and reward on the master, and heaped reproaches on the youth, saying, "Thou hast presumed to encounter him who educated thee, and thou hast failed." He replied, "Sire! my master overcame me, not by strength or power, but a small point was left in the art of wrestling which he withheld from me; and by this trifle he has to-day gotten the victory over me." The preceptor said, "I reserved it for such a day as this; for the sages have said, 'Give not thy friend so much power that if one day he should become a foe, thou mayst not be able to resist him.' Hast thou not heard what once was said by one who had suffered wrong from a pupil of his own?

STANZA.

'On earth there is no gratitude, I trow;
Or none, perhaps, to use it now pretend.
None learn of me the science of the bow,
Who make me not their target in the end.'"

Story XXVIII.

A solitary darwesh had fixed himself in the corner of a desert. A king passed by him. The darwesh, inasmuch as cessation from wordly pursuits is the kingdom of content, raised not up his head, and heeded him not. The king, through the domineering character of royalty, was offended, and observed, "This tribe of tatterdemalions is on a level with brutes." The vazīr said, "The king of earth's surface passed near thee; why didst thou not do him homage, and perform thy respects?" He replied, "Tell the king to look for service from one who expects favours from him, and let him also know that kings are for the protection of their subjects, not subjects for the service of kings: as they have said,

STANZA.

'Kings are but guardians, who the poor should keep;
Though this world's goods wait on their diadem.
Not for the shepherd's welfare are the sheep:
The shepherd rather is for pasturing them.

CONCLUDING STANZA.

To-day thou markest one flushed with success;
Another sick with struggles 'gainst his fate:
Pause but a little while, the earth shall press
His brain that did such plans erst meditate.
Lost is the difference of king and slave,
At the approach of destiny's decree:
Should one upturn the ashes of the grave,
Could he discern 'twixt wealth and poverty?'"

The discourse of the darwesh made a strong impression on the king. He said, "Ask a boon of me." The darwesh replied, "I request that thou wilt not again disturb me." On this the king rejoined, "Give me some piece of advice." He said,

STANZA.

"Now that thy hands retain these blessings, know—
This wealth, these lands, from hand to hand must go."

Story XXIX.

A vazīr went to Z̲ū'l-nūn,[122] of Egypt, and requested the

[122] Gentius tells us that there were two Z̲ū'l-nūns: one, the prophet Jonah, who lived about 862 B.C.; and the other,

aid of his prayers, saying, "I am day and night employed in the service of the Sulṭān, hoping for his favour, and dreading his wrath." Ẕū'l-nūn wept, and said, "If I had feared the Most High God as thou dost the Sulṭān, I should have been of the number of the just."

STANZA.

Could the holy darwesh cease from worldly joy and sorrow,
On the sky his foot would be;
And the vazīr for himself angelic light would borrow,
Served he God as royalty.[123]

Story XXX.

A king gave an order to put an innocent person to death. He said, "O king! for the anger which thou feelest against me, seek not thine own injury!" The king asked, "How so?" He replied, "I shall suffer this pang but for a moment, and the guilt of it will attach to thee for ever."

QUATRAIN.

Circling on, life's years have fled, as flies the breeze of morn;
Sadness and mirth, and foul and fair, for aye have passed away.
Dream'st thou, tyrant! thou hast wreaked on me thy rage and scorn?
The burthen from my neck has passed, on thine must ever stay.

Ṣuban, who, being in a vessel, was accused of stealing a very valuable pearl, and invoked God's aid to establish his innocence, whereupon the pearl was discovered in a fish. The person here alluded to is Abū Faẓl Ṣuban bin Ibrāhīm, a celebrated Muḥammadan saint, chief of the Ṣūfīs, who died in Egypt, A.H. 245.

[123] There is a very elegant turn in the original, which cannot be imitated in English: مَلِك *malik* is "a king," and مَلَك *malak* "an angel."

This admonition of his operated advantageously on the king, and he forbore to shed his blood, and asked pardon of him.

Story XXXI.

The vazīrs of Nūshīrwān were consulting on a matter connected with State affairs, and each delivered his opinions in accordance with what he judged best. The king also took part in their deliberations. Buzurchimihr adopted the opinion of the king. The vazīrs said to him privately, "What superiority didst thou discern in the king's opinion above the counsels of so many sage persons?" He replied, "In that the end of the affair is unknown, and the opinions of all depend on the will of the Most High God, whether they turn out just or erroneous. Wherefore it is better to conform to the monarch's opinion, that, should it turn out unfavourably, our obsequiousness will secure us from his reproaches.

DISTICHS.

Opinions, differing from the king, to have;
Is your own hands in your own blood to lave.
Should he affirm the day to be the night,
Say you behold the moon and Pleiads' light."

Story XXXII.

A traveller[124] twisted his ringlets,[125] saying, "I am a

[124] In my edition, I read in accordance with four MSS. سیّاحي *saiyāḥī*, instead of the شیّادي *shaiyādī*, which M. Semelet, Gladwin, and Ross prefer. The sense of the latter, "an impostor," is certainly more suitable to the context, but then it does not occur in the dictionaries, and is contrary to the MSS.

[125] This implies merely a swaggering air, as we say, "twirled his moustache." I do not believe that the descendants of Âlī have any particular way of wearing the hair, though there is a difference in their turbans and the colour of their clothes.

descendant of Ȧlī," and entered the city along with the caravan from Ḥijāz, giving out that he had come from the pilgrimage to Makkah; and produced an idyl before the king, affirming it to be his own. One of the king's counsellors had that year returned from travelling. He said, "I saw him in Baṣrah,[126] at the festival of Aẓḥa;[127] how, then, can he have come from the pilgrimage to Makkah?" Another said, "His father was a Christian in Malāṭiyah;[128] how should he be a descendant of Ȧlī?" His verses were found in the Dīwān[129] of Anvarī.[130] The king ordered him to be beaten and sent him away, saying, "Why hast thou uttered so many falsehoods?" He replied, "Lord of earth's surface! I will speak one word more, and if it be not true, I am worthy of any punishment that thou mayest command." The king inquired, "What is that?" He replied,

STANZA.

"Curds,[131] which to thee a poor man brings, will prove,
Water, two cups; and buttermilk, one spoon.
Let not my idle tales thine anger move,
For, from a traveller, lies thou'lt hear full soon."

[126] A seaport town in the Persian Gulf.

[127] The Ȋd, or festival of Aẓḥa, is held by the Muḥammadans on the tenth day of the month Ẕi'l-ḥajj, which is the last of the Musalmān year. It is celebrated in honour of the offering up of Ishmael by Abraham, for the Muḥammadans pretend that he, and not Isaac, was to be the sacrifice.—*Vide* Kānūn-ī Islām, p. 226.

[128] Malta.

[129] A poem, consisting of a series of odes, of which the first class terminate with ا *a*, the second with ب *b*, and so on through the alphabet.

[130] A celebrated Persian poet, who died A.H. 577=A.D. 1200. He was patronized by Sulṭān Sanjār, of the Saljuk family.

[131] This alludes to the practice in Persia of breakfasting on a cup of curds and bread, with a slice of cheese or melon.

The king laughed and said, "In thy life thou never saidst a truer word than this." He then commanded the usual allowance for descendants of the Prophet to be got ready for him.

Story XXXIII.

They have related that a certain vazīr was compassionate to his inferiors, and studied the welfare of all. It happened that he fell under the king's displeasure. All exerted themselves to obtain his release; and those who had the custody of him alleviated his punishment; and the other nobles spoke of his good qualities to the king, so that the king forgave his fault. A sage heard of this, and said,

STANZA.

"To gain thy friends' affection,
Sell the garden of thy sire;
To give them food, protection,
With thy goods go feed the fire.
Shew kindness even to thy foes;
The dog's mouth with a morsel close."[132]

Story XXXIV.

One of the sons of Hārūnu'r-rashīd[133] came to his father in a passion, saying, "Such an officer's son has insulted me, by speaking abusively of my mother."

[132] I have been compelled to translate these lines freely, *metri causâ*. The literal version is, for the third and fourth lines, "to cook the pot of thy well-wishers, it is better to burn all thy household furniture." The other lines are more literally rendered, save that each second line ends with a rhyming participle, which cannot be carried out in English.

[133] That is, "Hārūn the Just." He began to reign A.H. 170, and was the fifth Khalīfah of the house of Åbbās. He sent presents to Charlemagne, and, like him, divided his empire among his three sons.

Hārūn said to his nobles, "What should be the punishment of such a person?" One gave his voice for death, and another for the excision of his tongue, and another for the confiscation of his goods and banishment. Hārūn said, "O my son! the generous part would be to pardon him, and if thou canst not, then do thou abuse his mother, but not so as to exceed the just limits of retaliation, for in that case we should become the aggressors."

STANZA.

They that with raging elephants make war
Are not, so deem the wise, the truly brave;
But in real verity, the valiant are
Those who, when angered, are not passion's slave.[134]

DISTICHS.

An ill-bred fellow once a man reviled,
Who patient bore it, and replied, "Good friend!
Worse am I than by thee I could be styled,
And better know how often I offend."

Story XXXV.

I was seated in a vessel along with some persons of distinction. A barge, which was in our wake, went down, and two brothers were plunged into the vortex. One of the great personages said to the boatman, "Save those two, and I will give thee a hundred dīnārs." The boatman plunged into the water and rescued one. The other perished. I said, "He was destined not to survive, wherefore thou camest too late to get hold of him." The boatman laughed, and said, "What thou sayest is most true, and, besides, my mind was more set on saving this one, because once when I was exhausted in the desert he set me on his camel, and I had been flogged by the other in my childhood." I

[134] More literally, "do not speak intemperately."

replied, "*The Great God is righteous! for every one who does well benefits his own soul; and every one that sinneth, sinneth against himself.*"

STANZA.

Strive not to pain a single heart,
Nor by that thorny pathway move.
But with the needy aye take part;
To thee, too, this will succour prove.

Story XXXVI.

There were two brothers, one of whom served the Sulṭān, and the other obtained his bread by his manual labour. Once on a time the rich one said to the poor one, "Why dost thou not serve the Sulṭān, by which thou mayst escape from thy toilsome work?" He replied, "Why dost thou not work in order to free thyself from the disgrace of being a servant? since the sages have said, 'It is better to eat barley bread, and sit on the ground, than to gird oneself with a golden girdle, and stand up to serve.'"

COUPLET.

Better from lime make mortar with thy hand,
Than before chiefs with folded arms to stand.

STANZA.

Life, precious life, has been in pondering spent
On summer clothing and on winter food.
O glutton belly! let one loaf content
Thee, rather than the back [in slavish mood]
Be to the ground in others' service bent.

Story XXXVII.

A person brought to Nūshīrwān the Just good news, saying, "God [may he be honoured and glorified!] has removed such and such an enemy of thine." He replied, "Hast thou heard at all that he will spare me?"

COUPLET.

In my foe's death, what joy is there for me?
For my life, too, cannot eternal be.

Story XXXVIII.

A council of wise men at the court of Kisrạ[135] was discussing a certain matter. Buzurchimihr was silent. They said, "Why dost thou not deliver thy opinion with us in this consultation?" He replied, "Vazīrs are like physicians: and the physican does not give medicine save to the sick. Wherefore, when I see that your opinion is right, it would not be wise for me to interfere therein with my voice."

STANZA.

Without my meddling, if a thing succeed,
For me to give advice therein, what need?
But if I see a blind man and a pit,
Why, then, I'm guilty if I silent sit.

Story XXXIX.

When Hārūnu'r-rashīd had conquered Egypt, he said, "In contradiction to that impious rebel[136] who, through pride of having Egypt for his kingdom, laid claim to divine honours, I will give this province to none but the lowest of my slaves." He had a black slave of great stupidity, whose name was Khuṣaib; on him he bestowed the land of Egypt. They say that his intellect and capacity were so limited that when a body of Egyptian cultivators complained to him that they had sown cotton on the banks of the Nile, and that, owing to an unseasonable fall of rain, it had been destroyed; he replied, "You

[135] Kisrạ or Chosroes, as the Arabs styled the Persian kings of the Sassanian race, is here used for Nūshīrwān.

[136] Pharaoh is here meant.

ought to sow wool, that it might not be swept away." A sage heard it and said,

DISTICHS.

"If with your wisdom grew your store,
The fool would be the truly poor;
But Heaven to the fool supplies
Such wealth as would amaze the wise."[137]

DISTICHS.

Fortune and wealth are not to merit given:
None can obtain them but by aid from Heaven.
In this world oft a marvel meets our eyes;
The undiscerning honoured, scorned the wise.
The alchymist expires with grief and pain,
And fools a treasure 'neath a shed obtain.

Story XL.

They had brought a Chinese girl, of surpassing beauty and loveliness, to an Arabian king. In a moment of intoxication he attempted to embrace her. The damsel resisted him. The king was enraged, and bestowed her on one of his slaves, who was a negro, and whose upper lip ascended above his nostrils, and whose lower lip hung down on his collar. His form was such that the demon Ṣakẖr would have fled at his appearance.

COUPLET.

In him th' extreme of ugliness was found,
As beauty to all time fair Joseph crowned.

STANZA.

Not such his person that description can
His hideous aspect typify;
The fetor [save us!] from him foully ran
Like carrion sun-baked in July.

At that season the passions of the negro were roused,

[137] In the original it is "a hundred wise men."

and he was overpowered by lust. Agitated by desire he deflowered her. In the morning, the king sought for the girl and could not find her. They told him what had happened. He was incensed, and commanded that they should bind the negro and the girl fast together by their hands and feet, and cast them from the roof of the palace into the fosse. One of the vazīrs, who was of a benevolent disposition, bent down his face in intercession to the ground and said, "The negro is not to blame in this matter; for all your Majesty's slaves and attendants are accustomed to your royal bounty." The king said, "What great difference would it have made had he forborne to meddle with her for a night?" The vazīr replied, "Sire! hast thou not heard what they have said,

STANZA.

'When to a limpid fountain one parched with thirst advances,
Think not a raging elephant him would scare;
Or, when alone, an infidel sees meat with famished glances,
Can reason think he'd pause for the fast-day there.'"

The king was pleased with this pleasantry, and said, "I give thee the negro; but what shall I do with the girl?" He replied, "Give the girl to the negro; for his leavings are fit only for himself."

STANZA.

Never take him for thy friend
Who goes where it beseems him not:
The purest water will offend
The thirstiest lips, if it be got
From one whose breath is foul and hot.

STANZA.

Ne'er will the orange from the Sulṭān's hand
Once in the dunghill fallen, more there rest:
Though thirsty, none will water e'er demand,
When ulcerated lips the jar have pressed.

Story XLI.

They said to Alexander of Rūm, "How didst thou conquer the eastern and western worlds, when former kings surpassed thee in treasures, and territory, and long life, and armies, and yet did not obtain such victories?" He replied, "By the aid of the Most High God. Whenever I subdued a country I did not oppress its inhabitants, and I never spoke disparagingly of its kings."

COUPLET.

Ne'er will he be called great among the wise,
Who to the truly great their name denies.

STANZA.

These are no more than trifles, swiftly sped,
Fortune and throne, command and conquest—all.
Destroy not thou the good name of the dead,
That thy fame, too, may last and never fall.

CHAPTER II.

ON THE QUALITIES OF DARWESHES.

Story I.

A person of distinction asked a holy man, "What sayest thou with regard to a certain devotee; for others have spoken sneeringly of him?" He replied, "In his outward conduct I discern no fault, and I know nothing of his secret defects."

STANZA.

When thou dost one in saintly vestments find,
Doubt not his goodness or his sanctity.
What though thou knowest not his inmost mind?
Not within doors need the Muḥtasib[138] pry.

Story II.

I once saw a darwesh, who, with his head resting on the threshold of the temple at Makkah, called the Kâbah, was weeping and saying, "O Thou merciful and compassionate One! Thou knowest what homage can be offered by a sinful and ignorant being worthy of thee!"[139]

[138] The Muḥtasib is the Muḥammadan superintendent of police, who prevents drunkenness, gaming, and other disorders; but, as appears from this passage, his business is rather to enforce external decency, than to suppress latent immorality.

[139] That is, "The homage of a sinful being cannot be worthy of God."

STANZA.

For my scant service I would pardon crave,
Since on obedience I can ground no claim.
Sinners, of sin repent; but those who have
Knowledge of the Most High, at pardon aim
For worthless worship [which they view with shame].

The pious seek the reward of their obedience, and merchants look for the price of their wares, and I, thy servant, have brought hope, not obedience, and have come to beg, not to traffic. "*Do unto me that which is worthy of Thee, and not that of which I am worthy.*"

COUPLET.

Whether Thou wilt slay or spare me, at Thy door my head I lay;
To the creature will belongs not, Thy commandment I obey.

STANZA.

A supplicant at Makkah's shrine who wept
Full piteously and thus exclaimed, I saw;
"I ask Thee not my homage to accept,
But through my sins Thy pen absolving draw."

Story III.

Âbdu'l-Ḳādir Gīlānī[140] laid his face on the pebbles in the sanctuary of the Kâbah, and said, "O Lord! pardon me; but if I am deserving of punishment, raise me up at the resurrection blind, that I may not be ashamed in the sight of the righteous."

STANZA.

Humbly in dust I bow each day
My face, with wakening memory,
O Thou! whom I forget not, say,
Dost Thou bethink Thee e'er of me?

[140] This saintly personage was a celebrated Ṣūfī of Baghdād, under whom Sâdī embraced the doctrine of the Mystics.

Story IV.

A thief entered the house of a recluse. However much he searched, he found nothing. He turned back sadly and in despair, and was observed by the holy man, who cast the blanket on which he slept in the way of the thief, that he might not be disappointed.

STANZA.

The men of God's true faith, I've heard,
  Grieve not the hearts e'en of their foes.
When will this station be conferred
  On thee who dost thy friends oppose?

The friendship of the pure-minded, whether in presence or absence, is not such that they will find fault with thee behind thy back, and die for thee in thy presence.

COUPLET.

Before thee like the lamb they gentle are:
Absent, than savage wolves more ruthless far.

COUPLET.

They who the faults of others bring to you.
Be sure they'll bear to others your faults too.

Story V.

Certain travellers had agreed to journey together, and to share their pains and pleasures. I wished to join them. They withheld their consent. I said, "It is inconsistent with the benevolent habits of the eminent to avert the countenance from the society of the lowly, and to decline to be of service to them; and I feel in myself such power of exertion and energy that in the service of men I should be an active friend, not a weight on their minds.

COUPLET.

What though I'm borne[141] *not in the camel throng,*
Yet will I strive to bear your loads along."

One of them said, "Let not thy heart be grieved at the answer thou hast received, for within the last few days, a thief came in the guise of a darwesh, and linked himself in the chain of our society."

COUPLET.

What know men of the wearer, though they know the dress full well?
The letter-writer only can the letter's purport tell.

Inasmuch as the state of darweshes is one of security,[142] they had no suspicion of his meddling propensities, and admitted him into companionship.

DISTICHS.

Rags are th' external sign of holiness;
Sufficient—for men judge by outward dress.
Strive to do well, and what thou pleasest, wear;
Thy head a crown, thine arm a flag[143] may bear.
Virtue lies not in sackcloth coarse and sad;
Be purely pious, and in satin clad:

141 There is an attempt here at a pun in the words راكب *rākib*, "I am riding," and حامل *ḥāmil*, "I am bearing."

142 This word سلامت *salāmat*, is variously rendered. M. Semelet translates it by "une assurance"; Ross by "reverence"; Gladwin by "everywhere approved," renderings sufficiently free, one would think, and all of them objective. I prefer giving the word a subjective meaning, when it may take its natural signification and yet make good sense.

143 M. Semelet, from a note of M. de Sacy, conjectures علم *ālam* to mean "a rich dress, worn by the great;" or, "a piece of rich stuff worn by kings on the left shoulder." Gladwin and Ross translate as above, and I am content to follow them.

True holiness consists in quitting vice,
The world and lust,—not dress;—let this suffice.
Let valiant men their breasts with iron plate:
Weapons of war ill suit the effeminate.

"In short, one day, we had journeyed till dusk, and slept for the night under a castle's walls. The graceless thief took up the water-pot of one of his comrades, saying that he was going for a necessary purpose, and went, in truth, to plunder.

COUPLET.

He'd fain with tattered garment for a darwesh pass,
And makes the Kabah's[144] pall the housings of an ass.

As soon as he had got out of sight of the darweshes he scaled a bastion,[145] and stole a casket. Before the day dawned, that dark-hearted one had got to a considerable distance, and his innocent companions were still asleep. In the morning they carried them all to the fortress and imprisoned them. From that day we have abjured society, and kept to the path of retirement, for, *in solitude there is safety.*"

STANZA.

When but one member of a tribe has done
A foolish act, all bear alike disgrace,
Seest thou how in the mead one ox alone
Will lead astray the whole herd of a place?

I said, "I thank God (may He be honoured and glorified!) that I have not remained excluded from the

[144] First the Khalīfahs, then the Sulṭāns of Egypt, and lastly those of Constantinople, have been in the habit of sending annually to Makkah a rich covering of brocade for the temple there, called the Kâbah.

[145] I must confess I consider this reading unsatisfactory, and much prefer Dr. Sprenger's برخي برفت *barkhī baraft,* "he went a little distance." The Doctor has a misprint directly after: دِ جي for درجي *durjī.*

beneficial influences of the darweshes, although I have been deprived of their society, and I have derived profit from this story, and this advice will be useful to such as I am through the whole of life."

DISTICHS.

Be there but one rough person in their train,
For his misdeeds the wise will suffer pain.
Should you a cistern with rose-water fill,
A dog dropped in it would defile it still.

Story VI.

A religious recluse became the guest of a king. When they sate down to their meals, he ate less than his wont; and when they rose up to pray, he prayed longer than he was accustomed to, that they might have a greater opinion of his piety.

COUPLET.

O Arab! much I fear thou at Makkah's shrine wilt never be,
For the road that thou art going is the road to Tartary.

When he returned to his own abode he ordered the cloth to be laid that he might eat. He had a son possessed of a ready wit, who said, "O my father! didst thou eat nothing at the entertainment of the Sulṭān?" He replied, "I ate nothing in their sight to serve a purpose." The son rejoined, "Repeat thy prayers again, and make up for their omission, since thou hast done nothing that can serve any purpose."

STANZA.

Thy merits in thy palm thou dost display;
  Thy faults beneath thy arm from sight withhold.
What wilt thou purchase, vain one! in that day,
  The day of anguish, with thy feigned gold? [146]

[146] Literally, "Base silver or coin."

Story VII.

I remember that, in the time of my childhood, I was devout, and in the habit of keeping vigils, and eager to practise mortification and austerities. One night I sate up in attendance on my father, and did not close my eyes the whole night, and held the precious Ḳur'ān in my lap while the people around me slept. I said to my father, "Not one of these lifts up his head to perform a prayer.[147] They are so profoundly asleep that you would say they were dead." He replied, "Life of thy father! it were better if thou, too, wert asleep; rather than thou shouldst be backbiting people."

STANZA.

Naught but themselves can vain pretenders mark,
For conceit's curtain intercepts their view.
Did God illume that which in them is dark,
Naught than themselves would wear a darker hue.[148]

Story VIII.

In a certain assembly they were extolling a person of eminence, and going to an extreme in praising his excellent qualities. He raised his head, and said, "I am that which I know myself to be."

COUPLET.

Thou who wouldst sum my virtues up, enough thou'lt find
In outward semblance; to my secret failings blind.

[147] Literally, "A double prayer," "binæ precationes," as M. Semelet remarks, like "deux Pater et deux Avé."

[148] This translation is free. The nominative is throughout in the singular, and the last line is literally, "He would see no one more wretched than himself."

STANZA.

My person, in men's eyes, is fair to view;
But, for my inward faults, shame bows my head.
The peacock, lauded for his brilliant hue,
Is by his ugly feet discomfited.

Story IX.

One of the holy men of Mount Lebanon, whose discourses were quoted, and whose miracles were celebrated throughout the country of Arabia, came to the principal mosque of Damascus, and was performing his ablutions on the side of the reservoir of the well. His foot slipped, and he fell into the basin, and got out of it with the greatest trouble. When prayers were finished, one of his companions said, "I have a difficulty." The Shekh inquired what it was. He replied, "I remember that thou didst walk on the surface of the western sea without wetting thy feet, and to-day thou wast within a hair's breadth of perishing in this water, of but one fathom depth; what is the meaning of this?" He bent his head in the lap of meditation, and after much reflection, raised it, and said, "Hast thou not heard that the Lord of the World, Muḥammad Muṣṭafa (may the blessing and peace of God be upon him!) said, '*I have a season with God, in which neither ministering angel, nor any prophet that has been sent, can vie with me*,' but he did not say that this season was perpetual. In such a time as he mentioned, he was wrapt beyond Gabriel and Michael; and, at another time, he was contented with Ḥafṣah [149] and Zainab, for the vision of the pious is between effulgence and obscurity; at one moment He shews Himself, at another snatches Himself from our sight."

[149] These are the names of two of Muḥammad's wives, of which the latter was a Jewess who poisoned him.

COUPLET.

Thou dost Thy face now shew and now conceal,
Thy worth enhancest, and inflam'st our zeal.

STANZA.

I'll with unintercepted gaze survey
Him whom I love, and, wildered, lose my way.
One while a flame He kindles—bright in vain,
For soon He quenches it with cooling rain;
'Tis thus thou seest me burnt, then drowned again.

Story X.

VERSE.

To that bereaved father[150] one once said,
"Aged sire! on whose bright soul truth's light is shed,
From Egypt his coat's scent thy nostrils knew;
In Canaan's pit why was he hid from view?"
"My state," he said, "is like heaven's flashing light:
One moment shewn, the next concealed in night;
Now on the azure vault I sit supreme;
In darkness now my own feet hidden seem.
Did but the darwesh in one state abide,
He might himself from both worlds aye divide."[151]

Story XI.

I once, in the principal mosque of Baâlbak,[152] addressed a few words, by way of exhortation, to a frigid assembly,

[150] Jacob,—to the story of whose son Joseph, perpetual reference is made by the Musalmān.

[151] That is, he might attain re-union with the Deity.

[152] Baâlbak, by the Greeks called Heliopolis, is a city now in ruins, situated at the foot of Anti-Libanus, in the direct route between Tyre and Palmyra, by traffic with which cities it greatly profited. The principal temple, which is of extraordinary size and beauty, seems to have been built by Antoninus Pius. It contains now but 1200 inhabitants.

whose hearts were dead, and who had not found the way from the material to the spiritual world. I saw that my speech made no impression on them, and that the flame of my ardour did not take effect on their green wood. I felt repugnance to continue instructing such mere animals, and to holding up a mirror in the district of the blind; however, the gate of my spiritual discourse continued open, and the chain of my address was prolonged in explanation of the verse, "*We are nearer to him than the jugular vein.*"[153] I had brought my discourse to this point, when I exclaimed,

STANZA.

"Not to myself am I so near as He,
My friend; and stranger still, from Him I'm far.
What can I do? where tell this mystery?
He's in our arms, yet we excluded are."

I was intoxicated with the spirit of this address, and the remainder of the cup was in my hands, when, a traveller passing by the assembly, my last words[154] made an impression upon him. He gave such an applauding shout that the others, in sympathy with him, joined in the excitement, and the most apathetic of the assembly shared his enthusiasm. I exclaimed, "Praise be to God! Those at a distance who have knowledge of Him are admitted into His presence, while those who are at hand, but are deprived of vision, are kept aloof."

153 This verse of the Ḳur'ān occurs in ch. L., l. 27, of Sale's Translation.

154 The translators, in my opinion, have missed the sense of دور *daur*, which I take to mean not "ondulation," according to M. Semelet, but "circle of the cup"; the metaphor being still kept up, and the last sentence being compared to the last time the cup is sent round.

STANZA.

Expect not from that speaker eloquence,
Whose words his audience cannot value well.
With a wide field of willingness commence,
Then will the orator the ball[155] propel.

STORY XII.

One night, in the desert of Makkah, from excessive want of sleep, I was deprived of the power of proceeding. I reclined my head, and bade the camel-driver leave me alone.

STANZA.

What distance can the tired footman go,
When Bactria's camel faints beneath the load?
In the same time that fat men meagre grow,
The lean will perish on affliction's road.

The camel-driver said, "O brother! the sanctuary[156] is before thee, and the robber behind; if thou goest on, thou wilt obtain thy object; if thou sleepest, thou wilt die."

COUPLET.

Sweet is slumber in the desert under the acacia-tree,
On the night when friends are marching, but it bodeth death to thee.

STORY XIII.

I saw a devotee on the sea-shore, who had received a wound from a leopard, and had been for a long time thus

155 There is an equivoque here which cannot be retained in English: گوي *gūī* signifies both "speech," and "the ball used in the game of Chaugān."

156 There is a pun here, impossible to render in English, on the words حرم *ḥaram*, "sanctuary," and حرامي *ḥarāmī*, "a robber."

afflicted, but could obtain no relief from any medicine, and yet incessantly returned thanks to God Most High. They asked him, saying, "How is it that thou, who art suffering from this calamity, art returning thanks?" He replied, "Praise be to God! that I am suffering from a calamity, and not from a sin."

STANZA.

If that loved One should slay me cruelly,
Thou shouldst not say, e'en then, I feared to die.
I'd ask, What fault has Thy poor servant done?
'Tis for Thine anger that I grieve alone.

Story XIV.

A darwesh, having some pressing occasion, stole a blanket from the house of a friend. The judge ordered his hand to be cut off. The owner of the blanket interceded for him, saying that he had pardoned him. The judge said, "I shall not desist from carrying out the law on account of thy intercession." He replied, "Thou hast spoken the truth, but it is not necessary to punish with amputation one who steals property dedicated to pious purposes, for '*the faḳīr does not possess anything, and is not possessed by any one.*' Whatever the darwesh possesses is for the benefit of the necessitous." The judge released him, and said, "Was the world too narrow for thee, that thou must steal nowhere but from the house of such a friend?" He replied, "My Lord! hast thou not heard the saying, 'Make a clean sweep in thy friend's house, but do not even knock at the door of thy enemies.'"

COUPLET.

Art thou distressed? yield not to weak despair;
Uncloak thy friends, but strip thy foemen bare.[157]

[157] Literally, "strip off their skins." The second sentiment does not agree with the first.

Story XV.

A king said to a holy man, "Dost thou ever remember me?" He replied, "Yes! whenever I forget my God."

COUPLET.

Those He repels, to every side direct
Their course—whom he invites, all else reject.

Story XVI.

A certain pious man in a dream beheld a king in paradise and a devotee in hell. He inquired, "What is the reason of the exaltation of the one, and the cause of the degradation of the other? for I had imagined just the reverse." They said, "That king is now in paradise owing to his friendship for darweshes, and this recluse is in hell through frequenting the presence of kings."

STANZA.

Of what avail is frock, or rosary,
Or clouted garment? Keep thyself but free
From evil deeds, it will not need for thee
To wear the cap of felt: a darwesh be
In heart, and wear the cap of Tartary.

Story XVII.

A man on foot, with bare head and bare feet, came from Kūfah[158] with the caravan proceeding to Ḥijāz, and

[158] Kūfah is a city on the Euphrates, four days' journey from Baghdād, and so near Baṣrah that the two towns are called the two Baṣrahs, or the two Kūfahs. The Persians assert that it was built by Hūshang, the second king of the Pīshdādyan, or second dynasty of Persia. Khondemīr, however, affirms that it was founded by Sâd, a general of the Khalīfah Omar, A.H. 17. The first Âbbāsī Khalīfah made it his capital, and it became so extensive that the Euphrates was called نهرِ كوفه *nahar-i Kūfah,* "the river of Kūfah." The oldest Arabic characters are called Kūfic, from this city.

accompanied us. I looked at him, and saw that he was wholly unprovided with the supplies requisite for the journey. Nevertheless, he went on merrily, and said,

VERSE.

"I ride not on a camel, but am free from load and trammel;
To no subjects am I lord, and I fear no monarch's word;
I think not of the morrow, nor recall the gone-by sorrow,
Thus I breathe exempt from strife, and thus moves on my tranquil life."

One who rode on a camel said to him, "O darwesh! whither art thou going? turn back, or thou wilt perish from the hardships of the way." He did not listen, but entered the desert and proceeded on. When we reached "the palm-trees of Maḥmūd," fate overtook the rich man and he died. The darwesh approached his pillow, and said, "I have survived these hardships, and thou hast perished on the back of thy dromedary."

COUPLET.

A person wept the livelong night beside a sick man's bed:
When it dawned the sick was well, and the mourner, he was dead.

STANZA.

Fleet coursers oft have perished on the way,
While the lame ass the stage has safely passed;
Oft have they laid the vigorous 'neath the clay,
While the sore-wounded have revived at last.

Story XVIII.

A king sent an invitation to a religious man. The latter thought to himself, "I will take a medicine to make me look emaciated; perhaps it may increase the good opinion entertained of me." They relate that he swallowed deadly poison, and died.

STANZA.

He who, pistachio-like, all kernel seemed,
An onion was; for fold on fold was there.
The saint who turns to man to be esteemed,
Must on the Kiblah [159] turn his back in prayer.

COUPLET.

Who calls himself God's servant must forego
All else, and none besides his Maker know.

Story XIX.

In the country of the Greeks some banditti attacked a caravan, and carried off immense riches. The merchants made lamentations and outcries, and called upon God and the Prophet to intercede for them, without avail.

COUPLET.

When the dark-minded robber finds success,
What cares he for the caravan's distress?

The philosopher Luḳmān was among them. One of those who composed the caravan said, "Say some words of wisdom and admonition to them; perchance they may restore a portion of our goods; for it would be a pity that such wealth should be lost." Luḳmān said, "It would be a pity to address the words of wisdom to them."

[159] The Kiblah is the point to which men turn in prayer. This, among Jews and Christians, is Jerusalem; and when Muḥammad first ordered his followers to turn to the temple at Makkah, it occasioned such discontent that he added a verse, to the effect that prayer is heard to whatever quarter the supplicant turns. However, Muḥammadans now all turn to Makkah when praying.

STANZA.

When rust deep-seated has consumed the steel,
Its stain will never a new polish own.
Advice affects not those who cannot feel:
A nail of iron cannot pierce a stone.

STANZA.

In prosperous days go seek out the distressed;
The poor man's prayer can change misfortune's course.
Give when the beggar humbly makes request,
Lest the oppressor take from thee by force.

Story XX.

However much the excellent Sheikh Shamsu'd-dīn Abū'l-faraj-bin-Jauzī[160] commanded me to abandon music, and directed me towards retirement and solitude, the vigour of my youth prevailed, and sensual desires continued to crave. Maugre my will, I went some steps contrary to the advice of my preceptor, and enjoyed the delights of music and conviviality. When the admonitions of my master returned to my recollection, I used to exclaim,

COUPLET.

"E'en the Ḳāẓī would applaud us, could he of our party be;
Thou Muḥtasib! quaff the wine-cup, and thou wilt the drunkard free."

Till one night I joined the assembly of a tribe, and saw amongst them a minstrel.

[160] Ross reads Abū'l-faraḥ, as I felt inclined to do; but Gladwin, Semelet, and Sprenger read Abū'l-faraj. He was Sâdī's preceptor, and was the son of an eminent poet and sage, who died A.H. 597.

COUPLET.

Thou'dst say that through his fiddle-bow thy arteries
would burst,
Than tidings of thy father's death wouldst own his voice
more curst.

The fingers of his friends were at one time stopping their ears, at another pressed on their lips, to bid him be silent.

VERSE.

We haste to music's sound with stirred and kindling breast,
But thou a minstrel art, whose silence pleases best.

COUPLET.

One solitary pleasure in thy strains we find,
'Tis when they cease, we go, and thou art left behind.

DISTICHS.

When my shocked ear that lutist's voice had riven,
Straight to my host I cried, "For love of heaven,
Or with the quicksilver stop my ear, I pray,
Or ope thy door and let me haste away."

However, for the sake of my friends, I accommodated myself to the circumstances, and passed the night until dawn in this distress.

STANZA.

Mū'a<u>zz</u>in![161] why delay thy morning task?
Know'st thou not how much of the night is sped?
Wouldst know its length? it of my eyelids ask,
For ne'er has sleep its influence o'er them shed.

[161] I have here translated somewhat freely. Literally it is, "The mū'a<u>zz</u>in raised his voice unseasonably; he knows not how much of the night is passed. Ask the length of the night of my eyelashes, for not one moment has sleep passed on my eyes." The mū'a<u>zz</u>in is the summoner to prayer, or crier of the mosque. I am inclined to think that the free translation above represents what Sâdī really intended.

In the morning, by way of a blessing, I took my turban from my head, and some dīnārs [162] from my belt, and laid them before the minstrel, and embraced him, and returned him many thanks. My friends observed that the feeling I evinced towards him was contrary to what was usual, and ascribed it to the meanness of my understanding, and laughed at me privately. One of them extended the tongue of opposition, and began to reproach me, saying, "This thing thou hast done accords not with the character of the wise; thou hast given the tattered robe, which is the dress of darweshes, to such a musician as has never in his whole life had one diram [163] in his hand, nor a particle of gold on his drum.

DISTICHS.

Such minstrel (from this mansion far be he!)
As in one place none twice will ever see.
The moment that his strains his gullet leave,
The hairs upon his hearer's flesh upheave.
The sparrow flies from horror at his note;
Our brain he shatters, while he splits his throat."

I said, "It is advisable for you to shorten the tongue of reproach, for, to me, his miraculous powers have been clearly evinced." He replied, "Acquaint me with these circumstances, that we may approach him,[164] and ask forgiveness for the joke which has been passed." I replied, "It is by reason of this, because my preceptor

[162] The dīnār is nearly equal to a ducat or sequin, about nine shillings; but, according to the Ḳānūn-i Islām, only five.

[163] A silver coin, worth, according to some, twopence.

[164] Sprenger's reading of همچنین تقرّب نمائیم *hamchunīn taḳarrub numāīm*, seems better than همکنان تقرّب *hamkunān taḳarrub*. The izāfat under the ن *n*, of همکنان *hamkunān*, in my edition, is a misprint.

had repeatedly commanded me to give up music, and amply advised me, but his words had not entered the ear of my acceptance; to-night, however, my auspicious fortune and happy destiny conducted me to this monastery, where, by means of this musician, I have repented, vowing that I will never again betake myself to music [165] or conviviality."

STANZA.

When a sweet palate, mouth, lips, voice, we find,
Singing or speaking, they'll enchant the heart;
Ûshāḳ, Ṣifāhān, Ḥijāz,[166] all combined,
From a vile minstrel's gullet pain impart.

Story XXI.

They asked Luḳmān, "Of whom didst thou learn manners?" He replied, "From the unmannerly. Whatever I saw them do which I disapproved of, that I abstained from doing."

STANZA.

Not e'en in jest a playful word is said,
But to the wise, 'twill prove a fruitful theme.
To fools, a hundred chapters may be read
Of grave import; to them they'll jesting seem.

Story XXII.

They relate that a religious man, in one night, would

[165] The سماع *samā̃*, appears to be "the circular ecstatic dance of darweshes." In my edition, a و *wa* is omitted between سماع *samā̃*, and مخالطت *mukhālaṭat*.

[166] The names of three favourite musical modes; and not even these, says Sâdī, can please us if the musician be a bad one.

eat three pounds[167] of food, and before dawn go through the Ḳur'ān in his devotions. A holy man heard of this, and said, "If he were to eat half a loaf, and go to sleep, he would be a much better man than he is."

STANZA.

Keep thou thy inward man from surfeit free,
That thou, therein, the light of heaven may see.
Art thou of wisdom void? 'tis that with bread
Thou 'rt to thy nostrils over-surfeited.

Story XXIII.

The divine grace caused the lamp of mercy to shine on the path of one lost in sin, so that he entered the circle of men of piety. By the happy influence of the society of darweshes, and the sincerity of their prayers, his evil qualities were exchanged for good ones, and he withdrew his hand from sensuality; and, nevertheless, the tongue of calumniators was lengthened with regard to him, to the effect that he was, just as before, subject to the same habits, and that no confidence could be placed in his devotion and uprightness.

COUPLET.

By penitence thou mayst exempted be
From wrath divine: man's tongue thou canst not flee.

He was unable to endure the injustice of their tongues, and complained to the superior of his order, and said, "I am harassed by the tongues of men." His preceptor

[167] In my edition I read نیم من *nīm man,* "half a *man*," the *man* being, according to Chardin, 5 lb. 11 oz.; but the other editors, Sprenger, Semelet, etc., read ده من *daḥ man,* "ten *mans,*" or 58 lb. 12 oz., which is surely ridiculous. In India, the "man" is = 40 sers, or 80 lbs., which would prove too much even for the appetites of these gentlemen.

wept, and said, "How canst thou return thanks for this blessing, that thou art better than they think thee?

STANZA.

How oft, sayest thou, malignant enemies
Seek to find fault with wretched me!
What if to shed thy blood they furious rise,
Or sit in changeless enmity?
Be thou but good, and ill-report despise:
'Tis better thus than thou shouldst be
Bad whilst thou seemest good in others' eyes.

But, behold me, who am regarded by all as perfection, and yet am imperfection itself.

COUPLET.

Had but my deeds been like my words, ah! then,
I had[168] been numbered, too, with holy men.

COUPLET.

True, I may be from neighbours' eyes concealed:
God knows my acts, both secret and revealed.

STANZA.

I close the door before me against men,
That my faults may not stand to them confessed:
Of what avail its bar 'gainst Thee, whose ken
Sees both the hidden and the manifest!"

Story XXIV.

I complained to one of our elders that a certain person had testified against me that I had been guilty of mis-

[168] The بودمي *būdamī*, read by Sprenger and Semelet at the end of the second line of this couplet, is much better than the مردمي *mardumī*, in my edition.

conduct.[169] He replied, "Put him to the blush by thy virtuous conversation."

VERSE.

Walk well, that he who would calumniate
Thee may naught evil find of which to prate;
For when the lute a faithful sound returns,
It from the minstrel's hand, what censure earns!

Story XXV.

They asked one of the Shekhs of Damascus, "What is the true state of Ṣūfiism?"[170] He replied, "Formerly they were a sect outwardly disturbed, but inwardly collected; and at this day they are a tribe outwardly collected and inwardly disturbed."

STANZA.

While ever roams from place to place thy heart,
  No peacefulness in solitude thou'lt see;
Hast thou estates, wealth, rank, the trader's mart?
  Be thy heart God's—this solitude may be.

Story XXVI.

I remember that one night we had travelled all night in a caravan, and in the morning slept on the edge of a

[169] Ross and Gladwin, it appears to me, mistranslate this sentence. Sprenger reads, كه فلان بفسادِ من گواهي داد *kih fulān ba-fasād-i man guwāhī dād,* "That a certain person had borne witness to my misconduct," which is obviously not so good as the reading in the text.

[170] The Ṣūfīs are a sect of Muḥammadan mystics, whose opinions, with regard to the soul, the Deity, and creation, very much resemble the esoteric doctrines of the Brāhmaṇs. They look upon the soul as an emanation from the Deity, to be re-asorbed into its source, and regard that absorption as attainable by contemplation.

forest. A distracted person, who accompanied us on that journey, uttered a cry, and took the way to the wilderness, and did not rest for a moment. When it was day I said to him, "What state is this?" He replied, "I saw the nightingales engaged in pouring forth their plaintive strains from the trees, while the partridges uttered their cries from the mountains, the frogs from the water, and the beasts from the forests. I reflected that it would be ungrateful for me to slumber neglectful while all were engaged in praising God."

DISTICHS.

But yester morn, a bird with tender strain,
  My reason, patience, sense, endurance stole;
A comrade, one most near in friendship's chain,
  (Perhaps he heard th' outpourings of my soul),
Said, "My belief would ne'er have credited
  That a bird's voice could make thee thus distraught."
"It fits not well my state as man," I said,
  "That birds their God should praise, and I say nought."

Story XXVII.

Once on a time, in travelling through Arabia Petræa, a company of devout youths shared my aspirations[171] and my journey. They used often to chant and repeat mystic verses; and there was a devotee *en route* with us, who thought unfavourably of the character of darweshes, and was ignorant of their distress. When we arrived at the palm-grove of the children of Hallāl, a dark youth came out of one of the Arab families, and raised a voice which might have drawn down the birds from the air. I saw

[171] There is rather a neat pun in the Persian here, which I have made a poor attempt to preserve. همدم *hamdam*, signifies "breathing together;" *i.e.*, "a friend:" همقدم *hamḳadam*, "stepping together"; *i.e.*, "a companion."

the camel of the devotee begin to caper, and it threw its rider, and ran off into the desert. I said, "O Shekh! it has moved a brute, does it not create any emotion in thee?"

VERSE.

Knowest thou what said the bird of morn, the nightingale,
to me?
"What meanest thou that art unskilled in love's sweet
mystery?
The camels, at the Arab's song, ecstatic are and gay;
Feel'st thou no pleasure, then thou art more brutish far
than they!"

COUPLET.

When e'en the camels join in mirth and glee,
If men feel naught, then must they asses be.

COUPLET.

Before the blast the balsams[172] *bend in the Arab's garden*[173]
lone;
Those tender shrubs their boughs incline; naught yields the
hard firm stone.

DISTICHS.

All things thou seest still declare His praise;
The attentive heart can hear their secret lays.
Hymns to the rose the nightingale His name;
Each thorn's a tongue His marvels to proclaim.

Story XXVIII.

A king had reached the close of his life, and had no heir to succeed him. He made a will, that they should place the royal crown on the head of the first person who might enter the gates of the city in the morning,

[172] The بان *bān* is the myrobolan, whence is obtained the fine balsam, called Benjamin, or Benzoin.

[173] M. Semelet informs us that the حمي *ḥamą* is the space enclosed by the nomadic Arab for his use.

and should confide the government to him. It happened that the first person who entered the city-gate was a beggar, who throughout his whole life had collected scrap after scrap, and sewn rag upon rag. The Pillars of the State, and ministers of the late king, executed his will, and bestowed on him the country and the treasure. The darwesh carried on the government for a time, when some of the great nobles turned their necks from obeying him, and the princes of the surrounding countries rose up on every side to oppose him, and arrayed their armies against him. In short, his troops and his subjects were thrown into confusion, and a portion of his territory departed from his possession. The darwesh was in a state of dejection at this circumstance, when one of his old friends, who was intimate with him in the time of his poverty, returned from a journey, and, finding him in this exalted position, said, "Thanks be to God (may He be honoured and glorified!) that thy lofty destiny has aided thee, and thy auspicious fortune has led thee on, so that thy rose has come forth from the thorn, and the thorn from thy foot, and thou hast arrived at this rank, '*surely with calamity comes rejoicing.*' [174]

COUPLET.

The bud now blossoms; withered now is found:
The tree now naked; now with leaves is crowned."

He replied, "O brother! condole with me; for there is no room for felicitation. When thou sawest me, I was distressed for bread, and now I have the troubles of a world upon me."

DISTICHS.

Have we no wordly gear—'tis grief and pain:
Have we it—then its charms our feet enchain.
Can we than this a plague more troublous find,
Which absent, present, still afflicts the mind?

174 "After pain comes pleasure;" "Après la peine le plaisir."

STANZA.

Wouldst thou be rich, seek but content to gain;
For this a treasure is that ne'er will harm.
If in thy lap some Dives riches rain,
Let not thy heart with gratitude grow warm;[175]
For, by the wisest, I have oft been told,—
The poor man's patience better is than gold.

COUPLET.

A locust's leg, the poor ant's gift, is more
Than the wild ass dressed whole from Bahrām's [176] store.

Story XXIX.

A person had a friend who was filling the office of Dīwān.[177] A long interval had passed without his happening to see him. Some one said, "It is a long time since thou sawest such a one." He replied, "Neither do I wish to see him." By chance one of the Dīwān's people was there; he asked, "What fault has he committed that thou art indisposed to see him?" He answered, "There is no fault; but the time for seeing a Dīwān is when he is discharged from his office."

STANZA.

While office lasts, amid the cares of place,
The great can well dispense with friendship's train;
But in the day of sorrow and disgrace,
They come for pity to their friends again.

175 I have been obliged to render this line freely. Literally it is, "See that thou dost not regard his recompense."

176 Bahrām, the sixth of that name, was a king of Persia, called Gūr, from his fondness for hunting the wild ass. This couplet is a sort of Oriental version of the widow's mite.

177 Accountant-General, or superintendant of the imperial finances.

Story XXX.

Abū Hurairah[178] used every day to wait upon Muṣṭafa[179] (may the blessing and peace of God be upon him!). The latter said, "O Abū Hurairah! *visit me less often and thou wilt increase our friendship*;"[180] that is, "Come not every day, that our attachment may be augmented."

ANECDOTE IN ILLUSTRATION.

They said to a wise man, "Notwithstanding the kindly influence which the sun exerts, we have not heard that any one ever regarded it as a friend." He replied, "It is because we can see it every day except in winter, when it is concealed and beloved."

STANZA.

There is no harm in visiting a friend;
  But not so oft that he should say, "Enough!"
If thou wilt thyself only reprehend,
  Thou wilt not meet from others a rebuff.

Story XXXI.

Having become weary of the society of my friends at

[178] That is, "The father of the kitten." M. Semelet tells us Omar, who succeeded Abū-bakr as Khalīfah, was so called, because he always carried a kitten on his arm. It was a name given him by Muḥammad. But we are informed by the Ḳāmūs that the name is assigned, for no less than thirty different reasons, to Âbdu'r-raḥmān bin Sakhr. Abulfeda says, "Præterea quoque postremum hunc obiit Abu-Horaira de cujus et nomine et genere certum non constat. Fuit perpetuus comes et famulus prophetæ, tantumque ejus dictorum factorumque retulit, ut multi sint qui ob immanem traditionum, quas edidit, numerum suspectum fraudis eum habeant." Page 375, ed. Reiskii.

[179] "Chosen," a name of Muḥammad.

[180] This last sentence is in Arabic, and therefore the Persian interpretation is immediately added.

Damascus, I set out for the wilderness of Jerusalem, and associated with the brutes, until I was made prisoner by the Franks, who set me to work along with Jews at digging in the fosse of Tripolis, till one of the principal men of Aleppo, between whom and myself a former intimacy had subsisted, passed that way and recognised me, and said, "What state is this? and how are you living?" I replied,

STANZA.

"From men to mountain and to wild I fled
Myself to heavenly converse to betake;
Conjecture now my state, that in a shed
Of savages I must my dwelling make."

COUPLET.

Better to live in chains with those we love,
Than with the strange 'mid flow'rets gay to move.

He took compassion on my state, and with ten dīnārs redeemed me from the bondage of the Franks, and took me along with him to Aleppo. He had a daughter, whom he united to me in the marriage-knot, with a portion of a hundred dīnārs. As time went on, the girl turned out of a bad temper, quarrelsome and unruly. She began to give a loose to her tongue, and to disturb my happiness, as they have said,

DISTICHS.

"In a good man's house an evil wife
Is his hell above in this present life.
From a vixen wife protect us well,
Save us, O God! from the pains of hell."

At length she gave vent to reproaches, and said, "Art thou not he whom my father purchased from the Franks' prison for ten dīnārs?" I replied, "Yes! he redeemed me with ten dīnārs, and sold me into thy hands for a hundred."

DISTICHS.

I've heard that once a man of high degree
From a wolf's teeth and claws a lamb set free.
That night its throat he severed with a knife.
When thus complained the lamb's departing life,
"Thou from the wolf didst save me then, but now,
Too plainly I perceive the wolf art thou."

Story XXXII.

A king asked a religious man how his precious time was passed. He replied, "I pass the whole night in prayer, and the morning in benedictions and necessary requirements; and all the day in regulating my expenses."[181] The king commanded that they should supply him with food enough for his support, in order that his mind might be relieved from the burthen of his family.

DISTICHS.

Thou who art fettered by thy family!
Must ne'er again thyself imagine free.
Care for thy sons, bread, raiment, and support,
Will drag thy footsteps back from heaven's court.
All day I must the just arrangements make;
To God, at night, myself in prayer betake.
Night comes; I would to prayer my thoughts confine,
But think, How shall my sons to-morrow dine?

[181] Semelet and Sprenger, and also Ross and Gladwin, read, instead of ملک *malik*, ملک‌را مضمونِ اشارتِ عابد معلوم گشت *malik-rā mażmūn-i ishārat-i ʿābid maʿlūm gasht*, "The king perceived the drift of the devotee's hint;" but I think it much better to omit this, and suppose that the king gave the allowance of his own free will, without its being asked for.

Story XXXIII.

One of the Syrian recluses had for years worshipped in the desert, and sustained life by feeding on the leaves of trees. The king of that region made a pilgrimage to visit him, and said, "If thou thinkest fit I will prepare a place for thee in the city that thou mayest have greater conveniences for devotion than here, and that others may be benefited by the blessing of thy prayers,[182] and may imitate thy virtuous acts." The devotee did not assent to these words. The nobles said, "To oblige the king, the proper course is for thee to come into the city for a few days and learn the nature of the place; after which, if the serenity of thy precious time suffers disturbance from the society of others, thou wilt be still free to choose." They relate that the devotee entered the city, and that they prepared for him the garden of the king's own palace, a place delightsome to the mind, and suited to tranquillise the spirit.

DISTICHS.

Like beauty's cheek, bright shone its roses red;
Its hyacinths—like fair ones' ringlets spread—
Seemed babes, which from their mother milk ne'er drew,
In winter's cold so shrinkingly they grew.

COUPLET.

And the branches—on them grew pomegranate-flowers
Like fire, suspended there, 'mid verdant bowers.

The king forthwith despatched a beautiful damsel to him.

[182] Sprenger's reading of this passage is far the best, or, rather, it is correct; while the reading of all others, including my own, is ungrammatical and incorrect. As the sentence begins with the second person singular, the شما *shumā* after انفاس *anfās*, and اعمال *åmāl*, is a downright blunder. I saw this, but, unsupported by MSS., could not make an alteration, and am delighted to find that, on the best authority, Sprenger reads انفاست *anfāsat*, and بصلاحِ اعمالت *ba-ṣalāḥ-i åmālat*.

VERSE.

A young moon that e'en saints might lead astray,
Angel in form, a peacock in display,
When once beheld, not hermits could retain
Their holy state, nor undisturbed remain.

In like manner, after her, the king sent a slave, a youth of rare beauty and of graceful proportions.

STANZA.

Round him, who seems cupbearer, people sink;
Of thirst they die, he gives them not to drink.
The eyes that see him, still unsated crave,
As dropsy thirsts amid the Euphrates' wave.

The holy man began to feed on dainties and wear soft raiment, and to find gratification and enjoyment in fruits and perfumes, as well as to survey the beauty of the youth and of the damsel; and the wise have said, "The ringlets of the beautiful are the fetters of reason, and a snare to the bird of intelligence."

COUPLET.

In thy behoof, my heart, my faith, my intellect, I vow;
In truth, a subtle bird am I; the snare this day art thou.

In short, the bliss of his tranquil state began to decline; as they have said,

STANZA.

"All that exist—disciples, doctors, saints,
The pure and eloquent alike, all fail
When once this world's base gear their minds attaints,
As flies their legs in honey vainly trail."

At length the king felt a desire to visit him. He found the recluse altered in appearance from what he was before, with a florid complexion, and waxen fat, pillowed on a cushion of brocade, and the fairy-faced slave standing at his head, with a fan of peacock's feathers. The monarch was pleased at his felicitous state, and the conversation turned on a variety of subjects, till, at the close of it, the king said, "Of all the people in the world, I value these two sorts most—the learned and the devout." A philosophical and experienced vazīr was present. He said, "O king! friendship requires that thou shouldest do good to both these two orders of men—to the wise give gold, that they may study the more; and to the devout give nothing, that they may remain devout."

COUPLET.

To the devout, nor pence nor gold divide;
If one receive it, seek another guide.

STANZA.

Kind manners, and a heart on God bestowed
Make up the saint, without alms begged or bread
That piety bequeathes. What though no load
Of turquoise-rings on Beauty's fingers shed
Their ray, nor from her ear the shimmering gem
Depends; 'tis Beauty still, and needs not them.

STANZA.

O gentle darwesh! blest with mind serene,
Thou hast no need of alms or hermit's fare.
Lady of beauteous face and graceful mien!
Thou well the turquoise-ring and gauds canst spare.

COUPLET.

Seek I for goods which not to me belong;
Then if men call me worldly they're not wrong.[183]

Story XXXIV.

In conformity with the preceding story, an affair of

[183] Literally, "While I have, and seek for another's, if they do not call me hermit, perhaps they are right."

importance occurred to the king. He said, "If the termination of this matter be in accordance with my wishes, I will distribute so many dirams to holy men." When his desire was accomplished, it became incumbent on him to fulfil his vow according to the conditions. He gave a bag of dirams to one of his favourite servants, and told him to distribute them among devout personages. They say that the servant was shrewd and intelligent. He went about the whole day, and returned at night, and kissing the dirams, laid them before the king, saying, "However much I searched for the holy men I could not find them." The king replied, "What tale is this? I know that in this city there are four hundred saints." He answered, "O Lord of the earth! the devout accept them not, and he who accepts them is not devout." The king laughed and said to his courtiers, "Strong as my good intentions are towards this body of godly men, and much as I wish to express my favour towards them, I am thwarted by a proportionate enmity and rejection of them on the part of this saucy fellow, and he has reason on his side."

COUPLET.

When holy men accept of coin from thee,
Leave them, and seek some better devotee.

STORY XXXV.

They asked a profoundly learned man his opinion as to pious bequests. He said, "If the allowance is received in order to tranquillize the mind, and obtain more leisure for devotion, it is lawful; but when people congregate for the sake of the endowment, it is unlawful."

COUPLET.

For sacred leisure saints receive their bread,
Not to gain food that ease is furnished.

Story XXXVI.

A darwesh arrived at a place where the master of the house was of a beneficent disposition. A number of excellent persons, who were also endowed with eloquence, attended his circle, and each one of them, as is customary with men of wit, uttered some bon-mot or pleasantry. The darwesh had traversed the desert, and was fatigued, and had eaten nothing. One of them said in jest, "Thou, too, must say something." The darwesh said, "I have not the talent and eloquence of the others, and have not read anything; be satisfied with one couplet from me." All eagerly exclaimed, "Say on." He said,

COUPLET.

"Hungry I stand, with bread so near my path,
Like one unwedded by the women's bath."

All laughed and approved his wit, and brought a table before him. The host said, "Wait a little, friend! as my servants are preparing to roast some meat, cut small." The darwesh raised his head and said,

COUPLET.

"Not on my table let this roast meat be,
Baked as I am, dry bread is roast to me."

Story XXXVII.

A disciple said to his spiritual guide, "What shall I do, for I am harassed by people through the frequency of their visits to me, and my precious moments are disturbed by their coming and going." He replied, "Lend to all who are poor, and demand a loan of all who are rich, and they will not come about thee again."

COUPLET.

If Islām's van a beggar should precede,
To China infidels would fly his greed.

Story XXXVIII.

A lawyer said to his father, "No part of those facinating speeches of the orators makes an impression on me, for this reason, that I do not see their practice correspond with their preaching."

DISTICHS.

While men to leave the world they warn,
Themselves are hoarding pelf and corn.
The sage who does but preach, will ne'er,
With all his words, man's conscience stir.
Who does no evil, truly wise is he;
Not one whose acts and doctrines disagree.

COUPLET.

The sage, whom ease and pleasure lead aside,
Is himself lost; to whom can he be guide?

The father said, "O my son! it is not proper to avert one's countenance from the instruction of good advisers solely through this unfounded notion, and to take the path of idleness, and to tax the wise with error; and, while seeking for an immaculate sage, to remain deprived of the advantages of wisdom, like that blind man who one night fell into the mire and exclaimed, "O Musalmān! shew a lamp in my path!" A bold hussey heard him and said, "Thou who canst not see a lamp, what wilt thou see with a lamp?" In like manner, the congregation of preachers[184] is like the warehouse of mercers, for there, until thou give money, thou canst not get the goods; and here, unless thou bring good intentions, thou wilt not carry off a blessing."

[184] I prefer Dr. Sprenger's reading مجلسِ واعظان *majlis-i wāiẓān* to the old reading, مجلسِ وعظ *majlis-i wāẓ*.

STANZA.

Heed thou well the wise man's warning,
  Though his acts his words belie;
Futile is th' objector's scorning,
  "Sleepers ope not slumber's eye."
Heed thou then well the words of warning,
  Though on a wall thou them descry.

Story XXXIX.

(IN VERSE.)

A holy man left the monastic cell, his vow
Of sojourn with recluses broke, and now
A college sought. "How differ then?" I said,
"Sages and saints, that thou the one hast fled—
The other sought?" "This his own blanket saves,"
He said, "while that the drowning rescues from the waves."

Story XL.

A person had fallen asleep in a state of intoxication on the highway, and the reins of self-control had escaped from his hands. A devotee passed beside him, and noticed his disgraceful condition. The young man raised his head and said, "*And when they pass by the slips and shortcomings of others, they pass by absolvingly.*"[185]

VERSE.

When thou a sinner dost behold,
Shew mercy, nor his crimes unfold.
Seest thou my faults with scornful eye?
With pity rather pass me by.

[185] This is a quotation from the Ḳur'ān, chap. xxv. v. 72. I have altered Sale's words, and, with all due deference, I must confess I think his rendering of this passage execrable.

STANZA.

Turn not, O saint! thy face from sinful me;
But rather view me with benignity.
If I act not with honour, still do thou
So act, and pass me by with courteous brow.

Story XLI.

A band of dissolute fellows came to find fault with a darwesh, and used unwarrantable language, and wounded his feelings. He carried his complaint before the chief of his order, and said, "I have undergone such and such." His chief replied, "O son! the patchėd road of darweshes is the garment of resignation. Every one who in this garb endures not disappointment patiently is a pretender, and it is unlawful for him to wear the robe of the darwesh.

COUPLET.

A stone makes not great rivers turbid grow:
When saints are vexed their shallowness they shew.

STANZA.

Hast thou been injured? suffer it and clear
Thyself from guilt in pardoning other's sin.
O brother! since the end of all things here
Is into dust to moulder,[186] be thou in
Like humble mould, ere yet the change begin."

Story XLII.

(IN VERSE.)

List to my tale! In Baghdād once, dispute
Between a flag and curtain rose. Its suit
The banner, dusty and with toil oppressed,
Urged; and the curtain, angry, thus addressed:

[186] خاك *khāk*, signifies "dust," and خاك شدن *khāk shudan*, "to be humble." I have endeavoured to retain the equivoque.

"Myself and thou were comrades at one school;
Both now are slaves 'neath the same monarch's rule.
I in his service ne'er have rested,—still,
Whate'er the time, I journey at his will;
My foot is ever foremost in emprise;
Then why hast thou more honour in men's eyes?
With moon-faced slaves thy moments pass away;
With jasmine-scented girls thou mak'st thy stay.
I lie neglected still in servile hands,
Tossed by the winds my head, my feet in bands."
"The threshold is my couch," the curtain said,
"And ne'er, like thee, to heaven raise I my head:
He who exalts his neck with vain conceit,
Hurls himself headlong from his boasted seat."

Story XLIII.

A pious man saw an athlete who was exasperated, and infuriated, foaming at the mouth. He said, "What is the matter with this man?" Some one answered, "Such a one has abused him." "What!" said the holy man, "This contemptible fellow can lift a stone of a thousand mans'[187] weight, yet has not the power to support a word.

STANZA.

Boast not thy strength or manhood, while thy heart
Is swayed by impulse base;—if man thou art,
Or woman, matters naught;—but rather aim
All mouths to sweeten,—thus deserve the name
Of man; for manliness doth not consist
In stopping others' voices with thy fist.

STANZA.

Though one could brain an elephant, yet he
Is not a man without humanity.
In earth the source of Adam's sons began;
Art thou not humble? then thou art not man."

[187] A *man* varies in weight in different countries. M. Semelet fixes it 5lb.; but in India it is, in many places, 80lb.

Story XLIV.

They asked a person of eminence as to the character of the Brothers of Purity.[188] He replied, "The meanest of their qualities is, that they prefer the wishes of their friends to their own interests; and the wise have said, 'the brother whose aims are relative[189] to himself alone, is neither brother nor relative.'"

COUPLET.

Who goes too fast, cannot thy comrade be;
Fix not thy heart on one who loves not thee.

COUPLET.

If truth and faith sway not thy kinsman's breast,
To break off kinsmanship with him were best.

I remember that an opponent objected to the wording of this couplet, and said, "God, most glorious and most High, has, in the Glorious Book,[190] forbidden us to break the ties of blood, and has commanded us to love our relations; and what thou hast said is contrary to this." He replied, "Thou hast erred; it is in accordance with the Ḳur'ān. God most High has said, '*But if thy parents endeavour to prevail on thee to associate with me that concerning which thou hast no knowledge, obey them not.*'"[191]

[188] M. Semelet tells us, in his note on this passage, that in the third century of the Ḥijrah there was a college of that name, at Baghdād. There was also a monastery in Persia so called. The Ṣūfīs particularly affected the name, from the resemblance of صفا *ṣafā*, and صوفي *ṣūfī*, and they are designated in this passage by the said title.

[189] I have used this expression in order to retain the pun on خويش *kh'īsh*, "self," and خويش *kh'īsh*, "relation."

[190] That is, The Ḳur'ān.

[191] This quotation is from the Ḳur'ān, ch. xxxi. v. 15. I have given Sale's version.

COUPLET.

Thou, for one friendly stranger, sacrifice
A thousand kinsmen who their God despise.

Story XLV.[192]

(IN VERSE.)

In Baghdād once, an aged man of wit
His daughter to a cobbler gave;
The cruel fellow so the damsel bit,
That blood began her lips to lave.
Next morning, when the father saw her plight,
He sought his son-in-law and said,
"What mark of teeth is this? ignoble wight!
Her lip's not leather, that thou'st fed
Upon it thus. I speak this not in jest;
Take what is right, but cease to scoff.
When once ill habits have the soul possessed,
Till the last day they're not left off."

Story XLVI.

A lawyer had an extremely ugly daughter, who had arrived at maturity; but, notwithstanding her dowry and a superabundance of good things, no one shewed any desire to wed her.

COUPLET.

Brocade and damask but ill grace
A bride of loathly form and face.

In short, they were compelled to unite her in the nuptial bond with a blind man. They relate that at that time there arrived a physician from Ceylon, who restored the eyes of the blind to sight. They said to the

[192] This story and the next seem to belong rather to Chapter V.

lawyer, "Why dost thou not get thy son-in-law cured?" He replied, "I am afraid that he should recover his sight and divorce my daughter."

HEMISTICH.

An ugly woman's spouse is better blind.

Story XLVII.

A king was regarding a company of darweshes contemptuously. One of them, acute enough to divine his feelings, said, "O king! we, in this world, are inferior to thee in military pomp, but enjoy more pleasure, and are equal with thee in death, and superior to thee in the day of resurrection.

DISTICHS.

The conqueror may in every wish succeed;
Of bread the darwesh daily stands in need;
But in that hour when both return to clay,
Naught but their winding-sheet they take away.
When man makes up his load this realm to leave,
The beggar finds less cause than kings to grieve.

The outward mark of a darwesh is a patched garment and shaven head; but his essential qualities are a living heart and mortified passions.

STANZA.

Not at strife's door sits he; when thwarted, ne'er
Starts up to contest; all unmoved his soul.
He is no saint who from the path would stir,
Though a huge stone should from a mountain roll.

The darwesh's course of life is spent in commemorating, and thanking, and serving, and obeying God; and in beneficence and contentment; and in the acknowledgment of one God and in reliance on Him; and in resignation and patience. Every one who is endued with these qualities is, in fact, a darwesh, though dressed in a tunic. But a babbler, who neglects prayer, and is given to sensuality, and the gratification of his appetite; who spends his days till night-fall in the pursuit of licentiousness, and passes his night till day returns in careless slumber; eats whatever is set before him, and says whatever comes uppermost; is a profligate, though he wear the habit of a darwesh.

STANZA.

O thou! whose outer robe is falsehood, pride,
While inwardly thou art to virtue dead;
Thy curtain[193] of seven colours put aside,
While th' inner house with mats is poorly spread."

Story XLVIII.

(IN VERSE.)

I saw some handfuls of the rose in bloom,
With bands of grass suspended from a dome.
I said, "What means this worthless grass, that it
Should in the roses' fairy circle sit?"
Then wept the grass and said, "Be still! and know
The kind their old associates ne'er forego.
Mine is no beauty, hue, or fragrance, true!
But in the garden of the Lord I grew."
His ancient servant I,
Reared by His bounty from the dust;
Whate'er my quality,
I'll in His favouring mercy trust.
No stock of worth is mine,
Nor fund of worship, yet He will
A means of help divine;
When aid is past, He'll save me still.

[193] It is customary in Persia to have a curtain at the portal of the house, the richness of which depends on the circumstances of the owner.

Those who have power to free,
Let their old slaves in freedom live,
Thou Glorious Majesty!
Me, too, Thy ancient slave, forgive.
Sâdī! move thou to resignation's shrine,
O man of God! the path of God be thine.
Hapless is he who from this haven turns,
All doors shall spurn him who this portal spurns.

Story XLIX.

They asked a sage, "Which is better, courage or liberality?" He replied, "He who possesses liberality has no need of courage."

COUPLET.

Graved on the tomb of Bahrām Gūr we read,
"Of the strong arm the generous have no need."

STANZA.

Ḥātim[194] is dead; but to eternity
His lofty name will live renowned for good.
Give alms of what thou hast. The vineyard, see!
Yields more, the more the dresser prunes the wood.

[194] Abū Adi Ḥātim-bin-Âbdu 'llāh-bin-Sâdu'l Ṭāī, usually called Ḥātim Ṭāī, was an illustrious Arab, renowned for his generosity. He lived before Muḥammad, but his son Adi, who died at the age of 120, in the 68th year of the Hijrah, is said to have been a companion of the Prophet. Ṭāī is the name of a powerful Arabian tribe, to which Ḥātim belonged. One anecdote of Ḥātim's liberality is very celebrated. The Greek Emperor had sent ambassadors to him for a famous horse he possessed, whose swiftness and beauty were unrivalled, and which he valued with all an Arab's pride. When the envoys arrived, through some accident he had no food to give them; he, therefore, killed his favourite steed, and served up part of its flesh. When their hunger was satisfied, the envoys told the object of their mission, and were astounded at learning that the matchless courser had been sacrificed to shew them hospitality.

CHAPTER III.

ON THE EXCELLENCE OF CONTENTMENT.

Story I.

An African mendicant, in the street of the mercers of Aleppo, said, "O wealthy sirs! if *you* had but justice and *we* contentment, the custom of begging would be banished from the world."

STANZA.

Contentment! do thou me enrich; for those
  Who have thee not are blest with wealth in vain.
Wise Luḳmān for his treasure[195] patience chose:
  Who have not patience wisdom ne'er attain.

Story II.

There were in Egypt two sons of an Amīr.[196] One studied science; the other gained wealth. The former became the most learned man of the age; and the latter king of Egypt. The rich one then looked with scornful eyes on his learned brother, and said, "I have arrived at sovereign power, and thou hast remained in thy poverty

[195] Ross reads گنج *ganj*, "treasure," which I much prefer to كنج *kunj*, "corner," the reading of Gladwin, Semelet, and Sprenger. Luḳmān did not choose "retirement." His wisdom was φρόνησις picked up in the world, not ἐπιστήμη.

[196] Niebuhr, in his History of Arabia, tells us that the descendants of the Prophet are called Amīrs, but the general meaning of the word is "nobleman."

as at the first." He replied, "O brother! it behoves me to render thanks to God Most High, for His bounty, in that I have obtained the inheritance of the Prophets—that is to say, wisdom; and thou the inheritance of Firâun and Hāmān,[197] namely, the land of Egypt."

DISTICHS.

I am the ant which under foot men tread,
And not the hornet whose fierce sting they dread.
How, for this boon, shall I my thanks express?
That I, to injure man, am powerless.

STORY III.

I have heard of a darwesh who was consumed with the flames of hunger, and who sewed rag upon rag, and consoled himself with this couplet.

COUPLET.

I'm with dry bread contented, and with tatters; for 'tis better
To bear up under sorrow, than to be another's debtor.

Some one said to him, "Why dost thou sit here? for such a one in this city has a generous mind, and displays a munificence that extends to all, and his loins are ever girded to serve the distressed, and he sits at the gate of all hearts [waiting to fulfil their wishes]. If he should become acquainted with the state of thy circumstances, he would consider it an obligation to serve a man of worth, and regard it as a precious opportunity." The darwesh

[197] Dr. Sprenger omits the words و هامان, *wa hāmān*, and thus gets rid of the difficulty of the name Hāmān being associated with that of Pharaoh, the only Haman we know being the favourite of Ahasuerus. However, the names occur together in the Ḳur'ān, chaps. xxviii. and xl., where Hāmān appears to be the vazīr of Pharaoh, and therefore only of the same name as our Haman, not the same person.

replied, "Be silent! for it is better to die in indigence than to expose one's wants to another: as they have said,

STANZA.

'Better to suffer, and sew patch o'er patch,
Than begging letters to the rich to write.
Truly it doth hell's torments fairly match,
To mount by others to celestial light.'"

Story IV.

One of the kings of Persia sent a skilful physician to wait on Muṣṭafa[198] (on whom be peace!). He remained some years in the country of Arabia; but no one came to test his abilities, nor asked him for medicine. One day he presented himself before the Chief of the Prophets (on whom be peace!) and complained, saying, "They sent me to heal your companions, and during this long interval no one has addressed himself to me, that this slave might discharge the duty for which he was appointed." The Prophet (peace be upon him!) said, "This people have a custom of not eating anything till hunger compels them, and of withdrawing their hands from the repast while still hungry." "This," said the physician, "is the cause of their good health." He then kissed the ground respectfully and departed.

DISTICHS.

The wise will then begin their speech,
Then towards food their fingers reach,
When silence would with ills be rife,
When fasting would endange life:
Such speech were, certes, wisdom, too,
And from such food will health accrue.

198 A name of Muḥammad. *Vide* Note 179.

Story V.

A person made frequent vows of repentance and broke them again, till a venerable personage said to him, "I understand that thou hast the habit of gormandizing, and the bond of thy appetites—that is to say, thy vows of penitence—is finer than a hair; and thy appetites, as thou fosterest them, would break a chain; and a day will come when they will destroy thee."

COUPLET.

A wolf's whelp had been fostered till, one day,
Grown strong, it tore its master's life away.

Story VI.

In the annals of Ardshīr Bābakān,[199] it is related that he asked an Arabian physician how much food ought to be eaten daily. He replied, "A hundred dirhams' weight would suffice." The king replied, "What strength will this quantity give?" The physician answered, "*This quantity will carry thee; and that which is in excess of it thou must carry;*" or, "This quantity will support thee, and thou must support whatever thou addest to this."

COUPLET.

We eat to live, God's praises to repeat;
Thou art persuaded that we live to eat.

Story VII.

Two darweshes of Khurāsān, travelling together, united in companionship. One was weak, and was in the habit of breaking his fast after every two nights; and the other was strong, and made three meals a day. It happened

[199] This king was the first of the fourth Persian dynasty or Sassanides. He was the son of a shepherd, who married the daughter of one Bābak—hence the name. He was co-temporary with the Emperor Commodus.

that at the gate of a city they were seized, on suspicion of being spies, and were both imprisoned, and the door closed up with mud. After two weeks it was discovered that they were innocent. They opened the door, and found the strong man dead, and the weak man safe and alive. They were still in astonishment at this, when a wise man said, "The opposite of this would have been strange; for this man was a great eater, and could not support the being deprived of food, and so perished. But the other was in the habit of controlling himself; he endured, as was his wont, and was saved."

STANZA.

When to eat little is one's habit grown,
Then, should we want, we bear it easily;
Do we indulge when plenty is our own,
Then, when want happens, we of hardship die.

Story VIII.

A sage forbade his son to eat much, as satiety causes sickness. The son replied, "O my father! hunger kills. Hast thou not heard what the wits have said? 'That it is better to die of repletion than to endure hunger.'" The father answered, "Observe moderation; for God Most High has said, '*Eat and drink; but do not exceed.*'"

COUPLET.

Eat not so as to cause satiety;
Nor yet so little as of want tc die.

STANZA.

The sense by food is gratified; yet still
Th' excess of it brings sickness. Did you eat
Conserve of roses in excess, 'twere ill:
Eat late; then bread is as that conserve sweet."

Story IX.

They said to a sick man, "What does thy heart

desire?" He replied, "Only that it may desire something."[200]

COUPLET.

For stomachs loaded or oppressed with pain,
The costliest viands are prepared in vain.

Story X.

In the city of Wāsiṭ,[201] some Ṣūfīs had incurred a debt of a few dirams to a butcher. Every day he dunned them, and spoke roughly to them. The society were distressed by his reproaches, but had no remedy, save patience. A holy man among them said, "It is easier to put off the stomach with a promise of food, than the butcher with a promise of payment."

STANZA.

Better renounce the favour of the great,
  Than meet their porter's gibes at thy expense;
Rather through want of food succumb to fate,
  Than bear the butcher's dunning insolence.

Story XI.

A brave man had received a terrible wound in a war with the Tartars. Some one said to him, "Such a merchant possesses a remedy. If thou ask him, perhaps he may give thee a little." Now they say that that merchant was as notorious for his stinginess as Ḥātim Ṭāī for his liberality.

[200] The other translators read نخواهد *na khwāhad*, and render thus, "Only that it may not desire anything." This, I think, destroys the point of the story. The sick man wanted food, and being asked what he would wish to eat, replied, "That his wish was, that he could fancy *any*thing."

[201] Wāsiṭ [*lit.*, "middle"] is a city lying between Kūfah and Baṣrah, on the Tigris, built A.H. 83, by Hajjāj bin Yūsuf.

COUPLET.

If the sun upon his table-cloth instead of dry bread lay,
In all the world none would behold again the light of day.

The warrior replied, "If I ask him for the remedy, he may give it or he may not; and if he give it, it may do me good or it may not. In every case to ask of him is deadly poison."

COUPLET.

Whoe'er to beg of sordid persons stoops,
His flesh may profit, but his spirit droops.

And the wise have said, "Were they, for example, to sell the water of life at the price of honour,[202] a wise man would not buy it; since to die honourably is better than to live disgracefully."

COUPLET.

The colocynth from friends tastes better far,
Than sweets from those whose features scowling are.

Story XII.

One of the learned had a large family and small means. He stated his case to a great personage who entertained a favourable opinion of him. The great man was displeased with the request, and regarded with disapprobation this annoyance of begging on the part of a man of decorum.

STANZA.

Seekest thou thy friend? let not thy face be sad
With thy misfortunes, lest thou cloud his joy:
When asking favours let thy looks be glad;
For fortune's not to smiling brows more coy.

[202] There is a play on words here which cannot be preserved in English: آب روي *āb rūī*, literally, "water of the face," signifies "honour," and is here made to answer to آبِ حيات *āb-i ḥaiāt*, "water of life."

They relate that he increased his allowance a little, and diminished his regard for him much. After some days, when the learned man saw that the great man's wonted friendship was not continued to him, he said,

COUPLET.

"*Fie on that food which through base means you taste!*
The cauldron's 'stablished, but your worth's abased.[203]

COUPLET.

My bread increases; but my name's depressed:
Sure want is better than a base request."

Story XIII.

A darwesh was suffering from a pressing exigency. Some one said to him, "Such a one possesses incalculable wealth. If he were informed of your wants, he would probably not allow of any delay in relieving them." He replied, "I do not know him." The other answered, "I will conduct thee." He took his hand and brought him to that person's door. The darwesh beheld a man with a hanging lip, and sitting in an ill-tempered attitude: he said not a word and went back. The other said to him, "What hast thou done?" He replied, "I renounced his gift for the sake of his looks."

[203] There is a double equivoque in this Arabic couplet. قِدر *ḳidr*, is "a cauldron," and قدر *ḳadr*, is "worth," and منتصب *muntaṣab*, "established," signifies also inflected with نصب *naṣb*, this *naṣb* being the grammatical expression for *zabar*, or the short "a" vowel-sound. The قِدر *ḳidr*, "cauldron," is said then to be منتصب *muntaṣab*, made into قدر *ḳadr*, "worth;" and in the same way the قدر *ḳadr*, "worth," is said to be مخفوض *ma<u>kh</u>fūẓ* (which, as well as "abased," signifies also *kasrated*, or inflected with the vowel "ĭ") or made into قِدر *ḳidr*, "cauldron."

STANZA.

To one of scowling face tell not thy woes,
Lest that his evil temper should thee pain ;
But if thy griefs thou shouldst at all disclose,
Be it to one from whom thou mayst obtain,
In his kind countenance, a ready gain.

Story XIV.

One year there befel such a drought at Alexandria that the reins of endurance escaped from the hands of men, and the gates of heaven were closed against the earth, and the complaints of the terrestrial inhabitants ascended to heaven.

STANZA.

Nor beast, nor bird, nor fish, nor ant was there,
But to the sky arose its cry of pain.
Strange that the smoke-wreaths of the people's prayer
Became not clouds, their streaming tear-drops rain.

In such a year, an effeminate person (be he far from my friends!), to describe whom would be indecorous, especially in the august presence of the great; yet to pass over whom altogether in a careless manner would not be right, lest some party should impute it to the inability of the speaker: wherefore, we will sum up the matter with this couplet, that a little may be a sample of much, and a handful a specimen of an ass-load.

COUPLET.

A Tartar might that wretch effeminate
Slay, and not, therefore, merit a like fate.

Such a person, a partial description of whom thou hast heard, possessed that year incalculable wealth. He gave silver and gold to the necessitous, and kept a table for travellers. A party of darweshes, who were reduced to the last extremity by the violence of their hunger, formed the intention of accepting his invitation, and came to consult with me upon the matter. I withheld my consent, and said,

STANZA.

"Lions devour not food which dogs forego,
Of hunger though they perish in their den.
Give up thy frame to famine, want, and woe;
But stretch not forth thy hand to baser men.
A fool a second Farīdūn may be
In wealth; yet him you lightly should esteem.
Silk and brocade upon th' unworthy seem
Like gilding on a wall and lazuli."

Story XV.

They said to Ḥātim Ṭāī, "Hast thou seen or heard of any one in the world more magnanimous than thyself?" He replied, "Yes! One day I had sacrificed forty camels, and had gone out with the chiefs of the Arabs to a corner of the desert; there I saw a wood-cutter, who had collected a bundle of thorns. I said, 'Why dost thou not go to Ḥātim's entertainment? for the people have assembled at his board.' He replied,

COUPLET.

'By their own efforts those who earn their bread,
Need not by Ḥātim Ṭāī's alms be fed.'

I perceived that in magnanimity and generosity he was my superior.'"

Story XVI.

The Prophet Mūsạ[204] (on him be peace!) saw a darwesh who, to hide his nakedness, had concealed himself in the sand, and who said, "O Mūsạ! pray for me, that God Most High may give me wherewith to live, for I am so

[204] Moses.

weak as to be at the point of death." Mūsạ (peace be upon him!) prayed, so that God Most High granted him assistance. Some days after, when the Prophet was returning from his devotions, he saw the darwesh in custody, and surrounded by a crowd of people. He asked, "What has befallen him?" They replied, "He drank intoxicating liquor, raised a disturbance, and slew a man; now they are going to exact retaliation."

VERSE.

Had the poor cat but wings, it would erase
The sparrow's progeny from nature's face;
So, too, the feeble, could they but prevail,
Their fellow-impotents would soon assail.

Mūsạ (peace be on him!) acknowledged the wisdom of the Creator, and expressed contrition for his boldness, repeating the verse, "*And if God had plenteously afforded subsistence to His creatures, they would have rebelled on the earth.*"

COUPLET.

What, proud one! plunged thee in this hapless plight?
Would that the ant ne'er had the power of flight!

VERSE.

When to a blockhead riches, rank accrue,
His folly on his head a buffet brings.
Is not this proverb of the sages true?
"'Twere better for the ant not to have wings."

COUPLET.

Of honey hath the Sire a plenteous store;
But the son's feverish [and must not have more].[205]

COUPLET.

That Being, who increases not thy wealth,
Better than thou, knows what is for thy health.

[205] That is, our Heavenly Father has store of blessings; but man needs chastisement rather than indulgence.

Story XVII.

I once saw an Arab amid a circle of jewellers, at Baṣrah, who was relating the following story: "Once on a time I had lost my way in the desert, and had not a particle of food left, and I had made up my mind to perish, when, suddenly, I found a purse full of pearls. Never shall I forget the gratification and delight I felt when I imagined them to be parched wheat; nor again, the bitterness and despair when I found them to be pearls."

STANZA.

In the parched desert and the drifting sands,
What to the thirsty is or pearl or shell?
When the tired traveller foodless, powerless stands,
No more than sherds can gold his wants expel.

Story XVIII.

An Arab in the desert, from excess of thirst, exclaimed,

VERSE.

"*O would that, ere I die,*
I might at length one day obtain my will:
A river dashing by
Knee-deep, while I at ease my bucket fill."

In the same way a traveller had lost his way in a vast plain, and his food and strength were exhausted, and he had some dirams in his belt. He wandered about much, but could not regain the road, and perished of fatigue. A party arrived there, and saw the dirams spread out before his face, and these words traced on the ground,

STANZA.

"Though he all yellow gold, pure gold possessed,
His wishes still the foodless man would miss.
A turnip boiled, to the poor wretch distressed
In deserts, than crude silver better is."

Story XIX.

I never complained of the vicissitudes of fortune, nor suffered my face to be overcast at the revolution of the heavens, except once, when my feet were bare, and I had not the means of obtaining shoes. I came to the chief mosque of Kūfah[158] in a state of much dejection, and saw there a man who had no feet. I returned thanks to God and acknowledged his mercies, and endured my want of shoes with patience, and exclaimed,

STANZA.

"Roast fowl to him that's sated will seem less
Upon the board than leaves of garden cress.
While, in the sight of helpless poverty,
Boiled turnip will a roasted pullet be."

Story XX.

A certain king, with some of his principal officers, chanced to be in a hunting-park, at a great distance from any habitation, in time of winter. Night fell; they observed the house of a peasant, and the king said, "Let us go there for the night, that we do not suffer from the cold." One of his vazīrs said, "It would not be suitable to the dignity of a king to take refuge in the hut of a miserable peasant. Let us pitch our tent here and kindle a fire." The peasant learned what had taken place. He prepared what food he had ready and took it to the king, and, after kissing the ground respectfully, said, "The lofty dignity of the king will not be lowered by thus much condescension: but these are unwilling that the rank of the peasant should be exalted." The king was pleased with his address. He transferred himself to his cottage for the night, and in the morning gave him a robe of honour and other rich presents. I have heard that the villager ran by the king's stirrup for some distance, and said,

STANZA.

"Of the king's glorious attributes, not one
Was lost by honouring the hostelrie
Of the poor peasant, whose peaked cap the sun
Has reached, since on his head fell, shelteringly,
The shadow of a monarch great like thee."

Story XXI.

They relate that a horrible mendicant possessed great treasures. A king said to him, "It appears that thou possessest immense wealth, and I have an emergent occasion; if thou wouldst assist me with a little of it by way of loan, when the revenue of the country comes in it shall be faithfully repaid." He replied, "It would be unworthy of the lofty dignity of Earth's Lord to defile the hand of his nobleness with the property of a beggar like me, who has scraped it up grain by grain." The king replied, "There is no occasion to be distressed on that account, for I shall give it to the Tartars—*filth to the filthy.*"

COUPLET.

Mortar, they tell us, is by no means sweet;
'Tis then to stop foul drains with it more meet.

COUPLET.

A Christian's well may not be pure, 'tis true;
'Twill do to wash the carcase of a Jew.

I have heard that he bowed not to the king's command, and began to shuffle and be insolent. The king then ordered them to take out of his clutches, by force and intimidation, the amount under discussion.

DISTICHS.

When by kind means succeeds not an affair,
  Rough treatment then we must apply and force.
Whoever of himself will nothing spare,
  Others will him, too, nothing spare, of course.

Story XXII.

I met[206] with a merchant who had a hundred and fifty camels of burthen and forty slaves and servants. One night, in the island of Kīsh, he took me to his room, and did not cease the whole night from talking in a rhodomontade fashion, and saying, "I have such a correspondent in Turkistān, and such an agency in Hindūstan.; and this paper is the title-deed of such a piece of ground, and for such a thing I have such a person as security." At one time he said, "I intend to go to Alexandria, as the climate is agreeable." At another, "No! for the western sea is boisterous; O Sâdī! I have one more journey before me: when that is accomplished I shall retire for the rest of my life and give up trading." I said, "What journey is that?" He replied, "I shall take Persian sulphur to China, for I have heard that it brings a prodigious price there; and thence I shall take China-ware to Greece, and Grecian brocade to India, and Indian steel to Aleppo, and mirrors of Aleppo to Yaman,[207] and striped cloth of Yaman to Persia, and after that I shall give up trading and sit at home in my shop." He continued for some time rambling in this strain until he had no power to utter more. He then said, "O Sâdī! do thou say something of what thou hast seen and heard." I replied, "Thou hast not left me a single subject to talk about."

[206] Literally, "saw"; but here one may translate it, "was in the habit of seeing."

[207] Arabia Felix.

VERSE.

Hast thou not heard what once a merchant cried,
As in the desert from his beast he sank?
"The worldling's greedy eye is satisfied,
Or by contentment or the grave-yard dank."

STORY XXIII.

I have heard of a wealthy man who was as famous for his parsimony as Ḥātim Ṭāī for generosity. His outward estate was adorned with riches, but the baseness of his nature was so inherent in him that he would not have given a loaf to save a life, nor would have indulged the cat of Abū Hurairah[178] with a scrap, nor have cast a bone to the dog of the Companions of the Cave. In short, no one ever saw his mansion with the doors open, nor his table spread.

COUPLET.

No darwesh knew his viands save by smell,
Nor birds picked crumbs which from his table fell.

I have heard that he was voyaging to Egypt by the western sea with all the pride of Pharaoh, *according to the words of the Most High, "until his submersion arrived:"* All of a sudden an adverse wind sprang up round the vessel: as they have said,

COUPLET.

"Thy peevish mind all things must still displease.
The ship not always finds a favouring breeze."

He raised his hands in prayer, and began to make unavailing lamentations. *God Most High has said, "When they embark in a ship, they pray to God."*

COUPLET.

What will it avail the creature to stretch forth his hand
in grief ?
Raised in prayer to God in peril, but withheld from
man's relief.[208]

STANZA.

Go, with thy silver and thy gold, provide
Blessings to men ; nor from thyself withhold
Enjoyment due ; thus ever shall abide
Thy house, its bricks of silver and of gold.[209]

They relate that he had poor relations in Egypt, who were enriched by the residue of his property, and who, at his death, rent their old garments, and cut out others of silk and stuffs of Damietta. During the same week, too, I saw one of them mounted on a fleet courser, with a fairy-faced youth running at his stirrup. I said to myself,

STANZA.

"Ah ! could the dear defunct again
Back to his kin and friends repair,
Worse than his death would be the pain
Of restitution to his heir."

On the strength of a former acquaintance which existed between us, I pulled his sleeve and said,

COUPLET.

"Enjoy thy fortune, gentle sir ! for he,
Luckless, amassed ; th' enjoyment, left to thee."

[208] The literal translation of this impracticable couplet is—
"What avails the hand of entreaty to the needy creature,
Who in the hour of prayer raises it to God, but at the time
for liberality puts it under his armpit."

[209] The meaning of this is : Thou shalt obtain for thyself a heavenly dwelling, built, as it were, by the proper use of thy treasures in this world.

Story XXIV.

A strong fish fell into the net of a weak fisherman. He had not strength to secure it; the fish got the better of him, dragged the net from his hands, and escaped.

STANZA.

The slave went forth for water from the brook,
The streamlet rose and bore the slave away.
Each time the net its prize of fishes took,
But of the net the fish made prize to-day.

The other fishermen were vexed, and reproached him, saying, "Such a fish fell into thy net, and thou couldst not keep it!" He replied, "O brothers! what could I do? seeing that it was not my lucky day, and the fish had some days remaining."[210]

MAXIM.

A fisherman without luck cannot capture a fish in the Tigris; and unless his predestined time be come, a fish will not die on the dry land.

Story XXV.

One whose hands and feet had been cut off killed a millepede. A devout personage passed by and said, "Holy God! though it had a thousand feet, yet, when its time was come, it could not escape from one without either hands or feet."

[210] There is a play on the words here which cannot be well preserved in English. روزي *rūzī*, signifies "luck" as well as "days" [*i.e.* remnant of life].

DISTICHS.

When from behind speeds our last enemy,
Fate fetters us, how fleet soe'er we be.
And in that instant when comes up the foe,
'Tis vain to handle the Kaiānian bow.[211]

Story XXVI.

I saw a fat blockhead, with a gorgeous robe on his body, and an Arabian horse under him, and a turban of fine Egyptian linen on his head. Some one said, "O Sâdi! what thinkest thou of this splendid brocade on this animal who knows nothing?" I replied, "It is a villainous scrawl written in golden letters."

COUPLET.

He, among men, an ass appears to be,
Certes a very calf-like effigy.[212]

STANZA.

One cannot say this brute resembles man,
  Save by cloak, turban, outward garniture;
Go thou his goods, estates, possessions scan,
  Naught but his life is takeable, be sure.

STANZA.

Though one of birth illustrious should grow poor,
  This will his lofty station naught impair:
And though gold nails may stud his silver door,
  Think not a Jew can aught that's noble share.

[211] The Kaiānian is the second dynasty of Persian kings, of whom the first was Kaiḳubād or Darius the Mede. Archery is said to have reached perfection under these monarchs.

[212] There is a reference here to the Kur'ān, ch. vii. v. 148, "And the people of Moses, after his departure, took a corporeal calf, made of their ornaments, which lowed."

Story XXVII.

A thief said to a beggar, "Art thou not ashamed to hold out thy hand for the smallest particle of silver to every contemptible fellow?" He replied,

COUPLET.

"Better hold the hand for coin, though small,
Than lose, for one and half a dāng,[213] it all."

Story XXVIII.

They relate that an athlete had suffered so much from adverse fortune that he was reduced to despair, and bemoaned himself on account of his keen appetite and narrow means. He went to his father to complain, and asked his leave to set out on his travels, in order that by the strength of his arm he might succeed in grasping the skirt of his wishes.

COUPLET.

Merit and skill are weak while in the husk:
Aloes they cast on fire, and crush down musk.

The father said, "O son! put out of thy head this impracticable idea, and draw the feet of contentment under the skirt of security: as the wise have said, 'Riches are not to be gained by exertion; the best resource is to chagrin oneself less.'

COUPLET.

No one by strength of arm can fortune find:
'Tis labour lost—collyrium for the blind.

[213] A dāng is the sixth part of a dirham, or, according to some, the fourth part, and therefore equal to about one penny. M. Semelet remarks that this line shews that theft, in the time of Sâdī, was punished by amputation, if the thing stolen was worth one and a half dāng; I suppose, however, that this sum is used generally for any trifling value.

COUPLET.

Hast thou two hundred virtues on each hair?
With adverse fate thou still wilt badly fare.

COUPLET.

What can th' ill-starred athlete do? how thrive?
Can he, though strong, with stronger fortune strive?"

The son replied, "O father! the advantages of travel are manifold; in enlivening the mind, and acquiring advantages, and seeing wonderful things, and hearing marvels and in amusement, in passing through new countries, and in correspondence with friends, and in the acquisition of rank and courteous manners, and in the increase of wealth and profit, and as a means of obtaining companions, and making proof of different fortunes: as those who travel in the path of spirituality have said,

STANZA.

'Whilst thou art wedded to thy shop and home,
O simpleton! a man thou ne'er wilt be;
Go blithely forth, and in the wide world roam,
Ere thou roam'st from it to eternity.'"

The father answered, "O son! the advantage of travel in the manner thou hast mentioned is great; but it is secured to five kinds of persons. The first is the merchant, who, by the possession of riches and affluence, and active slaves, and enchanting damsels, and brave servants, enjoys all the luxuries of the world, being each day in a city, and each night at a halting-place, and each instant in an abode of pleasure.

STANZA.

In mountain-waste, or forest wild, the rich man is not strange;
Where'er he goes his tent is pitched, and there his court is made.
But he who has not this world's gear must ever friendless range,
Nor even in his fatherland will comfort find nor aid.

The second is the learned man, from whose sweetness of speech, and power of language, and stock of eloquence, wherever he goes, all hasten to serve him and do him honour.

STANZA.

The wise man's nature is like purest gold:
Where'er he comes all know his value, prize his worth.
But men will, cheap as leathern money, hold
The witless lord, save in the land that gave him birth.

The third is the beautiful person, being such that the heart[214] of persons of eminence inclines to friendship with him, and his society is regarded by them as a fortunate circumstance, and his service as a favour: as they have said: 'A little beauty is better than much wealth: a fair countenance is a salve for heart-sickness, and the key of closed doors.'

STANZA.

Let beauty travel where it will, it finds respectful greeting,
Though its own parents, wrathfully, should drive it from its home.
One day, amid the Ḳur'ān's leaves, a peacock's feather meeting,
I said, 'This place exceeds thy worth, thou dost it not become.'
'Peace!' it replied, 'for to each one who wears the charm of beauty,
Go where he will, all him receive with favour as a duty.'

VERSE.

When the son beauty has, and courtesy,
Let him not care how cold his sire may be.

[214] M. Semelet recommends کند *kunad* for کنند *kunand,* and Dr. Sprenger reads it; I do not, therefore, hesitate to adopt it in this translation.

He is a pearl, what if the shell be lost?
Who for a priceless[215] pearl will grudge the cost?

The fourth is he who possesses a sweet voice; who, with the throat of David, restrains the water from flowing, and arrests the bird in its flight; and, moreover, by means of this excellence, captivates the hearts of men, and spiritual persons eagerly desire his companionship.

COUPLET.

My ears attend his melody;
Who's this whose hands[216] *the lute-strings try?*

STANZA.

How winningly a soft and tender voice
Comes to the ears of friends, whom th' early bowl
Makes blithe! in it, more than in looks, rejoice
All hearts; these the sense gladden: that the soul.

The fifth is the artisan, who gains the means of support by the labour of his arm, so that his character is not jeoparded for bread: as the wise have said,

STANZA.

'If want from his own city should expel
A cotton-carder, he'd not feel distress;
But if the king of Nīmroz, ruined, fell
From his high place, he'd slumber supperless.'

Qualities such as I have described are a means of consolation in travel, and a sweet cause of enjoyment; but one

[215] There is a very good equivoque here which cannot be repeated in English: يتيم *yatīm*, signifies "unique, precious," and also "orphan."

[216] For the حُسْنُ المَثَانِي *ḥusn-u'l-maṣānī* in the second line, which is the common reading, Dr. Sprenger has the better (in my opinion) reading: جَسّ المَثَانِي *jassa-u'l maṣānī*, "he handled the strings."

who has no share in all these will enter the world with vain expectations, and no one will hear his name again, or see any more trace of him.

STANZA.

He, whom t' afflict upsprings revolving fate
Malevolent, is led by destiny
Against his will. The pigeon, who his mate
Shall ne'er revisit, follows fate's decree
Towards the net [in blind security]."

The son answered, "O father! how shall I act in opposition to the saying of the wise? who have pronounced that although a subsistence is allotted, yet it is on the condition of using the means of acquiring it; and though calamity is predestined, yet it is right to secure oneself against the portals by which it might have access.

STANZA.

Though, without doubt, fate will our want supply,
Reason requires it be sought from home;
'Tis true that none will unpredestined die,
Yet in a dragon's maw one should not come.

In my present condition I could encounter a furious elephant and contend with a devouring lion. My best course is to travel, for I am unable to endure my privations any longer.

STANZA.

Whene'er a man from home and country flies,
All earth is his; he has no further care.
Each night the rich man to his palace hies:
Where night descends, the poor man's home is there."

He spoke thus, and asking his father's blessing, took leave of him and set off, and at the time of his departure they heard him say,

COUPLET.

"The man of worth, whose fate is cross, will go
Where men have never learned his name to know."

So he travelled on till he came to the brink of a stream, by the violence of which stone was dashed upon stone, and whose noise resounded to the distance of a parasang.[217]

COUPLET.

A stream so dread, not birds were safe amid its waters' roar;
The smallest of its waves would sweep a mill-stone from its shore.

There he saw a party of men who had each of them obtained a seat in a ferry-boat, for a small piece of gold, and whose baggage was ready packed. The young man's hand was closed from payment, but he loosened the tongue of compliment. In spite of all his supplication they rendered him no assistance, but said,

COUPLET.

"Thou canst not make thy strength of arm the want of gold supply;
And hast thou gold, thou needest not to threaten or defy."

The rude boatman turned from him with a laugh, and said,

COUPLET.

"Gold thou hast not; the passage o'er by force may not be won;
What is the strength of ten men here? bring thou the gold for one."

The young man was incensed at this sarcasm, and

[217] Chardin explains this word as فارس سنگ *fārs sang*, "Persian stone;" a word written by Herodotus and other Greek authors, *Παρασαυγα, parasanga:* "Il paraît, par la signification du mot *Fars-seng*, qu'anciennement les lieues etaient marquées par de grandes et hautes pierres, tant dans l'Orient que dans l'Occident. On dit en latin, Ad primum vel secundum lapidem."

burned to revenge himself upon him. The boat had put off; he called out, "If thou wilt be content with this garment I am wearing, I will not refuse to give it." The boatman's avarice was roused; he put back the boat.

COUPLET.

The eyes of men, though sharp, are closed by avarice;
Greed will both bird and fish towards the net entice.

As soon as the young man's hand could reach the beard and collar of the boatman, he dragged him forward and knocked him down without mercy. His comrades[218] came out of the boat to help him, and meeting with the same rough treatment, turned their backs, finding it their best plan to make peace with him, and excuse him the passage-money.

DISTICHS.

Act thou forbearingly when discord's rife,
For gentleness will close the gates of strife.
When thou seest broils arise, use courtesy;
A sharp sword cuts not silk, though soft it be.
With honeyed words, good humour on thy side,
Thou, with a hair, an elephant mayst guide.

They fell at his feet, with excuses for their past conduct, and imprinted hypocritical kisses on his forehead and face, and brought him into the boat, and proceeded till they arrived at a pillar of a Grecian building which remained standing amid the waters. The boatman said, "The boat is in danger; let one of you, who is most courageous and valiant, and powerful, go to this pillar, and lay hold of the boat's hawser, that we may pass by

[218] Dr. Sprenger reads یارش آمدند *yārash āmadand*, M. Semelet یارش آمد *yārash āmad*. I must confess I prefer my own reading یارانش آمدند *yārānash āmadand*.

this building."[219] The young man, from the pride of valour which he felt, took no thought of his still smarting foe, and forbore to act in accordance with the saying of the wise, which they have uttered: "When thou hast wounded the heart of any one, even if thou shouldest subsequently do him a hundred favours, nevertheless deem not thyself safe from that one injury, for the shaft may have been extracted from the wound, yet the pang abide still in the heart."

COUPLET.

How truthfully to Khailtāsh, Yaktāsh[220] said;
Is thy foe hurt?—then live not free from dread.

STANZA.

Fancy not thyself safe, for thou shalt moan,
Who hast another treated cruelly.
Against the castle-wall hurl not a stone,
Lest from the walls a stone descend on thee.

He had no sooner twisted the hawser round his arm, and mounted the pillar, than the boatman twisted the rope from his hand, and urged on the boat. The athlete remained there helpless and astonished. For two days he endured his suffering and distress, and bore up against his hardships. On the third day sleep seized him by the collar, and plunged him in the water. After a night and a day[221] he was cast on the shore, with the breath of life

[219] Dr. Sprenger reads تا از عمارت عبور کنیم *tā az ʻimārat ʻubūr kunīm*, which, on the whole, I prefer to the reading in my edition. M. Semelet translates, "afin que nous fassions la réparation." Gladwin renders, "that we may save the vessel"; and Ross, "till we can swing her head round," all which translations are without the vestige of a foundation in the original.

[220] Of these two Gentius says, "duo nobilissimi sunt athletæ quos celebrat thesaurus regius."

[221] شبانروز *shabānrūz*, exactly the Greek *νυχθήμερον*.

just remaining. He began to eat the leaves of trees, and to pull up the roots of grass, until he recovered his strength a little. He then set his face toward the woods, and went on till he arrived, thirsty and hungry, and powerless, at the brink of a well. He saw a party of persons, who had assembled round it, and who were getting a draught of water for a small payment. The young man had no coin, not even the smallest; he asked for water, they refused it; he extended the hand of violence, but succeeded not. He struck down several of them; the men made a general attack upon him, beat him unmercifully, and wounded him.

STANZA.

Gnats will an elephant o'ercome, if they
Unite against their foe, so huge and grim.
And ants collected in one dense array,
Though fierce the lion be, will vanquish him.

Urged by necessity, he followed a caravan, sick and wounded, and proceeded on. At night they arrived at a place which was perilous on account of robbers. He saw that a tremor pervaded the frames of the people of the caravan, and that they had made up their minds to be slain. He said, "Be not troubled, for I am one among you who will answer for fifty men, and the other braves will assist me." The men's hearts were encouraged by his vaunt, and they were glad of his company, and ministered to him food and water. The fire was blazing up in the young man's stomach, and the reins of endurance had slipped from his hands. He devoured some mouthfuls with excessive voracity, and swallowed some gulps of water, till the demon within him was appeased, and slumber overcame him, and he slept. There was, in the caravan, an old man of experience, acquainted with the world, who said, "O my friends! I am more afraid of this guard of yours than of the robbers: as they tell that an Arab had amassed a few dirhams: he could not sleep when alone in his house from dread of the Lūrīs.[222] He brought one of his friends to be with him that he might get rid of the terrors of solitude by the sight of him. The friend remained some nights in his company, but as soon as he found out where his dirhams were, he carried them off and went on his travels. The next morning they saw the Arab despoiled and lamenting. They said, 'What is the matter? has some robber carried off those dirhams of thine?' He replied, 'No! by Heaven, the guard has taken them.'

STANZA.

With a companion I ne'er felt secure
  Until I learned his inward qualities.
Wounds from a foeman's tooth are worse t' endure
  When he has shown himself in friendship's guise.

How know ye, O my friends! whether this young man, also, be not of the number of the robbers, and sent among us through stratagem, in order that, on a favourable opportunity, he may communicate with his friends? I, therefore, think it expedient to leave him asleep, and proceed on our journey." The people of the caravan approved of the old man's advice, and felt a dread of the athlete arise in their hearts. They packed up their goods, and left the young man sleeping. He did not discover this until the sun was shining on his shoulders; he then raised his head, and saw that the caravan had departed. After wandering about a long time, he could not find his way, and thirsty and hungry, he placed his face on the ground, and fixed his thoughts on destruction, and said,

[222] The Lūrīs are the people of Lūrīstan, a mountainous province of Persia, to the north-east of Khuzistān, and having Kūrdistān to the north. The inhabitants are notorious thieves.

COUPLET.

"Gone[223] are the yellow camels now: who will address me more?
The poor man has no comrade—no comrade but the poor.

COUPLET.

With the poor wanderer they will harshly deal,
Who ne'er experienced what the friendless feel."

He was uttering these words when a prince, who, in pursuit of a quarry, had got to a distance from his retinue, came and stood over him. He heard what he said; and looking on his form, saw that his external shape was comely, while his appearance betokened wretchedness. He asked him whence he was, and how he had come there? He related a portion of what had befallen him. The prince pitied him, bestowed on him a dress and gifts, and sent a confidential servant along with him to see him back to his own city. His father was glad to see him, and returned thanks for his safety. At night, he told his father what had befallen him; of the adventure of the boat, and of the injurious conduct of the boatman, and of the peasants, and of the treachery of the people of the caravan. The father said, "O son! did I not tell thee at the time of thy departure that the hands of the empty-handed, however brave they may be, are fettered, and their lion's claws broken.

COUPLET.

That needy gladiator said right well,
A grain of gold doth pounds[224] of strength excel."

The son said, "O father! undoubtedly, until thou

[223] The word زمّ *zumm*, signifies "bridled," but in this place it refers to departure.

[224] Literally, "fifty *mans*," a weight which has been explained before.

endurest pain, thou wilt no treasure gain; and while thou riskest not thy life, thou wilt not subdue thy foe; and until thou scatterest abroad the seed, thou wilt not reap the harvest. Seest thou not, by a little matter of trouble which I have undergone, what an amount of treasure I have brought home; and by enduring the sting, what an abundance of honey I have obtained?"

COUPLET.

Though more than fate supplies we ne'er can gain,
Yet must we strive that portion to obtain.

COUPLET.

From the ravening monster's[225] jaw, should the diver pause and gasp,
He'd never hold the precious pearl, the bright pearl, in his grasp.

APOPHTHEGM.

The lower mill-stone revolves not, and hence, of necessity, supports the greater burthen.

STANZA.

On what would savage lions feed? if they
In their deep dens abode. The hawk would win
Small sustenance did it ne'er seek its prey.
And, like a spider's, will thy limbs grow thin,
If thine own house alone thou huntest in.

The father said, "O son! this time heaven has befriended thee, and thy good fortune has been thy guide, so that thy rose has come forth from the thorn, and the thorn from thy foot; and, accordingly, one who possessed wealth, found thee out and enriched thee, and he had compassion on thee, and repaired thy broken fortunes, inquiring kindly into them; and such an occurrence is

[225] Gladwin translates نهنگ *nihang*, "crocodile," but the danger to the pearl-diver would rather be from sharks.

rare, and one cannot govern one's conduct by events of rare occurrence. Beware lest thou be led by this greediness to hover a second time round this snare.

COUPLET.

The hunter does not always win the prey,
Perchance a tiger may him rend one day.

As, once a king of Persia had a very precious stone in a ring. On a certain occasion he went out with some of his favourite courtiers, to amuse himself, to the mosque near Shīrāz, called Muṣallā, and commanded that they should suspend the ring over the dome of Âẓad, saying that the ring should be the property of him who could send an arrow through it. It befell that four hundred archers, who plyed their bows in his service, shot at the ring. All of them missed. But a stripling, at play, was shooting arrows at random from a monastery, when the morning breeze carried his shaft through the circle of the ring. They bestowed the ring upon him, and loaded him with gifts beyond calculation. The boy, after this, burned his bow and arrows. They asked him why he did so. He replied, 'That my first glory may remain unchanged.'

STANZA.

The sage whose bright mind mirrors truth,
May sometimes wander wide of it:
While, by mistake, the simple youth,
Will, with his shaft, the target hit."

Story XXIX.

I have heard of a darwesh who had taken up his abode in a cave, and had closed the door before him on the world; while, in the eye of his lofty independence, kings and rich men had lost consideration.

STANZA.

Who, on himself, the door of begging opes,
Will, to his death, in want remain.
Quit greed, and as a monarch reign,
For proud his station who for nothing hopes.

One of the neighbouring princes signified to him that he relied on the condescension of his courteous character, that he would come and partake of his bread and salt. The Shekh consented, as to accept an invitation is enjoined by the authority of the Prophet. The next day the king went to apologize for the trouble[226] he had given him. The devotee arose and embraced the king, and treated him kindly. When the king was gone, one of the companions of the Shekh asked him, saying, "It is unusual with thee to display such tokens of regard to a king; what hidden meaning is there in this?" He replied, "Hast thou not heard that they have said,

COUPLET.

"If at another's table one has sat,
'Tis right, in turn, to rise and on him wait."

DISTICHS.

The ear may never through one's life
Hear sound of tabor, lute, or fife:
The eye abstain from floral show:
The brain the rose's[227] scent not know:
Though pillowed not on down, the head
May on a stone find sleep instead:
And when our arms no fair one hold,
On our own breast we may them fold.
But this vile belly, base and dull,
Will never rest unless 'tis full.

[226] Literally, "for excusing his service (*i.e.* lack of service) to him."

[227] I omit the Narcissus, *metri causâ*.

CHAPTER IV.

ON THE ADVANTAGES OF TACITURNITY.

Story I.

I said to one of my friends, "I have chosen to abstain from speaking, for this reason, because, on the majority of occasions, it happens that in speech there is evil as well as good, and the eye of enemies notes only the evil." He replied, "O brother! he is the best enemy[228] who does not observe our good qualities."

COUPLET.

No fault's like virtue to the foeman's eye,
Who, e'en in Sâdī's[229] self, would thorns descry.

COUPLET.

Ne'er the malignant pass a good man by,
But slander him with hateful villainy.

COUPLET.

The feeble-visioned mole perchance may scorn
The sun's bright fount, that doth the world adorn.

Story II.

A merchant met with the loss of a thousand dīnārs, and said to his son, "Thou must not tell any one of this

[228] Malice is comparatively quiet as long as the object of its hate is but an ordinary character. To be illustrious, provokes its bitterest wrath.

[229] Literally, "A rose is Sâdī, but in the eyes of enemies a thorn."

matter." The son replied, "O father! it is thy command; I will not tell; acquaint me, however, with the advantage to be derived from keeping the affair secret." The father answered, "In order that we may not have two misfortunes to encounter—first, the loss of our money; and secondly, the malignant rejoicings of our neighbours."

COUPLET.

Do not to foes thy sufferings impart,
Lest, while they seem to grieve, they joy at heart.[230]

Story III.

An intelligent young man, who possessed an ample stock of admirable accomplishments and a rare intellect, notwithstanding, uttered not a word whenever he was seated in the company of the wise. At length, his father said, "O son! why dost not thou also say somewhat of that thou knowest?" He replied, "I fear lest they should ask me something of which I am ignorant, and I should bring on myself disgrace."

STANZA.

One day a Ṣūfī (hast thou heard it told?)
By chance was hammering nails into his shoe:
Then of his sleeve an officer caught hold,
And said, "Come thou! and shoe my charger too!"

COUPLET.

Art silent? none can meddle with thee. When
Thou once hast spoken, thou must prove it then.

Story IV.

A learned man of high reputation had a dispute with a heretic, and did not get the better of him in argument.

[230] Literally, "While they repeat the deprecatory formula, There is no power or strength but in God."

He cast away his shield, and took to flight.[231] Some one said to him, "Hadst thou, notwithstanding all thy learning and address, and eminent qualities and sagacity, no argument left with which to combat an infidel?" He replied, "My knowledge is the Ḳur'ān, and the traditions of the Prophet and the doctrines of the fathers; and he believes not in these things, and will not attend to them; and in what shall I be benefited by listening to his impieties?"

COUPLET.

To those who doctrine and Ḳur'ān deny,
To answer nothing is the best reply.

Story V.

The physician Galen, on seeing a fool lay hold of the collar of a learned man and disgrace him, said, "Had this been a wise man, his dealings with a fool would not have reached this point."

DISTICHS.

The wise will not in hate or strife engage;
Nor with a simpleton contends the sage.
When fools, in savage words, their thoughts express,
The wise will soothe them by their gentleness.
Two men of judgment will not break a hair,
Thus 'twixt the headlong and the mild 'twill fare.
But should the band that parts them be a chain,
Two fools would quickly break its links in twain.

Story VI.

Saḥbān Wāil[232] has been regarded as unrivalled in eloquence, inasmuch as he could speak a whole year before an assembly without ever being guilty of repeti-

[231] Metaphorical expressions for giving up the dispute.
[232] Name of a celebrated Arabian poet.

tion; and should the same idea recur, he would express it in different language. And this is one of the accomplishments requisite for courtiers.

DISTICHS.

Thy speech may be attractive, just, and sweet,
Worthy to be approved by judgment nice;
But when once spoken, ne'er the same repeat,
For once to swallow sweetmeats will suffice.

Story VII.

I heard a sage say, "No one avows his ignorance but the man, who, while another is speaking, and has not yet finished, commences speaking himself."

DISTICHS.

Each several theme beginning has and end,
Therefore weave not discourse within discourse.
A man of judgment, wit, and sense, my friend!
Speaks not until thy words have had their course.

Story VIII.

Some of the servants of Sulṭān Maḥmūd asked Ḥasan Maimandī,[233] "What did the Sulṭān say to thee to-day about a certain affair?" He replied, "It will not have been concealed from you too?"[234] They answered,

[233] Khwājah Aḥmad-bin Ḥasan, called Maimandī, from the town of Maimand where he was born, was the vazīr of Sulṭān Maḥmūd of Ghaznī. His enemies, and particularly Altantush, the General of Maḥmūd's forces, endeavoured to ruin him with the king, but were constantly baffled through the Queen's influence. Fīrdausī, the author of the Shāh-nāmah, was introduced to the Sulṭān by Ḥasan.

[234] Dr. Sprenger reads نباشد *na bāshad* for my نماند *namānad*, and ظهيرِ سريرِ سلطانتي و مشيرِ تدبيرِ مملكت *ẓahīr-i sarīr-i sulṭānatī wa mushīr-i tadbīr-i mamlakat* for my دستورِ مملكت *dastūr-i mamlakat*.

"Thou art the Prime Minister of the State; the Sulṭān does not think of telling us what he tells thee." Ḥasan replied, "And he does this in the confidence that I will not repeat it. Wherefore, then, do ye ask me?"

COUPLET.

Not all they know will men of prudence tell;
Nor with kings' secrets sport, and life as well.

Story IX.

I was hesitating about a bargain for a house when a Jew said to me, "I am one of the old inhabitants of this quarter. Inquire of me the intrinsic value of the house, and purchase it, for it has not a fault." I replied, "None, except that thou livest near it."

STANZA.

A house with such a neighbour as thou art
Were worth ten silver dirhams—those, too, bad.
Yet hope we—shouldst thou from this life depart,
A thousand for it then might well be had.

Story X.

A poet went to the chief of a band of robbers and recited a panegyric upon him. He commanded them to strip off his clothes and turn him out of the village. The dogs, too, attacked him in the rear. He wanted to take up a stone, but the ground was frozen. Unable to do anything, he said, "What a villainous set are these, who have untied their dogs and tied up the stones." The chieftain heard this from a window, and said with a laugh, "Philosopher! ask a boon of me." He replied, "If thou wilt condescend to make me a present, bestow on me my own coat."

COUPLET.

From some a man might favours hope—from thee
We hope for nothing but immunity.

HEMISTICH.

We feel thy kindness that thou lett'st us go.

The robber chief had compassion on him. He gave him back his coat, and bestowed on him a fur cloak in addition, and further presented him with some dirhams.

Story XI.

An astrologer, on entering his own house, found a man sitting with his wife. He abused and reviled him, and a disturbance arose. A sagacious person, being informed of this, said,

COUPLET.

"Canst thou tell what goes on above the sky,
And not th' interior of thy house descry?"

Story XII.

A preacher, who had a shocking voice, fancied it was very agreeable, and employed it in shouting to no purpose. *The croaking of the raven* [you would say] was in his modulations; and that that verse was intended for him, "*Verily the most detestable of sounds is the voice of an ass.*"

COUPLET.

Preacher Abū'l-fawāris brays—from far
Persian Iṣṭakhar trembles at the jar.[235]

The people of the town, out of respect to the office he held, put up with the infliction, and did not think it right to annoy him: till at length, a preacher of that district, who had a secret spite against him, came to see him, and said, "I have seen a dream; I hope it will turn out well." The other asked, "What hast thou seen?" The visitor

[235] M. Semelet thinks this couplet a quotation. He does not, however, nor does any other author that I have seen, explain who Abū'l-fawāris [*lit.*, "father of the horsemen"] is.

answered, "I beheld that thy voice was pleasant, and that people were delighted with thy discourse." The preacher reflected a little on this, and said, "What a fortunate dream it is that thou hast seen, by which thou hast acquainted me with my failings. I now understand that I have an unpleasant voice, and that people are distressed by my delivery. I vow amendment, and, in future, will never read except in a low voice."

STANZA.

I wearied of my friend's society,
  Who my bad qualities as virtues shews;
Who, in my failings, can perfection see,
  And calls my thorns the jasmine and the rose.
Give me the pert and watchful enemy,
  Who will my faults to me with zest disclose.

Story XIII.

A person was performing gratis the office of summoner to prayer in the mosque of Sanjāriyah,[236] in a voice which disgusted those who heard him. The patron of the mosque was a prince who was just and amiable. He did not wish to pain the crier, and said, "O sir! there are Mūāzzins attached to this mosque to whom the office has descended from of old, each of whom has an allowance of five dīnārs, and I will give thee ten to go to another place." This was agreed upon, and he departed. After

[236] This mosque was built by Sulṭān Sanjār Saljūkī, sixth Sulṭān of the Saljūks, who was the son of Malik Shāh, and reigned over Persia and Khurāsān. He performed many exploits, and was called the second Alexander. As a mark of respect, prayers were read in his name in the mosques for a year after his decease. The Saljūks were originally Turkumāns, and entered Trans-oxiana A.H. 375. Sulṭān Sanjār succeeded his brother Muḥammad on the throne, A.H. 501.

some time he returned to the prince and said, "O my lord! thou didst me injustice in sending me from this place for ten dīnārs. In the place whence I have come they offered me twenty dīnārs to go somewhere else, and I will not accept it." The prince laughed and said, "Take care not to accept it, for they will consent to give thee even fifty dīnārs."

COUPLET.

No mattock can the clay remove from off the granite stone,
So well as thy discordant voice can make the spirit moan.

Story XIV.

A man with a harsh voice was reading the Ḳur'ān in a loud tone. A sage passed by and asked, "What is thy monthly stipend?" He replied, "Nothing." Wherefore, then," asked the sage, "dost thou give thyself this trouble?" He replied, "I read for the sake of God." "Then," said the sage, "for God's sake! read not."

COUPLET.

If in this fashion the Ḳur'ān you read,
You'll mar the loveliness of Islām's creed.

CHAPTER V.

ON LOVE AND YOUTH.

Story I.

They asked Ḥasan Maimandī, "How is it that, although Sulṭān Maḥmūd has so many handsome slaves, every one of whom is the wonder of the world, and the marvel of the age, he has not such a regard or affection for any one as for Ayāz,[237] who is not remarkable for beauty?" He replied, "Whatever pleases the heart appears fair to the eye."

DISTICHS.

The man for whom the Sulṭān shews esteem,
Though bad in every act, will virtuous seem.
But whom the monarch pleases to reject,
None of his retinue will e'er affect.

STANZA.

When with antipathy we eye a man,
We see in Joseph's beauty, want of grace:
And, prepossessed, should we a demon scan,
He'd seem a cherub with an angel's face.

Story II.

I remember that one night a dear friend of mine entered my door, and I rose from my seat with such impatience [to receive him] that I put out my lamp with my sleeve.

[237] Gladwin writes this name Iyaz, and I have followed him in my Vocabulary; but with Semelet, Ross, and Richardson on the other side, I feel bound to adopt the spelling given above.

VERSES.

By night a spectre came, and with its form lit up the gloom;
Methought it well would suit me for a guide throughout the night.[238]
"Hail!" I exclaimed, "Well art thou come! for thee is ample room;
I love thee, for the darkness flies before thy radiance bright."

COUPLET.

I said, astonished at my destiny,
"Whence has this happy fortune come to me?"

He sate down and began to remonstrate with me, saying, "Why, at the moment that thou sawest me, didst thou extinguish the lamp?" I replied, "I imagined that the sun had entered; and the witty have said,

STANZA.

'If one obscure the lamp with presence vile,
Arise and him before th' assembly smite:
But, if he have sweet lips and honeyed smile,[239]
Seize thou his sleeve, and then put out the light.'"

Story III.

A person had not seen his friend for a long interval. At last he met him and said, "Where wert thou? for I longed after thee." He replied, "Better longing than loathing."

[238] These three lines are not in Ross, Gladwin or Semelet. I inserted them in my edition, and am now glad to find my judgment confirmed by Dr. Sprenger, in whose edition they are likewise to be found, with some trifling difference of reading.

[239] They would be of no use in his radiant presence, which of itself would dispel the darkness.

COUPLET.

Gay idol of my soul! late comest thou!
Not soon will I release thy garment now.

VERSE.

'Tis better that our friend we seldom see,
Than to behold him to satiety.[240]

SENTIMENT.

When a fair one comes attended by companions, she comes only to torment us; because, in that case, there must arise the jealousy and discord of rivals.

COUPLET.

Comest thou attended, then thou comest me only to distress;
Thou comest truly to make war, though peace thy looks express.

STANZA.

But for an instant should my friend prefer
To be with others, envy would me slay.
"Sādī!" he smiling cried, "Would this deter
Me this assembly's beacon? what, I say,
Imports it that in me moths quench life's ray!"

Story IV.

I remember that, in former days, I and a friend of mine were so much associated together that we were like two kernels in one almond. All at once I happened to find it requisite to take a journey. When, after some time, I returned, he began to reproach me for not sending a messenger to him during such an interval. I replied, "I was unwilling that the eyes of the messenger should be brightened by thy beauty, while I remained excluded."

[240] I prefer the reading به *bih* to that of کم *kam* in my edition, which, however, if read, must be taken with سیر *ser*.

STANZA.

Friend of my youth! cease now me to reprove;
Thy love not steel could make me e'er repent.
That one should gaze his fill on thee does move
My envy, yet my heart would soon relent—
For seeing thee could ne'er his sight content.

Story V.

They shut up a parrot in a cage with a crow. The parrot was distressed at the ugly appearance of the other, and said, "What hateful form is this, and detested shape, and accursed face, and unpolished manners? *O crow of the desert! would that between me and thee were the space 'twixt east and west!"*

STANZA.

Should one at dawn arising thy face see,
'Twould change to twilight gloom that morning's mirth.
Such wretch as thou art should thy comrade be,
But where could such a one be found on earth!

But still more strangely the crow, too, was harassed to death by the society of the parrot, and was utterly chagrined by it. Reciting the deprecatory formula, "There is no power nor strength but in God,"[241] it complained of its fate, and, rubbing one upon the other the hands of vexation,[242] it said, "What evil fate is this, and unlucky destiny, and fickleness of fortune! It would have been commensurate with my deserts to have walked proudly along with another crow on the wall of a garden.

[241] This means, "There is no striving against fate." "Nisi Dominus frustra." *See* Ḳānūn-i Islām, p. 335, Gloss., 66.

[242] The only meanings given for تغابن *taghābun* in the Dictionary are, "Defrauding one another." "Neglecting, erring, straying." None of these can we apply here.

COUPLET.

'Twill for a prison to the good suffice,
To herd them with the worthless sons of vice.

What crime have I committed in punishment for which my fate has involved me in such a calamity, and imprisoned me with a conceited fool like this, at once worthless and fatuous?"

STANZA.

All would that wall with loathing fly
Which bore impressed thy effigy:
And if thy lot in Eden fell,
All others would make choice of Hell.

I have brought this example to show that, how strong soever the disgust a wise man may feel for a fool, a fool regards with a hundred times more aversion a wise man.

COUPLETS.

A pious man, 'mid dance and song, was seated with the gay;
One of Balkh's beauties saw him there, and marked the mirth decay:
"Do we, then, weary thee?" he said, "at least, uncloud thy brow;
For we, too, feel thy presence here is bitterness enow.

QUATRAIN.

This social band like roses is and lilies joined in one,
And 'mid them thou, a withered stick, upspringest all alone;
Like winter's cruel cold art thou, or like an adverse blast,—
Thou sittest there like fallen snow, ice-bound and frozen fast."

Story VI.

I had a companion with whom I had for many years travelled, and with whom I had partaken of bread and salt, and the rights of friendship were established between us without reserve. Afterwards, on account of some trifling advantage, he suffered me to be displeased, and our friendship was broken off. Yet, notwithstanding all this, there was a feeling of attachment existing on both sides; in accordance with which I heard that he one day repeated, in an assembly, these two couplets, taken from my works:—

STANZA.

"When my soul's idol to me comes with laughter arch yet kind,
She sprinkles salt upon my wound, and opes afresh the sore;
O would that I could fondly grasp her tresses unconfined!
As the skirt of the munificent is caught at by the poor."

A party of friends applauded the sentiment, not so much on account of the beauty of the verses as by reason of their own kind feeling. He, too, went beyond all of them in his eulogies, and expressed his regret for the extinction of our former intimacy, and confessed his fault. I saw that he, too, was eager for a renewal of our friendship. I sent him these verses, and effected our reconciliation.

STANZA.

Were we not plighted to fidelity?
Yet thou wert harsh and didst thyself estrange.
When I left all and fixed my thoughts on thee,
I knew not that so soon thou wouldest change!
Yet still, would'st thou make peace, return to me,
And then thou wilt more loved, more honoured, be.

Story VII.

A man had a beautiful wife, who died, and his wife's mother, a decrepit old woman, on account of the marriage-settlement,[243] took up her abode, and fixed herself in his house. The man was vexed to death by her propinquity, yet he did not see how to get rid of her by reason of the settlement. Some of his friends came to inquire after him, and one of them said, "How dost thou bear the loss of thy beloved one?" He replied, "The not seeing my wife is not so intolerable to me as the seeing her mother."

DISTICHS.

The tree has lost its roses, but retains
Its thorn. The treasure's gone, the snake[244] remains.
'Tis better on the lance-point fixed to see
One's eye, than to behold an enemy.
'Tis well a thousand friendships to erase
Could we thereby avoid our foeman's face.

Story VIII.

I remember that in my youth I was passing along a street when I beheld a moon-faced beauty. The season was that of the month July, when the fierce heat dried up the moisture of the mouth, and the scorching wind consumed the marrow of the bones. Through the weakness of human nature I was unable to support the power of the sun, and involuntarily took shelter under the shade of a wall, waiting to see if any one would relieve me from the pain I suffered, owing to the ardour of the sun's rays,

[243] As he could not pay what he had covenanted to pay, when he married, his wife's relations indemnified themselves by saddling him with the old lady, his wife's mother.

[244] It is a popular Oriental notion that treasures are guarded by serpents.

and cool my flame with water. All of a sudden, from the dark portico of a house, I beheld a bright form appear, of such beauty that the tongue of eloquence would fail in narrating her charms. She came forth as morn succeeding a dark night, or as the waters of life issuing from the gloom. She held in her hand a cup of snow-water, in which she had mixed sugar and the juice of the grape. I know not whether she had perfumed it with her own roses, or distilled into it some drops from the bloom of her countenance. In short, I took the cup from her fair hand, and drained its contents, and received new life. *"The thirst of my heart cannot be slaked with a drop of water, nor if I should drink rivers would it be lessened."*

STANZA.

Most blest that happy one whose gaze intense
Rests on such face at each successive morn;
The drunk with wine at midnight may his sense
Regain; but not till the last day shall dawn
Will love's intoxication reach its bourne.

Story IX.

Once, in the caravan of Ḥijāz, a darwesh accompanied us. One of the Arab chiefs had bestowed on him a hundred dīnārs, for the support of his family. All of a sudden the robbers of the tribe Khafāchah attacked the caravan, and spoiled it of everything. The merchants began to weep and lament, and pour forth unavailing complaints.

COUPLET

Thou mayest complain, or cry, Alack!
The thieves the gold will not give back.

But that darwesh, in his tattered garb, retained his composure, and his manner underwent no change. I said, "Perhaps they have not taken thy money?" He replied, "Yes! they have taken it. However, I had not such an attachment for that money[245] that I should break my heart at losing it."

COUPLET.

Thy heart from loving thing or person guard;
For to recall affection is most hard.

I said, "What thou hast uttered is à-propos of my condition; for in my youth I had formed a friendship with a young man, and entertained a sincere attachment for him to that degree that his beauty was the point of adoration of my eyes, and my intimacy with him as it were the interest on the capital of life.

STANZA.

It may be angels do not; man I trow
Ne'er did his beauty equal on this earth.
By friendship's self friends are forbidden now,
For after him his like shall ne'er find birth.

Suddenly the foot of his existence went down into the clay of death, and the smoke of separation arose from his family.[246] I watched for days at the head of his grave, and this is one of the many things which I uttered touching his loss:—

STANZA.

Death like a thorn transfixed thy foot. Ah! then,
Would that fate's cruel sword me too had slain;
Then I'd ne'er missed thee from thy fellow-men.
Thou on whose dust my head is laid—in vain!
Dust be on it! [thou ne'er shalt breathe again].

[245] The darwesh had only just got it as a present, and I imagine his words partly imply that he had not had time to grow fond of it.

[246] There is a play on words here which it is altogether impossible to retain in English. دود *dūd*, "smoke," also signifies "anguish;" and the word for "family" in Persian, دودمان *dūdmān*, strongly resembles it.

STANZA.

He who, before he slept or took repose,
Did roses and the jasmine round him fling;
Revolving time has shed his beauty's rose,
While from his ashes now the thorns upspring.

After separation from him, I made a determination and a steadfast vow that, for the remainder of my life, I would fold up the carpet of desire and abstain from social intercourse.

STANZA.

Pleasant were the gains[247] of ocean, were there of the waves no fear;
Pleasant with the rose to dwell, were the thorn not lurking there;
Peacock-like I walked exulting in love's garden yesternight;
Snake-like now I writhe in anguish—she no more will glad my sight."

Story X.

They told to one of the Arabian kings the story of Laila and Majnūn, and of the insanity which happened to him, so that, although possessed of high qualities and perfect eloquence, he betook himself to the desert and abandoned the reins of choice. After commanding them to bring him into his presence, the king began to rebuke him, saying, "What defect hast thou seen in the nobleness of man's nature that thou hast taken up the habits of an animal, and bidden adieu to the happiness of human society?" Majnūn wept and said,

VERSE.

"Oft have my friends reproached me for my love:
The day will come they'll see her and approve.

[247] That is, by traffic in ships.

STANZA.

Would that those who seek to blame me
  Could thy face, O fairest! see;
Theirs would then the loss and shame be:
  While amazed, intent on thee,
They would wound their hands while they
Careless with the orange[248] play:

That the truth of the reality might testify to the appearance I claim for her!" The king was inspired with a desire to behold her beauty, in order to know what sort of person it was who was the cause of such mischief. He commanded, and they sought for her, and, searching through the Arab families, found her, and brought her before the king, in the court of the royal pavilion. The king surveyed her countenance, and beheld a person of a dark complexion and weak form. She appeared to him so contemptible that he thought the meanest of the servants of his ḥaram superior to her in beauty and grace. Majnūn acutely discerned his thoughts and said, "O king! it is requisite to survey the beauty of Lailạ from the window of the eye of Majnūn, in order that the mystery of the spectacle may be revealed to you."

[248] I have amplified these lines a little. The allusion is to the story of Joseph and Zulaikhā, the wife of Potiphar. In the 12th chapter of the Ḳur'ān we read, "And certain women said publicly in the city, 'The nobleman's wife asked her servant to lie with her; he hath inflamed her breast with his love, and we perceive her to be in a manifest error.' And when she heard of this subtle behaviour she sent unto them, and prepared a banquet for them, and she gave to each of them a knife; and she said unto Joseph, 'Come forth unto them.' And when they saw him, they praised him greatly; and they cut their own hands, and said, 'This is not a mortal,'" etc.

DISTICHS.

Unmoved with pity thou me hear'st complain;
I need a comrade who can share my pain:
The livelong day I'd then my woes recite;
Wood with wood joined will ever burn more bright.

VERSE.

" *What passed within my hearing of the grove,*
O forest leaves! did ye but learn,
Ye'd mourn with me. My friends! tell him whom love
Has spared, I would he did but burn
With lover's flames; he'd then my grief discern."

VERSE.

Scars may be laughed at by the sound.
But to a fellow-sufferer reveal
Thy anguish. Of the hornet's wound
What reck they who did never feel
Its sting? Till fortune shall bring round
Thy woes to thee, they will but seem
The weak illusions of a dream.
Do not my sufferings confound
With those of others. Canst thou deem
One holding salt[249] can tell the pain of him
Who has salt rubbed upon his wounded limb?

Story XI.

(IN VERSE.)

A gallant youth there was and fair
Pledged to a maid beyond compare;
They on the sea, as poets tell,
Together in a whirlpool fell.

[249] This is a favourite comparison of Oriental poets. Rubbing salt on a wound is a proverbial expression with them.

The boatman came the youth to save—
To snatch him from his watery grave:
But, 'mid those billows of despair,
He cried, " My love! my love is there!
Save her, oh save!" he said, and died;
But with his parting breath he cried,
" Not from that wretch love's story hear
Who love forgets when peril's near."
Together thus these lovers died.
Be told by him who love has tried;
For Sådī knows each whim and freak
Of love,—as well its ways can speak
As Baghdād's dwellers Arabic.
Hast thou a mistress? her then prize,
And on all others close thine eyes.
Could Majnūn and his Laiḷa back return,
They might love's story from this volume learn.

CHAPTER VI.

ON DECREPITUDE AND OLD AGE.

STORY I.

I was engaged in a dispute with some learned men in the principal mosque of Damascus. Suddenly a young man entered the door, and said, "Is there any one among you who knows the Persian language?" They pointed to me. I said, "Is all well?"[250] He replied, "An old man, of a hundred and fifty years of age, is in the agonies of death, and says something to me in Persian, which is not intelligible to me. If thou wouldest be so kind as to trouble thyself so far as to step with me thou wilt be rewarded.[251] It may be that he wants to make his will." When I reached his pillow, he said this,

[250] M. Semelet translates "Cela est vrai," in which he appears to me to mistake the sense altogether. The expression خیر است *khair ast*, corresponds to our "What is the matter?" but I have translated it literally. A similar expression occurs in the 2nd book of Kings, chapter v. verse 21, "He lighted down from the chariot to meet him, and said, 'Is all well?'" Of M. Semelet's MSS., one reads خبر چیست *khabar chīst;* and another, چه خدمت است *chih khidmat ast,* "What is the news?" and, "What service can I do you?"

[251] That is, by God.

STANZA.

"Methought a few short moments I would spend
As my soul wished; alas! I gasp for air.
At the rich board, where all life's dainties blend,
I sate me down—partook a moment there,
When, ah! they bade me leave the scarcely tasted fare."

I repeated the meaning of these words to the Damascenes in Arabic. They marvelled at his having lived so long, and yet grieving for worldly life. I said to him, "How dost thou find thyself under present circumstances?" He replied, "What shall I say?"

STANZA.

"Hast thou ne'er marked his agony,
Out from whose jaw a tooth is wrenched?
Then think what must his feelings be,
Whose life, dear life, is being quenched!"

I said, "Dismiss from thy mind the idea of death, and let not thine imagination conquer thy nature; for the philosophers have said, 'Though the constitution may be vigorous, we are not to rely upon it as gifted with perpetuity, and, though a disease may be terrible, it furnishes no positive proof of a fatal termination.' If thou wilt give us leave, we will send for a physician, in order that he may use remedies for thy recovery." He replied, "Alas!

DISTICHS.

The master's bent on garnishing
His house, which, sapped, is falling in;
The skilful leech, in mute despair,
Together smites his hands as there
He marks, like broken potsherd, lie
The poor old man outstretched to die.

The old man groans in parting pain;
His wife the sandal[252] rubs in vain:
But once unpoise our nature frail,
Nor cure nor amulet avail."

Story II.

An old man, descanting about himself, said, "I had espoused a young maiden, and adorned my room with flowers, and, sitting alone with her, fastened on her my eyes and my heart. Through long nights I never slept, but passed the time in narrating witty jests and amusing stories, in order to dispel her coyness, and to make her attached to me. Among other things, I said to her one night, 'Thy lofty fate befriended thee, and the eye of thy happy destiny was open, that thou hast fallen into the arms of an old man, prudent and acquainted with the world; one who has tasted the vicissitudes of fortune, and experienced good and evil; who knows what is required in social intercourse, and performs all the conditions of friendship, and who is kind and considerate, cheerful and gentle in his language.

DISTICHS.

To win thy heart shall be my lot;
Though thou griev'st me, I'll grieve thee not.
Is sugar, parrot-like, thy food:
Be thou with my life's sweetness wooed.

Thou hast not fallen a prey to a young man, self-conceited and rude, headstrong and fickle, who each moment takes

[252] Preparations of sandal-wood are used by Orientals for rubbing the body, and are thought to be cooling and restorative. Thus in the *Prem Sāgar*, p. 85, l. 29, of my translation, "Thou hast removed my weariness; having met me, thou hast given to me cool sandal."

a new whim, and changes his opinion every instant, and sleeps every night in a different place, and gets a new mistress every day.

STANZA.

Young men are gay and fair to see,
But wanting in fidelity.
Who can the bulbul true suppose,
That, singing, flits from rose to rose?

But the class of old men pass their life according to the dictates of reason; not in those things which ignorant youth wishes for.

COUPLET.

A better than thyself seek out and prize;
For with one like thyself time vainly flies.' "

The old man said, "I spoke much more after this fashion, and I imagined I had got possession of her heart, and secured her affections. Suddenly she heaved a cold sigh from a heart full of melancholy, and said, 'All the words that thou hast uttered do not weigh so much in the balance of my reason as that one word which I heard from my nurse, "That to have her side pierced with an arrow was better for a young woman, than to have an old husband."' In short, it was not possible for us to agree, and a separation was decided upon. The period of probation after divorce[253] elapsed. They united her in the nuptial bands with a youth irascible and cross-looking, destitute of fortune, and on the watch for a pretext to quarrel. She had to endure harshness and violence, and to submit to annoyance and vexation, and, nevertheless,

[253] The period for which a woman must wait before marrying again, after her husband's death, is four months and ten days. After divorce, she must wait three menstrual periods. This is to see if she be pregnant by her former husband. *Vide* Ḳānūn-i Islām, p. 147; Ḳur'ān, ch. ii. ver. 229, 235.

she returned thanks to heaven for her blessings, saying, 'Praise be to God! that I have escaped from that excruciating torment and arrived at this blissful condition.

COUPLET.

Spite of thy passion and thy frowning brow,
I'll bear thy airs, for beautiful art thou!

STANZA.

Better with thee be tortured and consume,
Than with another Eden's bowers possess:
More sweet from beauty's mouth the onion's fume,
Than roses from the hand of ugliness.'"

Story III.

In the country of Diyārbakr,[254] I was the guest of an old man, who possessed great riches, and a handsome son. One night he told me that in his whole life he had never had but this one son. There was a tree, he said, in that valley to which pilgrimages were made, and whither persons resorted to pray for what they needed; and that he, too, had wept for many nights, at the foot of that tree, in prayer to God, who had bestowed on him this son. I heard his son whisper softly to his companions, "Would that I knew where that tree is, that I might pray there for my father's death!"

STANZA.

Long years, successive years have gone,
Since thou didst visit at thy father's grave;
What filial actions hast thou done,
That from thy son thou should'st like worship crave?

Story IV.

One day, in the pride of my youth, I had travelled hard, and at night stopped, much fatigued, at the foot

[254] Anciently called Mesopotamia.

of a mountain. An infirm old man, who followed the caravan, said to me, "Arise! this is not a place to slumber in." I replied, "How can I proceed, when I have not the power to stir a foot?" He rejoined, "Hast thou not heard that they have said, 'It is better to walk and rest, than to run and be oppressed?'"

STANZA.

Thou who wouldst reach the halting-place, haste not;
Be patient! and my counsel hear aright:
Two courses may be sped by charger hot;
The mule goes slowly, but goes day and night.

Story V.

In the circle of my acquaintance there was a sprightly and amiable youth, gay and soft-spoken, who had not a particle of melancholy in his composition, and whose mouth was never closed for laughter. An interval passed during which I did not happen to meet him. After that, I saw him when he had married a wife, and his children were growing up, and the root of his contentment was severed, and the rose of his desires withered. I asked him, "What is this state of thine?" He replied, "As soon as I had got boys I left off play."

COUPLET.

When thou art old thy pastimes put away:
Leave frolics to the young and mirthful play.

DISTICHS.

The youth's gay humour seek not from the old
The stream returns not which has onward rolled.
Not so elastic bends the yellow corn
As the young blade before the breeze of morn.

STANZA.

Youth's circling hours have passed for aye away;
  Ah me! alas that that gay time is spent!
The lion feels his strength of paw decay;
  Now, like a pard, with cheese-scraps I'm content.
An aged dame had dyed her locks of grey;
  "Granted," I said, "thy hair with silver blent
May cheat us now; yet, little mother! say,
  Canst thou make straight thy back, which time has
      bent?"

Story VI.

One day, in the ignorance and folly of youth, I raised my voice against my mother. Cut to the heart, she sate down in a corner and said, weeping, "Perhaps thou hast forgotten thy infancy, that thou treatest me with this rudeness?"

STANZA.

Well said that aged mother to her son
  Whose giant arm could well a tiger slay!
"Couldst thou remember days long past and gone,
  When in my arms a helpless infant lay,
And know thyself that babe, thou wouldst not now
Thus wrong me when I'm old; an athlete thou!"

Story VII.

The son of a rich miser was sick. The father's friends said to him, "The course to be adopted is to read through the Ḳur'ān from beginning to end, or to offer up a sacrifice. It may be that the Most High God will grant him recovery." He reflected for a short space, and said, "It is better to read the Ḳur'ān, as it is at hand; whereas the flock is at a distance." A devout person heard him, and said, "He made choice of the reading, because the Ḳur'ān is on the tip of his tongue, and the gold is in the centre of his heart."

DISTICHS.

In sooth, it is an easy task to do,
To bow the neck; but were alms needed too
'Twere hard indeed. One dīnār but require,
And, like an ass, he flounders in the mire;
But for a chapter of the Ḳur'ān call,—
Ask only one, he'll gladly give thee all.

Story VIII.

They asked an old man why he did not marry. He replied, "I don't think I could fancy an old woman." They rejoined, "Espouse a young one, since thou hast substance." "Nay," he rejoined, "when I, who am old, do not like old women, how is it possible for a young woman to like me, an old man?"

CHAPTER VII.

ON THE EFFECT OF EDUCATION.

Story I.

A certain vazīr had a stupid son, whom he sent to a wise man, saying, "Instruct him; perhaps he may become intelligent." The sage spent a long time in teaching him, without effect. At last he sent a person to his father, with this message, "This boy does not gain in understanding, and has driven me mad."

STANZA.

Is our first nature such that teaching can
  Affect it, soon instruction will take root:
But iron, which at first imperfect ran
  Forth from the furnace, who then can imbue it
With the capacity of polish? So
  In the seven[255] seas wouldst thou a dog make clean?
  When wet, 'tis fouler than it erst has been.

Story II.

A philosopher was advising his children as follows: "Dear to me as life! acquire knowledge; for there is

[255] The Orientals delight in the number seven. One list of the seven seas comprises the Chinese, the Indian, the Persian, the Red Sea, the Mediterranean, the Caspian, and the Euxine.

no reliance to be placed in worldly possessions, either of land or money. You cannot take rank abroad with you; and silver and gold on a journey occasion risk, and either the thief may carry it off at one swoop, or the owner will gradually expend it: but knowledge is an ever-springing fountain, and a source of enduring wealth, and if an accomplished person ceases to be wealthy it matters not, for his knowledge is wealth existing in his mind itself. Wherever the accomplished man goes he is esteemed, and is seated in the place of honour, while the man without accomplishments has, go where he will, to pick up scraps and endure raps.

COUPLET.

'Tis hard t' obey for those who have borne rule,
Or fortune's minions in rough ways to school.

STANZA.

In Syria once commotions so arose
That discord shook each person from his hearth.
Eftsoons the king his vazīrship bestows
On peasants' sons, wise, though of lowly birth:
The vazīr's dullard children in their stead,
Through town and hamlet humbly beg their bread.

COUPLET.

Learn what thy father knew, if thou wouldst hold
His place. In ten days thou wilt spend his gold."

Story III.

A learned man had the education of a king's son, and used to beat him unmercifully, and scold him incessantly. The boy, unable to endure it, complained to his father, and removed his dress from his body, which was aching with blows. The father's heart was troubled, and, sending for the instructor, he said, "Thou dost not think it right to treat the children of any one of my subjects with such cruelty and harshness as thou shewest to my son. What is the reason of this?" He replied, "All persons ought to speak with reflection, and act with propriety: but this is especially requisite for kings, for whatever comes from their hand or lips, will assuredly be the common topic of conversation; while the words and actions of common people have not so much weight.

STANZA.

A hundred evil acts the poor may do,
  Their comrades of the hundred know but one;
But region after region permeates through
  One evil action by a monarch done.

Wherefore, in correcting the manners of princes, we ought to use greater strictness than in reference to others.

STANZA.

They who in youth to manners ne'er attend,
  Will in advancing years small gain acquire:
Wood, while 'tis green, thou mayst at pleasure bend;
  When dry, thou canst not change it save by fire.

COUPLET.

Surely green branches thou mayst render straight;
Th' attempt to straighten dry wood comes too late."

The king approved of the sage counsel of the master, and of the manner in which he had spoken, and bestowed on him a robe of honour and rich presents, at the same time advancing him to a higher rank.

Story IV.

I saw, in Africa, a schoolmaster of a sour countenance and harsh address, ill-natured, cruel, mulish and intemperate; such that the very sight of him dispelled the pleasure of Muslims, and whose reading of the Ḳur'ān threw a gloom over men's hearts. A multitude of fair boys and young maidens were surrendered to his cruel grasp, who neither dared to laugh, nor durst venture on conversing. Sometimes he would box the silver cheeks of the latter, and put the crystal legs of the former in the stocks. In short, I heard that people came to the knowledge of some of his disloyal acts, on which they beat him, and expelled him, and gave his school to a man of conciliating temper—a pious, good and meek person, who never uttered a word but when compelled, and never said anything which could distress any one. The children forgot the awe they had been wont to feel for their former master, when they saw that the present one possessed the qualities of an angel, and became demons to each other, and, depending on his mildness, abandoned study, and spent the chief part of their time in play, and, without finishing their copies, broke their tablets on each other's heads.

COUPLET.

When the schoolmaster gentle is and sweet,
The boys will play at leap-frog in the street.

Two weeks after, I passed by the door of the mosque, and saw there the former master, whom they had pacified and reinstated in his former office. I was sadly vexed, and uttering the deprecatory formula, "There is no power but in God," I said, "Why have they a second time made Iblīs the instructor of angels?" An old man, who knew the world, heard me, and said, "Hast thou not heard that they have said:

DISTICHS.

'A monarch sent his son to school, and placed
A silver tablet round his neck, where, traced
In gold, appeared—"The fondness of thy sire
Will harm thee more than the schoolmaster's ire?"'"

Story V.

The son of a religious personage acquired incalculable riches by the bequest of his uncles. He began to indulge in licentiousness and impiety, and entered on a course of extravagance. In short, there was no sinful or criminal action that he failed to commit, nor intoxicating liquor that he abstained from drinking. At last I said to him, by way of admonition, "O my son! income is a passing current, and pleasure a revolving mill. In other words, a prodigal expenditure is safe only for one who has a permanent and settled revenue.

STANZA.

Hast thou no income—then thy wants restrain;
For ever sing the boatmen merrily:
'If on the mountain-summits fell no rain,
One year would make the Tigris channel dry.'

Betake thyself to a rational and moderate life, and give up thy follies; for, when thy wealth is exhausted, thou wilt have to endure hardship, and wilt suffer remorse." The youth, seduced by the delights of music and wine, was deaf to my advice, and rejected my counsel, saying, "It is opposed to the opinion of the wise to disturb, by forebodings of death, the pleasures of this transitory life.

DISTICHS.

Through fear of ill should fortune's favourites
Make for themselves ills that are premature?
Be happy thou in whom my heart delights!
Nor thus to-day to-morrow's pangs endure.

Much less should I do as thou sayest, I who hold the highest rank for generosity, and have made a compact to be liberal, and the fame of whose munificence is blazed abroad among all classes.

DISTICHS.

Whom mankind with the name of 'Generous' grace[256]
Must on his dirams no restriction place:
When our good fame pervades the public street,
We must no suitor with denial meet."

I saw that he did not accept my advice, and that my warm breath made no impression on his cold iron. I left off counselling him, and turned away from his society. I seated myself in the corner of security, and put in practice that saying of the sages, which they have uttered: "*Convey to them that which it behoves thee to say, and then, if they receive it not, what does it concern thee?*"

VERSE.

What though thou know'st they will not hearken, still
  Thy warning counsel give—'tis best.
Soon shalt thou see the man of headstrong will
  With his two legs by fetters pressed;
Smiting his hands, he cries, in accents shrill,
  "To hearken to the sage is best."

After some time, what I had anticipated as to his downfall, came to pass, for he had to sew rag to rag and beg scrap by scrap. My heart was pained at his wretched state. I thought it unkind, in his then condition, to irritate and scatter salt on the wound of the poor man by reproaches; but I said to myself,

DISTICHS.

"The profligate, in pleasure's ecstacy,
Dreads not the coming day of poverty:
Trees that in summer fruits profusely bear,
Stand, therefore, leafless in the wintry air."

[256] The first and fourth lines are freely rendered. The literal translation of the first is, "Whoever has become an ensign by his liberality and bounty;" and of the fourth, "Thou canst not close the door on any face."

Story VI.

A king handed over his son to a teacher, and said, "This is my son; educate him as one of thine own sons." The preceptor spent some years in endeavouring to teach him without success, while his own sons were made perfect in learning and eloquence. The king took the preceptor to task, and said, "Thou hast acted contrary to thy agreement, and hast not been faithful to thy promise." He replied, "O King! education is the same, but capacities differ."

STANZA.

Silver and gold 'tis true in stones are found;
Yet not all stones the precious metals bear:
Canopus shines to earth's most distant bound;
But here gives leather—scented leather there.[257]

Story VII.

I have heard of an old doctor who said to a pupil, "If the minds of the children of men were as much fixed on the Giver of subsistence as they are on the subsistence itself, they would rise above the angels."

STANZA.

Thou wast by God then not forgotten when
Thou wast a seed—thy nature in suspense;
He gave thee soul and reason, wisdom, ken,
Beauty and speech, reflection, judgment, sense;
He on thy hand arrayed thy fingers ten,
And thy arms fastened to thy shoulders. Whence
Canst thou then think, O thou most weak of men!
He'd be unmindful of thy subsistence?

[257] That is, the light of Canopus in one place causes the leather to be perfumed (a strange notion!), in another leaves it in its common state.

Story VIII.

I saw an Arab who was saying to his son, "*O my son! thou wilt be asked, in the day of resurrection, What hast thou acquired? not, From whom hast thou sprung?*"[258] or, in other words, they will demand of thee an account of thy actions, not of thy pedigree.

STANZA.

The pall suspended o'er the Kâbah's shrine
Not from the yellow worm[259] derives its fame;
But it has dwelt some days near the Divine,
And therefore do men venerate its name.

Story IX.

Philosophers tell us, in their writings, that scorpions are not engendered in the same way as other animals, but that they devour the entrails of their mothers, rend their bellies, and go forth to the desert; and the skins which men see in the holes of scorpions are the vestiges which are thus left. I mentioned this extraordinary circumstance to an eminent personage. He said, "My heart testifies to the truth of this legend, and it can hardly be otherwise; for since, when little, they behave thus to their mothers and fathers, they are, consequently, so pleasant and beloved when they grow old."

STANZA.

This counsel to his son a father gave:
"Dear youth! to recollect these words be thine,—
Who for their kinsmen no affection have,
On them the star of fortune ne'er will shine."

[258] This sentence, being in Arabic, is afterwards explained in Persian, which gives the appearance of tautology in English.

[259] The silk-worm.

WITTICISM.

They said to a scorpion, "Why dost thou not come abroad in winter?" He replied, "What respect is shewn to me in summer, that I should shew myself in winter also?"

STORY X.

The wife of a darwesh was pregnant, and her time was completed. The darwesh, throughout his life, had never had a son. He said, "If God (may He be honoured and glorified!) gives me a son, I will bestow on my brethren all that I possess, with the exception of the garb I wear." It happened that his wife did bear a son. He made rejoicings, and, in accordance with his vow, prepared an entertainment for his friends. After some years, when I returned from travelling in Syria, I passed by the quarter where that darwesh resided, and inquired as to his circumstances. They replied, "He is in the Government prison." I asked the cause. They told me that his son had drunk intoxicating liquors, and raised an uproar, and, after shedding a man's blood, had fled the city; and that, on account of this, they had put a chain round his father's neck and heavy fetters on his feet. I exclaimed, "It was this calamitous monster whom he besought God to grant to him."

STANZA.

Wise friend! 'tis better that the fruitful bride
  In parturition should a serpent bear
Rather than sons (for thus the wise decide)—
  Sons who respond not to a father's care.

STORY XI.

One year a quarrel arose among the pilgrims who were going on foot to Makkah. I also happened to be making the journey on foot. We fell upon one another tooth and nail with a vengeance, and did all that could be possibly expected from lewd fellows and combatants. I heard one who sate in a litter say to his companion, "Passing strange! the ivory[260] pawn, on completing its traverse of the chess-board, becomes a queen, that is to say, it becomes better than it was, and the foot-pilgrims to Makkah have crossed the desert and become worse!"

STANZA.

Go, tell for me the pilgrims who offend
Their brother men, and cruel would them flay,
To them none can the pilgrim's name extend;
The patient camel earns it more than they,
Who feeds on thorns, nor does his task gainsay.

Story XII.

A Hindū was teaching the art of making fireworks. A sage said to him: "For thee, with thy house of reeds, this sport is out of all rule."

COUPLET.

Speak not until thou knowest speech is best,
Nor that of which the answer is unblest.

Story XIII.

A fellow had a pain in his eyes, and went to a farrier, saying, "Give me medicine." The farrier applied to his eyes the remedies he was in the habit of using for animals, and blinded him, on which he complained to the magistrate, who pronounced that he could not recover damages; "For," said he, "if this fellow had not been an ass, he would not have consulted a farrier." The moral of the story is, that whoever commits an affair of

[260] There is a very good pun between عاج ʿāj, "ivory," and حاج ḥāj, "pilgrimage to Makkah," which cannot be retained in English.

importance to an inexperienced person will smart for it, and, in addition, will be considered an imbecile by persons of intelligence.

STANZA.

The prudent man of clear intelligence
  Not to the mean will weighty things commit:
Mat-makers weave, 'tis true, yet, hast thou sense,
  Thou'lt not think weaving silk robes for them fit.

Story XIV.

A certain great man had an amiable son, who died. They asked the father what they should write on his grave-stone. He replied, "The verses of the Holy Book are too venerable and sacred to be written on such places, where they may be effaced by the weather, and the trampling of men's feet, and desecrated by dogs. If ye must write something, these two couplets will suffice:—

STANZA.

Ah me! when in the garden freshly green
  Upsprang the verdure, how my heart was gay!
Wait, friend! till spring renascent tints the scene,
  And mark young rosebuds blossom from my clay.

Story XV.

A holy man passed by a wealthy personage, and observed that he had tightly bound one of his slaves hand and foot, and was engaged in torturing him. He said, "O son! God (may He be honoured and glorified!) has placed in bondage to thee a creature like thyself, and given thee the superiority over him; thank God Most High, therefore, for His blessings, and do not allow thyself to treat him with such cruelty. Beware, lest to-morrow, in the day of resurrection, this slave be better than thee, and thou carry off disgrace.

DISTICHS.

Not over ireful with thy servant be,
Nor plague his heart, nor practise tyranny.
Thou with ten dirams didst him purchase, true!
Not thine the Power from whence his breath he drew.
Soon must thou anger, rule, and pride resign:
There is a Lord whose sway surpasses thine.
Thou'rt master of Arslān and Āg͟hūsh[261] yet;
Beware, lest thine own Master thou forget."

It is related of the Prophet (on whom be peace!) that he said, that the bitterest of all regrets will be when they transport the good slave to paradise and convey the impious master to hell.

STANZA.

Not 'gainst the slaves that in thy service bow
  Rage thou without restraint, or madly chafe:
In the last day of reckoning wouldst thou
Mark, with shamed soul and agonised brow,
  The master fettered and the bondsman safe?

Story XVI.

In a certain year I journeyed from Balkh with some Syrians, and the road was replete with peril from robbers. A young man accompanied us as guide, skilled in the use of the buckler and the bow, trained to arms, and of prodigious strength, so that ten powerful men could not string his bow, nor the greatest athletes in the world bring his back to the ground; but he had been delicately brought up, and reared in indulgence, and had neither seen the world nor travelled. The thundering drum of the warrior had not reached his ears, nor the flash of the horseman's scymitar glittered in his eyes.

[261] Names of slaves, used generally to denote any bondsmen.

COUPLET.

To a stern foe ne'er captive had he been,
Nor iron rain of arrows round him seen.

It happened that I and this young man were running one after the other. Every old wall that came in the way he cast down with the strength of his arm, and tore up with the force of his wrist all the large trees that he beheld, and he boastingly exclaimed,

COUPLET.

Where is the elephant, to see the arms and shoulders of the strong?
The lion where, to feel the powers which to men of might belong?"

We were thus engaged when two Hindūs[262] lifted up their heads from behind a rock, and seemed prepared to slay us. One had a stick in his hand, and the other a sling under his arm. I said to the young man, "Why dost thou stop?"

COUPLET.

Now what thou hast of strength and courage shew;
For of himself to death comes on thy foe.

I beheld the bow and arrows drop from the hand of the young man, and a tremor pervade his frame.

COUPLET.

Not all whose forceful shaft could strike a hair,
Where warriors charge, would stand unshaken there.

[262] There is little doubt that Afghānistān was, at no very remote æra, peopled by Indians who were driven out by the Afghāns, and other northern tribes, and this passage seems to me a proof of it. Otherwise, whence could come these Hindūs on the road between Balkh and Syria.

We saw no remedy but to give up our clothes and arms and get free with our lives.

STANZA.

A veteran choose for deeds of high emprise
He the fierce lion in his noose will tame;
The youth may mighty be, of giant size,
But in the fight fear will unnerve his frame:
War to the well-trained warrior is the same
As some nice quillet of the law is to the wise.

Story XVII.

I saw the son of a rich man seated at the head of his father's sepulchre, and engaged in a dispute with the son of a poor man, and saying, "My father's sarcophagus is of stone, and the inscription coloured with a pavement of alabaster and turquoise bricks. What resemblance has it to that of thy father? which consists of a brick or two huddled together, with a few handfuls of dust sprinkled over it." The son of the poor man heard him, and answered, "Peace! for before thy father can have moved himself under this heavy stone, my sire will have arrived in paradise. This is a saying of the Prophet: '*The death of the poor is repose.*'

COUPLET.

Doubtless the ass, on which they do impose
The lightest burthen, also easiest goes.

STANZA.

The poor man, who the agony has borne
Of famine's pangs, treads lightly to the door
Of death. While one from blessings torn—
From luxury and ease—will grieve the more
To lose them. This is certain. Happier he
Whom, like a captive, death from bonds sets free,
Than great men, whom it hurries to captivity."

Story XVIII.

I asked an eminent personage the meaning of this traditionary saying, "*The most malignant of thy enemies is the lust which abides within thee.*" He replied, "It is because every enemy on whom thou conferrest favours becomes a friend, save lust; whose hostility increases the more thou dost gratify it."

STANZA.

By abstinence, man might an angel be;
By surfeiting, his nature brutifies:
Whom thou obligest will succumb to thee—
Save lusts, which, sated, still rebellious rise.

Story XIX.

THE DISPUTE OF SÅDĪ WITH A PRESUMPTUOUS PRETENDER AS TO THE QUALITIES OF THE RICH AND THE POOR.

I once saw seated in an assembly a person in the garb of a darwesh—not with the character of one—engaged in pouring out a disgraceful tirade, and uttering a volume of abuse and reproachful language against the rich. His discourse, moreover, had reached this point, that the hands of poor men are tied from doing anything, while the feet of rich men's intentions are lame.

COUPLET.

The merciful are ever moneyless;
Hardhearted they who have the power to bless.

I, who have been supported by the munificence of the great, disapproved of this speech. I said, "O friend! the rich are a revenue to the poor, and storehouses for the recluse; the pilgrim's goal; the traveller's refuge; and the supporters of heavy burthens for the gratification of others. When they stretch forth their hands to their repast, their dependents and inferiors partake with them, and what is left of their bounty comes to the widowed and the old, and to their relatives and neighbours.

VERSE.

Offerings to God, bequests to furnish ease
To the worn traveller, enfranchisement
Of slaves, alms, gifts, and sacrifices—these
Are rich men's works. Say, when wilt thou invent
Like merits for thyself, who canst but pray,
With twice a hundred wanderings,[263] twice a day?

If the question be as to the power of doing liberal actions and the discharge of religious duties, they are seen to be possessed in a higher degree by the rich, because they possess wealth hallowed by the usage of giving alms, pure garments, a reputation intact, and a heart free from care. And good meals greatly facilitate worship, just as clean garments have no little weight in sanctifying our devotions, for what strength is there in an empty stomach, or what liberality in an empty hand? How can the fettered feet walk, or the hungry belly bestow alms?

STANZA.

The man at night uneasy sleeps,
Who knows not how to gain to-morrow's bread:
The ant in summer corn upheaps;
'Tis thus in winter with abundance fed.

It is certain that leisure and poverty will not combine, and the mind of the indigent cannot be at ease. The rich man hallows the evening in prayer, and the poor man seats himself on the look-out for his supper. The former will admit of no comparison with the latter.

[263] That is, of mind. Ross and Gladwin translate پريشاني *parīshānī*, "difficulties," which is hardly the meaning. Semelet is nearer the sense with "*distractions*." I have altered the "hundred" to "twice a hundred," to render the line more forcible.

COUPLET.

The rich man is with thoughts of God impressed :
The needy is for such thoughts too distressed.

Wherefore the worship of the former is more likely to be accepted, inasmuch as their minds are collected and attentive, not distracted and wavering; for, as they are prepared with the means of subsistence, they can betake themselves to their devotions. The Arabians say, '*God defend me from humiliating poverty, and from the neighbourhood of one I do not love!*' And tradition tells us that it was a saying of the Prophet, '*Poverty blackens the countenance in both worlds.*'" My opponent replied, "Hast thou not heard that the Prophet (on whom be peace!) said, '*Poverty is my glory*'?" I answered, "Be silent! for the allusion of the Lord of the world is to the poverty of those who are the warriors of the battle-field of resignation and who receive with submission the arrows of destiny—not to that of those who put on the patched robe of the devout, and sell the scraps bestowed on them in charity.

QUATRAIN.

O noisy drum, all emptiness within,
How without food wilt thou thy march begin!
Be manly, and from cringing cease: for this
Than thousand-beaded rosaries better is.[264]

A darwesh without spirituality will not pause until his

[264] I have translated the last three lines rather freely. The literal version is, "Without provisions, what plan wilt thou devise at the time of marching? Turn the face of greediness from people, if thou art a man. Do not turn in thy hand the rosary with a thousand beads." In the second line پسیچ *pasīch* clearly means "a journey," and rhymes to هیچ *hīch;* but, in Richardson's Dictionary, we find only پسیج *pasīj*, with the meanings "ready, prepared, provision for a journey."

poverty ends in infidelity, for '*Poverty borders on the denial of God.*' Moreover, without the possession of riches we cannot clothe the naked or exert ourselves in liberating the captive. Who can compare the position of such as we are with the dignity of the rich? or what resemblance is there between the hand that gives and that which receives? Dost thou not perceive that the most glorious and most high God announces, in a clear passage of the Ḳur'ān,[265] regarding the blessings of the inhabitants of Paradise, that, '*To them there is an assured allowance of fruits, and they are honoured in the gardens of Paradise?*' in order that thou mayest know that he who is occupied in gaining a subsistence is excluded from the happiness of this degree of holiness, and that the kingdom of contentment is dependant[266] on a fixed income.

COUPLET.

To those athirst the whole world seems
A spring of water—in their dreams.

Wherever thou seest one who has endured hardship and tasted the bitterness of misfortune, thou wilt find him precipitate himself with avidity into enormities without fear of the consequences or dread of punishment in a future life, inasmuch as he discriminates not between things lawful and unlawful.

STANZA.

A dog leaps up with joy when on his head
A clod descends—he thinks a bone to spy.
So, when two men bear forth the coffined dead
Upon their shoulders, greedy miscreants eye
The bier, and think they then a tray of meat descry.

[265] Ross refers for this passage to the 28th chapter of the Ḳur'ān; but the only verse that is at all similar in that chapter is v. 57, "a secure asylum, to which fruits of every sort are brought, as a provision of our bounty."

[266] *Literally*, "under the signet."

But the wealthy man is regarded with an eye of favour, and, by the possession of that which is lawful, is preserved from committing that which is unlawful. But, even supposing that I have not proved what I have adduced, nor demonstrated the truth of my arguments, I yet expect justice from thee. Hast thou ever seen the hand of a suppliant tied behind his back? or an indigent person imprisoned? or the veil of chastity rent? or the hand amputated at the wrist?[267] except by reason of poverty? Driven by necessity, brave men are taken in the act of undermining houses,[268] and are punished by having their heels bored; and it is likely that, when the passions of the poor man are roused and he has not the means of gratifying them, he will be involved in sin. And it is one among the causes of the tranquillity and content that rich men enjoy, that they each day renew their youth, and each night embrace a beauty[269] such that bright morn is ashamed[270] in her presence, and the graceful cypress, in modest acknowledgment of her superiority, finds its feet imbedded in the clay of bashfulness.

COUPLET.

Her hands in gore of hapless lovers dipped,
Her fingers with the ruddy jujube tipped.

It is impossible that, in despite of the beauty of such countenance, they should hover round that which is forbidden or engage in depravities.

[267] The punishment for theft.

[268] Burglars in the East effect their entrance into the houses they intend to rob by mining under the walls. This is easy enough where, as in India, the soil is light and no one is on the alert.

[269] I cannot at all agree with M. Semelet's reading of this passage, and infinitely prefer my own, by which the extreme indelicacy of the French and other editions is avoided.

[270] *Literally*, "Places its hand on its heart at her beauty."

COUPLET.

A heart that Houris charmed and made its prey,
To Yaghmā's[271] beauties when will devious stray?

COUPLET.

Who holds the dates he loves his hands between,
Contented, pelts the clusters not, I ween.

The majority of the necessitous stain the garment of chastity with sin, as those who are hungry steal bread.

COUPLET.

So when a ravenous cur finds meat—small care has he
If Ṣāliḥ's camel or if Dajjāl's[272] ass it be.

Many decent persons have fallen into abominable wickedness through poverty, and have given their precious honour to the winds of disgrace.

COUPLET.

With hunger abstinence will scarce remain,
And want will wrest away devotion's rein."

At the moment that I uttered these words the darwesh lost his hold of the reins of endurance, and he unsheathed the sword of his tongue and let loose the steed of eloquence in the plain of shamelessness, and attacked me furiously,

[271] يغما *Yag͟hmā* is said to be a city of Turkestān, famous for its beautiful women. It also signifies "prey," whence arises an equivoque which cannot be preserved in English.

[272] صالح *Ṣāliḥ*, "good, just;" the Patriarch Ṣāliḥ, son of Arphaxad, who is said in the Ḳur'ān (ch. vii.) to have been a prophet sent to the tribe ثمود *S̤amūd*, who inhabited Arabia Petræa, and were descended from Aram, brother of Arphaxad. To convince them of his mission he miraculously brought a camel out of a rock, but they continued still in their unbelief, on which they were slain by the Angel Gabriel. Dajjāl is Anti-christ, who is to appear riding on an ass and to lead men astray, until killed by Mahdī, the twelfth Imām, at his coming.

saying, "Thou hast employed such exaggeration in praising them, and talked so extravagantly on the subject, that one would imagine the rich to be the antidote to the poison of poverty, or the key of the stores of Providence. They are a handful of proud, arrogant, conceited, repulsive persons, who are taken up with their wealth and their luxuries, and led away by their rank and opulence, and who can only talk insipidly and look disdainfully. They treat the learned like mendicants, and reproach the poor with their distresses. Through the pride of their wealth and the assumption of their supposed dignity, they take their seats above all others and imagine themselves better than any. They never take it into their heads to notice[273] any one, in ignorance of that saying which has been uttered by the wise, 'Whoever is inferior to others in devotion, but surpasses them in wealth, is outwardly rich but inwardly poor.'

COUPLET.

When a fool would exalt himself, for his wealth, above
the wise,
Though he be an ox of ambergris,[274] him as a fool despise."

I replied, "Suffer not thyself to blame them, for they are the possessors of beneficence." He rejoined, "Thou hast

[273] M. Semelet thinks سر بر دارند *sar bar dārand*—the reading of Gladwin and Gentius—an error, and substitutes سر فرو دارند *sar farū dārand*. But surely the former expression may mean "they lift up the head," *i.e.*, "they notice."

[274] The Orientals think that ambergris is produced by sea-cows. M. Barbier tells us, "Ambergris is found in the sea on the coasts of India, Africa, and Brazil. It is gray striped with yellow, brownish, and white. It appears to be a concretion that, in some diseased states, is formed in whales and principally in their cæcum." It is a medicinal substance, rarely used now-a-days by the physician, but in great request among perfumers, as it increases and draws out the odour of their essences.

spoken wrongly, for they are the slaves of money. Of what use is it that they are the clouds of the month Āẕar[275] and do not rain on any one; or that they are the fountains of the sun, and yet shine on none; and that they ride on the steed of power, if they will not let him go on. They will not move a step in God's service, nor bestow a diram without making you feel painfully the obligation. They amass, too, their hoards drudgingly, and protect them grudgingly; and the sages have said, 'The silver of the miser is disinterred when he is interred.'

COUPLET.

With toil and trouble one does riches gain,
Another comes and reaps them without pain."

I replied, "Thou hast gained no knowledge of the parsimony of the rich save by begging; otherwise every one who lays aside covetousness sees no difference in the liberal and the miserly. The touchstone discerns what is gold, and the beggar knows who is stingy." He said, "I speak from experience that they place their menials at their gate, and commission coarse ruffians not to admit respectable persons, and these officials of theirs lay their hands on the breasts of men of knowledge and say, 'There is nobody at home,' and, in point of fact, they speak the truth.[276]

COUPLET.

The soulless, stingy, dull, and senseless wight,
Bids thee go say, 'There's no one in,'—he's right!"

I replied, "There is an excuse for their doing this, in that they are driven to extremity by the petitions of those

[275] According to Gladwin, "August;" according to Richardson's Dictionary, "November."

[276] This is said as a sneer, and means that the rich are "nobodys," "persons of no worth or value."

who expect aid from them and are harassed by begging letters, and it cannot reasonably be supposed that, if the sand of the desert should become pearls, the eyes of beggars would be satisfied.

COUPLET.

No wealth could fill the eye of avarice,
As dew to brim a well would ne'er suffice.

Had Ḥātim Ṭā'ī, who lived in the desert, dwelt in a city, he would have been driven to desperation by the importunity of beggars, and the very clothes would have been torn off his back." The darwesh said, "I pity[277] their condition." I replied, "Not so; thou enviest their wealth." We were disputing thus and mutually opposed; when he advanced a pawn I endeavoured to repel it, and when he called out check to my king I covered it with the queen, until he had spent all the coin of his wit and discharged all the arrows of the quiver of argument.

STANZA.

Beware, lest at that speaker's onset, who
Has but a borrowed and a vain tirade,
Thou should'st thy shield fling down. Keep thyself true
To faith and virtue, and be not afraid
Of empty posts with arms above the door displayed.

At length he had not a word to say and was utterly overthrown by me. He then became outrageous and began to talk at random. It is the way with the ignorant that, when inferior to an opponent in argument, they betake themselves[278] to violence. As, when the idol-worshipper Āẕur could not succeed with his son[279] in argument, he rose up to attack him, for *God most High*

[277] A sneer.
[278] *Literally*, "They shake the chain of enmity."
[279] Abraham.

has said, "Of a truth if thou wilt not yield this point, then I will stone thee." He began to abuse me and I answered him in the same strain. He seized my collar and I his chin.

STANZA.

O'er him I tumbled, he o'er me,
A crowd with laughter us pursued,
And wondered at our colloquy
With fingers in their mouths fast glued.[280]

In short we carried our dispute before the Ḳāẓī, and agreed to abide by his just decision, so that the judge of the Musalmān might examine as to what was best, and pronounce on the points of difference between the rich and the poor.

When the Ḳāẓī beheld our faces and heard our address, he allowed his head to sink down into his vest in meditation, and, after much reflection, raised it and said, "O thou! who hast extolled the rich and thought fit to speak with severity of the poor, know that wherever there is a rose there is a thorn, and with wine is intoxication, and over a treasure is coiled a serpent, and where there are royal pearls there are also devouring monsters. So over the enjoyments of the world impends the terror of death, and between the blessings of Paradise intervenes a wall of difficulties.[281]

COUPLET.

Who would have friends, a foe's hate must sustain,
Linked are snakes, gold; thorns, flowers; joy and pain.

Seest thou not that in the garden are found together musk-willows and dry logs? so, too, among the rich are those who are thankful and unthankful, and among the poor are the patient and impatient.

[280] The Oriental way of denoting surprise is to bite the finger.
[281] *Vide* Ḳur'ān, ch. vii., v. 47, ed. Maracci.

COUPLET.

Could every hailstone to a pearl be turned,
Pearls in the mart like oyster shells were spurned.

The beloved of the Almighty (may He be honoured and glorified!) are the rich who have the humility of the poor, and the poor who have the magnanimity of the rich; and the prince of rich men is he who compassionates the poor, and among the poor men he is the best who depreciates the rich least. *God most High has said, 'Whosoever trusteth in God, He is sufficient for him.'*" The Ḳāẓī then turned the face of rebuke from me towards the darwesh, and said, "O thou! who hast said that the rich are absorbed in forbidden enjoyments and intoxicated with profane delights; it is true that there are a number of persons such as thou hast said, deficient in liberality and unthankful for their blessings, who gather money and hoard it, and who enjoy it but give none away. If, for example, the rain should not fall, or a deluge overwhelm the world, in the security of their own abundance they would not ask after the poor man nor fear the Most High God.

COUPLET.

What though another die of want? my bread
Fails not: to water-fowls floods cause no dread.

COUPLET.

Borne aloft in camel-litters, what, I pray, do women care
For the tired pilgrim struggling through the sand-heaps drifted there?

COUPLET.

The base who've saved their own vile wrappers cry,
'What matters though the universe should die?'

There are persons of the character I have described; but there is another numerous body who prepare a hospitable table and proclaim a liberal invitation, and whose countenances expand with affability while they in this manner pursue the path of fame and divine acceptance, and thus enjoy both this present world and a future recompense. Of these is his Majesty the King of the world, *the aided by God, the victorious and triumphant over his enemies, the holder of the reins of the human race, defender of the passes of Islām, heir to the throne of Sulaimān, the most just of the monarchs of the age, Muẕaffaru'd-dīn Abū Bakr bin Sād bin Zangī (may God prolong his days and grant victory to his banners!)*

STANZA.

No sire e'er showed such kindness to his child
As thy all-bounteous hand hath heaped on man.
Heaven on this world with favouring mercy smiled,
And by its Providence thy reign began."

When the Ḳāẕi had extended his discourse thus far, and had urged the steed of his rhetoric beyond the limits of our expectation, we acquiesced in the necessity of obeying his decree, overlooked what had passed, and, banishing our past differences, entered on the road of reconciliation; and, in amends for what we had mutually done, bowed our heads at each other's feet and kissed each other's head and faces. The discord ceased and our enmity terminated in peace, and our disagreement concluded with these two couplets:

STANZA.

Complain not, darwesh! of vicissitude:
Hapless if in such train of thought thou die!
And thou, rich man! while yet thou art endued
With a kind heart and riches, gratify
Thyself and others: thus on earth make sure
Of joys; and thy reward in heaven secure.

CHAPTER VIII.

ON THE DUTIES OF SOCIETY.

MAXIM I.

Riches are for the sake of making life comfortable, not life for the sake of amassing riches. I asked a wise man, "Who is fortunate and who unfortunate?" He replied, "The fortunate is he who sowed[282] and reaped; the unfortunate he who died and abandoned."

COUPLET.

Not for that worthless one a prayer afford,
Who life in hoarding spent—ne'er spent his hoard.

MAXIM II.

The holy Mūsạ (Peace be on him!) advised Ḳārūn,[283] saying, "*Do good unto others, as God has done good unto thee!*" He did not listen, and thou hast heard his end.

STANZA.

He who by wealth no good deeds has upstored,
For it has marred his future destiny.
Wouldst thou derive advantage from thy hoard?
Do good to others, as God has to thee.

[282] I have transposed خورد و کشت *kh'urd wa kisht*, as it is evident that "*kisht*" is put last only to rhyme with هشت *hisht*.

[283] Ḳur'ān, chap. xxviii., page 296, l. 6. Sale's Translation.

The Arabs say, "*Do good, and do not speak of it, and assuredly thy kindness will be recompensed to thee;*" that is to say, "Give and be liberal, and do not impute the obligation, and the benefit will revert to thee."

STANZA.

Where'er the tree of gracious deeds takes root,
Its towering top and branches reach the sky:
Do not, if thou wouldst wish to taste its fruit,
By boasting of those deeds, the axe apply.

STANZA.

Thank God that He vouchsafes to succour thee,
And has not left thee void of grace.
Thou serv'st the king—well! do not boastful be,
But rather thankful for thy place.

Maxim III.

Two men have laboured fruitlessly and exerted themselves to no purpose. One is the man who has gained wealth without enjoying it; the other he who has acquired knowledge but has failed to practise it.

DISTICHS.

How much soe'er thou learn'st, 'tis all vain;
Who practise not, still ignorant remain.
A quadruped, with volumes laden, is
No whit the wiser or more sage for this:
How can the witless animal discern,
If books be piled on it? or wood to burn?

Maxim IV.

Science is for the cultivation of religion, not for worldly enjoyments.

COUPLET.

Who makes a gain of virtue, science, lore,
Is one who garners up, then burns his store.

Maxim V.

A learned man who does not restrain his passions is like a blind man holding a torch; *he guides others but not himself.*

COUPLET.

Who life has wasted without doing aught,
His gold has squandered, and has purchased nought.

Maxim VI.

A country is adorned by wise men, and religion is perfected by the virtuous. Kings stand more in need of the counsel of the wise, than wise men do of propinquity to kings.

STANZA.

King! let my words with thee find grace;
My book than this can nought more sage advise:
The wise alone in office place;
Though office truly little suits the wise.

Maxim VII.

Three things lack permanency, uncombined with three other things: wealth without trading; learning without instruction;[284] and empire without a strict administration of justice.

STANZA.

By courteous speech, politeness, gentleness,
Sometimes thou mayest direct the human will:
Anon by threats; for it oft profits less
With sugar twice a hundred cups to fill,
Than from one colocynth its bitters to distil.

[284] The other translators take "controversy" to be the meaning of دراست *dirāsat;* I confess I am at a loss for authority to justify this sense. But the meaning I have given above is simple enough:—If the learned do not teach others, learning must soon come to an end.

MAXIM VIII.

To shew pity to the bad is to oppress the good, and to pardon oppressors is to tyrannise over the oppressed.

COUPLET.

When thou to base men giv'st encouragement,
Thou shar'st their sins, since thou them aid hast lent.

MAXIM IX.

No reliance can be placed on the friendship of princes, nor must we plume ourselves on the sweet voices of children, since that is changed by a caprice, and these by a single slumber.

COUPLET.

On the mistress of a thousand hearts, do not thy love bestow;
But if thou wilt, prepare eftsoons her friendship to forego.

MAXIM X.

Reveal not to a friend every secret that thou possessest. How knowest thou whether at some time he may not become an enemy? Nor inflict on thy enemy every injury that is in thy power, perchance he may some day become thy friend. Tell not the secret that thou wouldest have continue hidden to any person, although he may be worthy of confidence; for no one will be so careful of thy secret as thyself.

STANZA.

Better be silent, than thy purpose tell
To others; and enjoin them secresy.
O dolt! keep back the water at the well,
For the swoll'n stream to stop thou'lt vainly try.
In private, utter not a single word
Which thou in public wouldst regret were heard.

MAXIM XI.

A weak enemy who submits and makes a shew of friendship, does so only with the intention of becoming more dangerous; and they have said, "There is no reliance to be placed in the friendship of friends; how much less in the professions of enemies!" Whosoever despises a small enemy is like him who is careless about a little fire.

STANZA.

To-day extinguish, if thou can'st, the fire,
Which for its victims will a world require,
If not arrested. And ere yet his bow
Be strung, thy arrow should transfix the foe.

Maxim XII.

Let thy words between two foes be such that if they were to become friends thou wouldest not be ashamed.

DISTICHS.

Like fire is strife betwixt two enemies:
The luckless mischief-maker wood supplies.
Struck with confusion and ashamed is he,
If e'er the two belligerents agree.
Can we in this aught rational discern—
To light a fire which will ourselves first burn?

STANZA.

In talk with friends speak soft and low,
  Lest thy bloodthirsty foeman thee should hear:
A wall may front thee—true! but dost thou know
  If there be not behind a listening ear?

Maxim XIII.

Whoever comes to an agreement with the enemies of his friends, does so with the intention of injuring the latter.

COUPLET.

Eschew that friend, if thou art wise,
Who consorts with thy enemies.

Maxim XIV.

When, in transacting business, thou art in doubt, make choice of that side from which the least injury will result.

COUPLET.

Reply not roughly to smooth language, nor
Contend with him who knocks at peace's door.

Maxim XV.

As long as a matter can be compassed by money, it is not right to imperil life. The Arabs say, "*The sword is the last resource.*"

COUPLET.

When thou hast failed in every known resource,
Then to the sword 'tis right to have recourse.

Maxim XVI.

Compassionate not the weakness of a foe, for were he to become powerful he would have no pity on thee.[285]

COUPLET.

Twist not thy moustaches boastful, nor with pride thy weak foe scan:
Every bone contains some marrow, every garment cloaks a man.

APOPHTHEGM.

He who slays a bad man, rids mankind of annoyance from him, and the man himself from an increase of punishment [which his future misdeeds would have merited] from God (may He be honoured and glorified!).[286]

[285] These maxims are a very good index of Oriental feeling; and all who know the East will admit that they are most religiously observed.

[286] An unlucky maxim for a criminal. So, in taking off his head, you are in fact consulting not only the public weal, but the welfare of the criminal himself.

STANZA.

Pity is commendable—that we own ;
Yet on the tyrant's wound no ointment place.
He that has mercy to a serpent shown,
Has acted cruelly to Adam's race.

MAXIM XVII.

To act in accordance with an enemy's advice is foolish, but it is permissible to hear it, in order to do the opposite, for that will be exactly the right course.

DISTICHS.

Beware of what thy foeman bids thee do,
Lest on thy knees thou smite thy hands, and grieve.
Straight as a dart may be the road—'tis true—
He points to ; yet 'twere better it to leave.

MAXIM XVIII.

Anger that has no limit causes terror, and unseasonable kindness does away with respect. Be not so severe as to cause disgust, nor so lenient as to make people presume.

DISTICHS.

Sternness and gentleness are best combined :
The leech both salves and scarifies, you find.
The sage is not too rigorous, nor yet
Too mild, lest men their awe of him forget :
He seeks not for himself too high a place ;
Nor will himself too suddenly abase.

DISTICHS.

Once to his sire a shepherd said, " O Sage !
Teach me one maxim worthy of thy age."
" Use gentleness," he said, " yet not so much,
That the wolf be emboldened thee to clutch."

MAXIM XIX.

Two persons are the foes of a state and of religion; a king without clemency, and a religious man without learning.

COUPLET.

Ne'er to that king may states allegiance own,
Who bows not humbly at th' Almighty's throne.

MAXIM XX.

A king ought not to indulge his resentment against his enemies to such an extent as to shake the confidence of his friends; for the fire of wrath falls first on the wrathful man himself, and after, its flame may or may not reach the enemy.

DISTICHS.

It suits not Adam's children, earthly-born,
T' indulge in pride, ferocity, and scorn.
When I behold in thee such heat and ire,
I cannot think thee sprung from earth, but fire.

STANZA.

In Bailḳān[287] once a devotee I saw,
"From folly purge me by thy words," I said.
"Go!" he replied, "thou who art skilled in law,
Be as earth humble, or what thou hast read
Might in the earth as well be buried."

MAXIM[288] XXI.

The wicked man is overtaken in the grasp of an enemy from whose torturing clutches he can never escape, go where he will.

COUPLET.

Though bad men seek in heaven to flee from ill,
E'en there their vices will pursue them still.

[287] A city in Armenia Major, near the ports of the Caspian Sea.

[288] This is headed مطايبه *muṭāyabah*, "pleasantry," as the next is پند *pand*, "advice," as others are ملاطفه *mulāṭafah*, "facetiæ," and تنبيه *tambīh*, "admonition;" but, as it is difficult to see how these differ from حكمت *ḥikmat*, and from one another, I have rendered them all "Maxim."

Maxim XXII.

When thou seest discord arise among the forces of the enemy, take courage; and when they are united[289] beware then of rout.

STANZA.

Go! with thy friends sit free from care,
  If thou thy foes shouldst see with discord rent.
But if thou mark'st agreement there,
Go string thy bow, thyself prepare,
  And pile thy missiles on the battlement.

Maxim XXIII.

When an enemy has tried every expedient in vain, he will pretend friendship,[290] and then, by this pretext, execute designs which no enemy could have effected.

Maxim XXIV.

Crush the serpent's head with the hand of an enemy, which must result in one of two good things. If the latter be successful, thou hast killed a snake; and if the former, thou hast freed thyself from an enemy.

COUPLET.

Though thy foe be feeble, be not in the battle void of care;
He will dash the lion's brains out when he's driven to despair.

Maxim XXV.

When thou knowest tidings that will pain the heart of any one, be silent, so that another may be the first to convey them.

[289] There is a play on words here, which I have not been able to preserve in English. جمع شدن *jamā shudan* signifies "to be collected, united," and also, "to be of good cheer."

[290] *Literally*, "Agitate the chain of friendship."

COUPLET.

O nightingale! spring's tidings breathe,
Ill rumours to the owls bequeath.

Maxim XXVI.

Do not acquaint a king with the treason of any one, unless when thou art assured that the disclosure will meet with his full approval, else thou art but labouring for thy own destruction.

COUPLET.

Then, only then, to speak intend
When speaking can effect thy end.

Maxim XXVII.

He who gives advice to a conceited man is himself in need of counsel.

Maxim XXVIII.

Be not caught by the artifice of a foe, nor purchase pride of a flatterer; for the one has set the snare of hypocrisy, and the other has opened the mouth of greediness. The fool is puffed up with flattery, like a corpse whose inflated heels appear plump.

STANZA.

Heed not the flatterer's fulsome talk,
He from thee hopes some trifle to obtain;
Thou wilt, shouldst thou his wishes baulk,
Two hundred times as much of censure gain.

Maxim XXIX.

Until some one points out to an orator his defects, his discourse will never be amended.

COUPLET.

To vaunt of one's own speaking is not meet,
At fools' approval and one's own conceit.

Maxim XXX.

Every one thinks his own judgment perfect, and his own son beautiful.

VERSE.

A Jew and Musalmān once so contended
That laughter seized me as their contest grew.
The true believer thus his cause defended:
"Is this bond false, then may I die a Jew!"
The Jew replied: "By Moses' books I vow that
'Tis true, or else a Musalmān am I!"
So from earth's face were Wisdom's self to fly,
Not one could be amongst us found t' allow that
He judgment lacked, or himself stultify.

Maxim XXXI.

Ten men can eat at one board, but two dogs cannot satisfy themselves at one carcase. The greedy man continues to hunger, though a world supply his wants; and the contented man is satisfied with a crust.

COUPLET.

A single loaf the stomach will supply;
But not earth's richest gifts the greedy eye.

DISTICHS.

When my sire's age had reached its latest day,
He gave me this advice, and passed away:—
"Lust is a fire;—from it thyself keep well;
Nor kindle 'gainst thyself the flames of Hell.
Thou hast not patience to endure that flame, I trow;
With patience, as with water, quench it now."

Maxim XXXII.

Whosoever does no good when he has the ability to do it, in the time of inability to aid others will himself suffer distress.

COUPLET.

Ill-starred, indeed, is he who injures men :
Is fortune adverse, he is friendless then.

Maxim XXXIII.

Life hangs on a single breath; and the world of existence is between two non-existences. Those who barter religion for the world are asses; they sell Joseph and get what in return? *Did I not covenant with you, O sons of Adam! that ye should not serve Satan? for verily he is your avowed enemy.*

COUPLET.

With thy friend thou faith hast broken at the bidding of thy foe:
See with whom thou'st joined alliance, and from whom thou'st sought to go.

Maxim XXXIV.

Satan prevails not against the righteous; nor a king against the poor.

DISTICHS.

Lend not to him who prayer neglects, though he
Gasping with want and inanition be;
For he who renders not to God His due,
What will he care for that he owes to you?

STANZA.

I've heard that they so temper Eastern clay [291]
That they in forty years one cup prepare:
Hundreds are made in Baghdād in a day,
And hence the lowness of the price they bear.

[291] The other translators render خاک مشرق *khāk-i mashrik*, "in the land of the East," "dans le pays d'Orient," etc.; but surely the translation I have given is at least as defensible.

VERSE.

The young bird from its egg comes forth and meets at
once its fate,
While infant man is destitute of reason and of sense:
Too soon matured the first arrives at nothing high or great;
The second with slow steps attains a proud pre-eminence.
Crystal is everywhere beheld, and hence contemned its
state;
But since the ruby's rarely found, its worth's the
consequence.

Maxim XXXV.

Affairs succeed by patience; and he that is hasty falleth headlong.

DISTICHS.

I've in the desert with these eyes beheld
The hurrying pilgrim to the slow-stepped yield:
The rapid courser in the rear remains,
While the slow camel still its step maintains.

Maxim XXXVI.

There is no better ornament for the ignorant than silence, and did he but know this he would not be ignorant.

STANZA.

Hast thou not perfect excellence, 'tis best
To keep thy tongue in silence, for 'tis this
Which shames a man; as lightness does attest
The nut is empty, nor of value is.

STANZA.

Once, in these words, a fool rebuked an ass,—
"Go, thou who all thy life hast lived in vain!"
A sage said to him, "Blockhead! why dost pass
Thy time in this? Gibes will be all thy gain.
To learn of thee a brute no power has:
Learn thou of brutes in silence to remain."

DISTICHS.

Whoe'er his answer does not ponder, will,
In most affairs, be found to answer ill;
Thy speech embellish with man's sense and wit,
Or learn in silence like a brute to sit.

MAXIM XXXVII.

Whoever disputes with a man more wise than himself, to make people think him wise, will be thought ignorant.

COUPLET.

When one more wise than thou begins to speak,
Do not, tho' skilful, to oppose him seek.

MAXIM XXXVIII.

Whoso sits with bad men will not see aught good.

DISTICHS.

With demons did an angel take his seat,
He'd learn but terror, treason, and deceit:
Thou from the bad wilt nothing learn but ill;
The wolf will ne'er the furrier's office fill.

MAXIM XXXIX.

Divulge not the secret faults of men; for at the same time that thou disgracest them thou wilt destroy thy own credit.

MAXIM XL.

He that has acquired learning and not practised what he has learnt, is like a man who ploughs but sows no seed.

MAXIM XLI.

Worship cannot be performed by the body without the mind, and a shell without a kernel will not do for merchandise.

Maxim XLII.

Not every one who is ready at wrangling is correct in his dealings.

COUPLET.

Forms enow beneath the mantle wear the outward signs
of grace;
But if thou shouldst them unwimple, thou wouldst find
a grandam's face.

Maxim XLIII.

If every night was a night of power,[292] the Night of Power would lose its value.

COUPLET.

Were each stone such ruby as is found in Badakhshānyan
earth,
How would then the ruby differ from the pebble in its
worth?

Maxim XLIV.

Not every one whose outward form is graceful possesses the graces of the mind; for action depends on the heart, not on the exterior.

[292] Gladwin seems to me to destroy the pith of this sentence by rendering شبِ قدر *shab-i ḳadr*, "many of such nights;" to say nothing of making a singular noun plural. Chapter xcvii. of the Ḳur'ān is as follows: "Verily, we sent down the Ḳur'ān in the night of Al Ḳadr. And what shall make thee understand how excellent the night of Al Ḳadr is? The night of Al Ḳadr is better than a thousand months. Therein do the angels descend, and the spirit Gabriel also, by the permission of their Lord, with his decrees concerning every matter. It is peace until the rising of the morn." The Moslem doctors are not agreed when to fix this night; but most think it one of the last nights of Ramazān, and the seventh reckoned backwards, whence it will fall between the 23rd and 24th days of that month.

STANZA.

From a man's qualities a day's enough
To make us of his learning's limit sure.
Plume not thyself as though the hidden stuff
Thou of his heart hast reached; nor be secure,
For not e'en long revolving years can tell
The foul things which in man unnoticed dwell.

Maxim XLV.

He who joins battle with the great sheds his own blood.

STANZA.

Say'st thou, "Behold! how great I am!"
The squint-eyed even thus of one makes two;
Who play at butting with a ram
Will quick enough a broken forehead rue.

Maxim XLVI.

It is not the part of wise men to grapple with a lion, or strike the fist against a sword.

COUPLET.

Not in contention with the furious stand,
And near the mighty humbly clasp thy hand.[293]

Maxim XLVII.

A weak man, who has the fool-hardiness to contend with a strong one, assists his adversary in destroying himself.

STANZA.

He who was nursed in soft repose
Cannot with warriors to the battle go;
Vain with his weakly arm to close,
And struggle with an iron-wristed foe.

[293] *Literally*, "Put thy hand under thy armpit;" *i.e.* "Put thyself in a peaceful attitude."

Maxim XLVIII.

Whoso will not listen to advice aims at hearing himself reproached.

COUPLET.

He who will not to friends' advice attend,
Must not complain when they him reprehend.

Maxim XLIX.

Persons devoid of virtue cannot endure the sight of the virtuous; just as market-curs, when they see dogs of the chase, bark at them, but dare not approach them.

Maxim L.

When a base fellow cannot vie with another in merit, he will attack him with malicious slander.

COUPLET.

Weak envy absent virtue slanders,—Why?
Since it is dumb, perforce, when it is by.

Maxim LI.

But for the tyranny of hunger no bird would fall into the snare—nay, the fowler himself would not set the snare.

COUPLET.

The belly binds the hands, the feet unnerves;
He heeds not heaven who his belly serves.

Maxim LII.

Wise men eat late; devout men but half satisfy their appetites; and hermits take only enough to support life; the young eat till the dishes are removed, and the old till they sweat; but the Ḳalandars[294] stuff till they have no room in their stomachs to breathe, and not a morsel is left on the table for any one.

[294] A sort of faḳīr.

COUPLET.

The glutton for two nights no sleep can get;
The first from surfeit, the next from regret.[295]

MAXIM LIII.

To consult with women is ruin, and to be liberal to the mischievous is a crime.

COUPLET.

To sharp-toothed tigers kind to be
To harmless flocks is tyranny.[296]

MAXIM LIV.

Whoso slays not his enemy when he is in his power is his own enemy.

COUPLET.

When a stone is in the hand; on a stone the serpent's pate;
He is not a man of sense who to strike should hesitate.

There are, however, persons who think the opposite of this advisable, and have said, "It is better to pause in the execution of prisoners, inasmuch as the option [of slaying or pardoning them] is retained. Whereas, if a prisoner

[295] *Literally*, "One who is a captive in the bonds of the belly." Gladwin translates the دل تنگي *dil tangī*, in the second line, "want." M. Semelet, more literally, "inquiétude de cœur." I suppose it to be "regret," for having eaten the supplies for the next day. Dr. Sprenger reads معدهٔ خالي *mi'dah-i khālī*, for معدهٔ سنگي *mi'dah-i sangī*, which I cannot approve.

[296] As the couplet in my edition occurs, and has been already translated under Maxim VIII., I prefer rendering Dr. Sprenger's and M. Semelet's reading, which is as follows:—

ترحّم بر پلنگِ تيز دندان
ستمگاري بود بر گوسفندان

and which occurs in my edition after the next couplet.

be put to death without deliberation, it is probable that the best course will be let slip, since the step is irremediable."

COUPLETS.

'Tis very easy one alive to slay;
Not so to give back life thou tak'st away:
Reason demands that archers patience show,
For shafts once shot return not to the bow.

Maxim LV.

The sage who engages in controversy with ignorant people must not expect to be treated with honour; and if a fool should overpower a philosopher by his loquacity, it is not to be wondered at, for a common stone will break a jewel.

COUPLET.

What marvel is it if his spirits droop?
A nightingale—and with him crows to coop!

COUPLETS.

What if a vagabond on merit rail?
Let not the spirits of the worthy fail:
A common stone may break a golden cup;
Its value goes not down, the stone's not up.

Maxim LVI.

If in a company of dissolute fellows the discourse of a wise man is not received with attention, be not astonished; for the sound of the lute is drowned by that of the drum, and the perfume of ambergris is overpowered by the fœtor of garlic.

VERSE.

Proud has the loud-voiced wittol grown,
That impudence the wise has overthrown;
Know'st thou not Ḥijāz' strains too low-toned are
To mingle with the brazen drum of war.

If a jewel fall into the mire it remains as precious as

before: and though dust should ascend to heaven, its former worthlessness will not be altered. A capacity without education is pitiable, and education without capacity is thrown away. Ashes, though akin to what is exalted, inasmuch as fire is essentially noble, yet, not possessing any intrinsic worth, are no better than dirt; and the value of sugar is not derived from the cane, but from its own inherent qualities. Musk is that which of itself yields a sweet smell, not that which the perfumer says is musk.[297] The wise man is like the tray of the druggist—silent, but evincing its own merits; and the ignorant man resembles the drum of the warrior—loud-voiced, and empty, and bragging vainly.

VERSE.

A learned man, as sages state,
Among the dull illiterate,
Is like a beauty 'mid the blind,
Or Ḳur'ān to the impious mind.
In Canaan's land, when sin prevailed,
The Prophet's birth no fruit entailed.
If innate worth is in thee born,
[Thy origin deserves not scorn,]
The rose aye blossoms on the thorn;
[The worthless may engender worth,]
And Āẕur gave to Abraham birth.

Maxim LVII.

It is not right to estrange in a moment a friend whom it takes a lifetime to secure.

TRIPLET.

'Tis years before the pebble can put on
The ruby's nature.—Wilt thou on a stone
In one short moment mar what time has done?

[297] He may call that which is adulterated or counterfeit "musk."

Maxim LVIII.

Reason is a captive in the hands of the passions, as a weak man in the hands of an artful woman.

COUPLET.

Shut on that house the door of sweet content,
Where woman can aloud her passions vent.

Maxim LIX.

Purpose without power is mere weakness and deception; and power without purpose is fatuity and insanity.

COUPLET.

Have judgment, counsel, sense, and then bear rule;
Wealth, empire, are self-murder[298] to the fool.

Maxim LX.

The liberal man, who enjoys and bestows, is better than the devotee, who fasts and lays by. Whoso abandons lust in order to gain acceptance with the world has fallen from venial desires into those which are unpardonable.

COUPLET.

Hermits, who are not so through piety,
Darken a glass and then attempt to see.

COUPLET.

Little to little added much will grow:
The barn's store, grain by grain, is gathered so.

Many littles make a mickle, many drops a flood.

Maxim LXI.

It is not right for a learned man to pass over leniently

[298] I prefer Gladwin's and Gentius' renderings of this passage to those of Semelet and Ross. Literally, the sense of the second line is, "For the territories and wealth of the ignorant are the weapons of warfare against himself."

the foolish impertinencies of the vulgar, for this is detrimental to both parties: the awe which the former ought to inspire is diminished, and the folly of the latter augmented.

COUPLET.

Art thou with fools too courteous and too free,
Their pride and folly will augmented be.

Maxim LXII.

Wickedness, by whomsoever committed, is odious: but most of all in men of learning; for learning is the weapon with which Satan is combated; and when a man is made captive with arms in his hand, his shame is more excessive.

COUPLET.

Better an ignorant and wretched state
Than to be learned and yet profligate;
That from the path his blindness did beguile;
This saw, and in a pitfall slipped the while.

Maxim LXIII.

People forget the name of him whose bread they have not tasted during his lifetime. Joseph the just (Peace be on him!), during the famine in Egypt, would not eat so as to satisfy his appetite, that he might not forget the hungry. It is the poor widow that relishes the grapes, not the owner of the vineyard.[299]

COUPLETS.

He who in pleasure and abundance lives,
What knows he of the pang that hunger gives?
He can affliction best appreciate,
Who has himself experienced the same state.

[299] That is, We estimate blessings when we are deprived of them, and value highly what is beyond our reach.

STANZA.

O thou! who rid'st a mettled courser, see
How toils, 'mid mire, the poor thorn-loaded ass!
From poor men's houses, let no fire for thee
Be brought. The wreaths which from their chimney pass,
Are sighs wrung from their hearts by destiny.[300]

Maxim LXIV.

Inquire not of the distressed darwesh in his destitution and time of want, "How art thou?" save on the condition that thou puttest ointment on his wound and settest money before him.

STANZA.

The ass has fallen with its burthen—well!
Thou mark'st it—then be pitiful, nor tread
It down; but if thou askest how it fell,
[Let not thy help to this be limited],
But bravely strive to drag it forth instead.[301]

Maxim LXV.

Two things are impossible: to obtain more food than what Providence destines for us; and to die before the time known to God.

STANZA.

Fate is not altered by a thousand sighs;
Complain or render thanks—arrive it will:
The angel at whose bidding winds arise
Cares little for the widow's lamp, if still
It burns, or by the storm extinguished dies.

[300] That is, do not wring from the poor the smallest trifle. The comparison between smoke and a sigh has occurred twice before. It is a simile in which Orientals delight, inept as it appears to us.

[301] *Literally*, "Gird up thy loins and, like brave men, lay hold of the ass's tail."

Maxim LXVI.

O thou! who seekest subsistence, sit down, that thou mayest be fed; and thou who desirest to die! go not [in pursuit of death]; for thou canst not preserve thy life [beyond the destined term].

STANZA.

Wouldst thou by toil or not thy wants supply,
The Glorious and High God will give thee food.
Nor, mortal! canst thou unpredestined die,
Didst thou in maw of ravenous tigers lie,
Or savage lions thirsting for thy blood.

Maxim LXVII.

It is impossible to lay hands on that which is not predestined for us, and that which is predestined will reach us wherever we are.

TRIPLET.

Hast thou not heard with what excess of pain
Sikandar sought the shades? nor yet could gain
Life's water, which he strove thus to attain.

Maxim LXVIII.

A fisherman cannot catch fish in the Tigris without the aid of destiny; nor can a fish perish on dry land unless fated to do so.

COUPLET.

Poor greedy wretch! where'er he drags himself,
Death him pursues, while he's pursuing pelf.

Maxim LXIX.

A wicked rich man is a gilded clod, and a pious darwesh is a beauty soiled with earth. The latter is the tattered garment of Moses patched together, and the former is the ulcer of Pharaoh[302] covered with jewels. The sufferings of the good have a joyful aspect, while the prosperity of the wicked looks downward.

STANZA.

Tell those to whom rank, wealth are given,
Who care not for the sons of pain;
That in the bright abodes of Heaven
They neither wealth nor rank will gain.

Maxim LXX.

The envious man begrudgeth God's blessings, and is the foe of the innocent.

STANZA.

A wretched crack-brained fellow once I saw,
Who slandered one of lofty dignity;
I said, "Good sir! I grant thee that a flaw
May in thy fortunes be observed,—but why
Impute it to the man who lives more happily?

SECOND STANZA.

Oh! on the envious man invoke no curse,
For of himself, poor wretch! accursed is he;
On him no hatred can inflict aught worse
Than his self-fed, self-torturing enmity.

Maxim LXXI.

A student without the inclination to learn is a lover without money; and a pilgrim without spirituality is a

[302] Ross translates ريش *rīsh*, in this passage, "embroidered mantle," a strange freedom. M. Semelet renders it "la barbe," which is downright nonsense. Gladwin seems to me to have expressed the right meaning. One of the seven plagues was a boil and blain breaking out on the Egyptians.

bird without wings; and a devotee without learning[303] is a house without a door.

MAXIM LXXII.

The intent of revealing the Ḳur'ān was, to give men the means of learning good morality, not that they should employ themselves in the mere recitation of the text. The man who is devout but illiterate, is one who performs his journey though it be on foot; while the man who is learned but negligent, is a sleeping rider. A sinner who lifts up his hand [in prayer] is better than a devotee who lifts up his head [in pride].

COUPLET.

Better the kind and courteous man of arms
Than lawyer who his fellow-creatures harms.

MAXIM LXXIII.

A learned man without practice is a bee without honey.

COUPLET.

Go, tell the hornet—fierce, ungentle thing,
We want no honey: but at least don't sting!

MAXIM LXXIV.

A man without courage is a woman,[304] and a devotee with covetous desires is a robber.

303 علم *ïlm*, here, is "learning" rather than "knowledge," as Gladwin renders it. The devotee may have knowledge of spiritual things; but, not having learning, he may be unable to teach others, and thus resemble a house well furnished and spacious, but inaccessible.

304 There is an equivoque in the Persian which cannot be preserved in English. زن *zan* is "a woman," ره زن *rah-zan* "a robber." Gladwin translates مروت *muruwat*, in my opinion, incorrectly.

STANZA.

Thou! who t'appease the crowd and win repute
Hast made the robe of outward actions white;
Know, to resign the world doth better suit
The pious, and to be regardless quite
Whether the sleeve be long or short to sight.

Maxim LXXV.

Two sorts of persons cannot cease to feel regret at heart, nor can they extricate the foot of remorse from the mire: one is the merchant, whose vessel has been wrecked; and the other, the heir who has become the associate of Ḳalandars. In accordance with this they have said: "Though the robe bestowed by the Sulṭān is precious, people's own clothes are more regarded; and though the tray of dishes at the table of the great is full of delicacies, yet the scraps of one's own wallet are better relished."

COUPLET.

Than the mayor's kid and loaf more dainty far
Are our poor herbs—self-earned—and vinegar.

Maxim LXXVI.

It is contrary to right reason, and a violation of the precepts of the wise, to take medicine about which we are in doubt; and to travel by a road we do not know, save in the company of a caravan.

Maxim LXXVII.

They asked the Imām and spiritual guide—Muḥammad bin Muḥammad Ghizālī—(may the mercy of God be upon him!) by what means he had attained such a degree of learning. He replied, "In this way: I was not ashamed to ask whatever I did not know."

STANZA.

Hope thou with reason for good health, when thou
Dost to the skilful leech thy pulse present;
Ask what thou know'st not—with the stigma, now,
(If shame there be) of asking be content;
And thus in learning grow pre-eminent.

MAXIM LXXVIII.

Whenever thou art certain of being informed of a thing, be not precipitate in inquiry; for this will lessen thy credit and respectability.

VERSE.

When Luḳmān marked how wax-like iron grew,
Moulded in David's hands; though wondrous, he
Forbore to ask his secret; for he knew
He of himself would learn the mystery.

MAXIM LXXIX.

It is one of the essentials of society that thou either play the part of host thyself, or act so as to conciliate the host.[305]

STANZA.

Let thy story aye befit
The hearer's taste, wouldst thou that he approve;[306]
They who would with Majnūn sit,
Must still of Lailạ talk—still talk of love.

[305] Gladwin translates, "Amongst the qualifications for society, it is necessary either that you attend to the concerns of your household, or else devote yourself to religion." This is, no doubt, the implied meaning. Life is compared to an entertainment, where, if you choose the part of host, you must entertain religious men; or, if you would be a guest, be a religious man yourself, and so please the Great Host, that is, God.

[306] I should wish to read, in the second line of this stanza, اگر خواهي *agar khwāhī*, instead of اگر داني *agar dānī*, which appears to me to be nonsense. If a man knew that another was well disposed to him, he might presume, on that, to say unpalatable things; but if he wished to ingratiate himself, he would choose a pleasing subject.

Maxim LXXX.

Whoso associates with the wicked will be accused of following their ways, though their principles may have made no impression upon him; just as if a person were in the habit of frequenting taverns, he would not be supposed to go there for prayer, but to drink intoxicating liquors.

DISTICHS.

Thyself thou'lt surely stigmatise,
In choosing for thy friends th' unwise.
I asked a sage for one sound rule;
He said, "Consort not with a fool,
For this of wise men fools will make,
And even fools deteriorate."

Maxim LXXXI.

So tractable is the camel that, as is well known, if a child took hold of its bridle and led it a hundred parasangs, it would not withdraw its neck from obeying him: but if they came to a dangerous road which might cause its destruction, and the child, through ignorance, wished to go that way, it would wrest the reins from his grasp, and would not after that obey him: for, in the time when rough dealing is required, kindness is blameable; and they have said: "An enemy will not become friendly by being treated with kindness; but, on the contrary, his avarice will be increased."

STANZA.

Thou to the courteous humble be, as dust;
  But rough to those with whom thou hast a feud;[307]
A soft file will not cleanse deep-seated rust:
  Then use not gentle language with the rude.

[307] I have translated this line freely. Literally, it is, "If he oppose thee, fill his two eyes with mud."

Maxim LXXXII.

Whoever interrupts the conversation of others to display the extent of his wisdom, will assuredly discover the depth of his folly: and the wise have said:

STANZA.

"Until they him interrogate,
The prudent man will aye continue mute;
For though his words might be sedate,
Men would to folly the display impute."

Maxim LXXXIII.

I had once a sore under my robe. My religious superior (on whom be the mercy of God!) every day asked me, "How art thou?" and he did not inquire, "On what part is thy wound?" forbearing, because it is not right to mention every member: and the wise have said: "Whoever does not weigh his words, will receive an answer that will vex him."

STANZA.

Until thou knowest that a speech is sooth,
Thou shouldest not unclose thy lips to speak:
Better to be confined for speaking truth
Than, by false speaking, thy release to seek.

Maxim LXXXIV.

The uttering of a falsehood is like a violent blow; for, even should the wound be healed, the scar will remain. Thus, when the brothers of Joseph (peace be on him!) had acquired the character of telling untruths, their words were not believed, even when they said that which was true. *God Most High has said, "But your passions have suggested this to you."*[308]

[308] *Vide* Sale's Ḳur'ān, II. 35. Jacob is speaking.

STANZA.

When 'tis one's habit aye the truth to say,
A slip is pardoned readily;
But should one be renowned the other way,
Even in his truth we error see.

Maxim LXXXV.

The most glorious of created things, in outward form, is man; and the most vile of living things, is a dog; yet, by the unanimous consent of the wise, a grateful dog is better than an ungrateful man.

STANZA.

The scrap thou on a dog bestowest, it—
Though pelted oft—will yet remember still;
But though thro' life the base thou benefit,
They for the merest trifle would thee kill.

Maxim LXXXVI.

The sensual ne'er can eminence attain;
And those who have not merit should not reign.

DISTICHS.

Spare not the glutton ox, for know that he
Who much devours will also slothful be:
If thou must needs be fatted like the ox,
Then like the ass submit to people's knocks.

Maxim LXXXVII.

It is said, in the Gospel,[309] "O son of Adam! if I give thee wealth, thou wilt occupy thyself with riches and

[309] This is probably a quotation from some spurious Gospel. Ross refers to Proverbs, chap. xxx. ver. 7, 8, 9, "Two things have I required of thee; deny me them not before I die: Remove far from me vanity and lies: give me neither poverty nor riches; feed me with food convenient for me: Lest I be full and deny thee, and say, Who is the Lord? or lest I be poor, and steal, and take the name of my God in vain."

neglect me; and, if I make thee poor, then thou wilt cower down in distress. Wherefore, in what state wilt thou find the happiness of praising me? or when wilt thou hasten to serve me?"

STANZA.

With riches now thou art too proud, elate;
Or sinkest down too low beneath the rod:
Since this in joy and sorrow is thy state,
When wilt thou turn from selfishness to God?

Maxim LXXXVIII.

The will of Him who has no like brings down one man from a royal throne, and preserves another in the belly of a fish.

COUPLET.

He who parts not from Thy praises will enjoy tranquillity,
Though—as was the Prophet Jonas—in the fish-maw he should be.

Maxim LXXXIX.

When God draws the sword of His wrath, prophets and saints draw back their heads [in fear of the stroke], and if He smile graciously with His eyes, He raises the bad to an equality with the good.

STANZA.

If in judgment He should, wrathful, words severe of anger say,
What pardon e'en for saints were there?
Pray Him, therefore, from His mercy's face the veil to take away,
And free e'en sinners from despair.

Maxim XC.

Whoso learns not from this world's lesson to take the right way, will be overtaken by the punishments of the next. *God Most High has said,* "*And we will cause them to taste the lesser punishment of this world, besides the more grievous punishment of the next; peradventure they will repent.*"[310]

COUPLET.

The great admonish first—observant be!
Lest, if thou heed not words, they shackle thee.

Those endued with a happy disposition are warned by the anecdotes and precedents of former generations, so as not to become themselves a warning to those who follow them.

STANZA.

No bird will settle on the grain,
That sees another bird already snared;
Take warning then from others' pain,
Or else to point a moral be prepared.

Maxim XCI.

How can one, the ear of whose choice has been made heavy, hear? and how can he, who is drawn by the noose of happy destiny, decline to proceed.[311]

STANZA.

The dark night of the friends of Heaven
Shines with the brilliant light of day;
Not to man's might is this rich blessing given,
It comes from God—no other way.

QUATRAIN.

To whom, save Thee, shall I complain? Thou only
Rulest; and no arm equals thine in might;
Guided by Thee, none are e'er lost or lonely;
Whom Thou forsakest, none can guide aright.

[310] *Vide* Ḳur'ān, chap. xxxii. ver. 22; Sale's Translation, p. 311.

[311] This seems to be the doctrine of Predestination. Ross and Gladwin both omit to translate the word ارادت *irādat*, and the latter omits also سعادت *saădat*.

MAXIM XCII.

A beggar whose end is blest is better than a king who dies miserably.

COUPLET.

Better feel sorrow ere we gladness know,
Than to be happy and then suffer woe.

MAXIM XCIII.

The sky supplies the earth with showers, while the earth renders back dust. *Every vessel allows that to permeate through it which it contains.*[312]

COUPLET.

My temper seems unpleasing in thy eyes;
Change not for that thy better qualities.

God Most High sees [our sins], but casts a veil over them; and our neighbour blazes abroad [our offences], though he sees them not.

COUPLET.

Save us, good Lord! could men in secret see,
None were from others' interference free!

MAXIM XCIV.

Gold is procured from the vein by digging the mine, and from the miser's clutches by digging out his mind.[313]

STANZA.

Base men enjoy not, and to lonely haunts
Slink sullen, and they say, "On hope to feed
Is better than to gratify one's wants."
One day thou'lt see the victim of his greed
A corse,—his foes exulting and his money freed.[314]

[312] In other words, "That which exudes from a vessel is of the same nature as its contents." Our proverb is, "You cannot make a silk purse out of a sow's ear."

[313] جان کندن *jān kandan*, means, literally, "to dig out the soul," and is generally applied to the agonies of death.

[314] That is, from his clutches.

MAXIM XCV.

Whoso shews no compassion to the weak will suffer from the violence of the strong.

DISTICHS.

Not every arm that is of might possessed,
Can crush the poor or ruin the distressed:
Grieve not the feeble, lest in turn thou, too,
Th' oppressor's power and injustice rue.

MAXIM XCVI.

The prudent man, when he beholds contention arising, steps aside; and when he sees that peace prevails, casts anchor there: for, in the one case, safety lies in withdrawing, and, in the other, he is assured of tranquillity.

MAXIM XCVII.

The gamester wants three sixes, but three aces turn up.

COUPLET.

Far better is the pasture than the plain[315]
But the horse guides not for himself the rein.

MAXIM XCVIII.

A darwesh said in his prayers, "O God! have mercy on the wicked, for Thou hast already had mercy on the good, in that Thou hast created them good!"

MAXIM XCIX.

The first person who introduced distinctions of dress, and the habit of wearing rings on the finger, was Jamshīd.[316] They asked him, Why he had conferred all these ornaments on the left arm, while the right was the more excellent? He replied, "The right arm is completely adorned in being the right."

[315] میدان *maidān*, "plain," is used for the "parade-ground," "place of exercise," "battle-field."

[316] An ancient king of Persia, being the fourth monarch of the first or Pīshdādyan dynasty. He built Istakhar or Persepolis, and was dethroned by Ẓaḥḥāk.

STANZA.

Said Farīdūn to China's men of art,
"Round my pavilion's walls embroider this,—
'If thou art wise, to bad men good impart;
The good enough of honour have and bliss.'"

Maxim C.

They asked an eminent personage why, when the right hand was so superior to the left, men were in the habit of placing the signet-ring on the left hand? He rejoined, "Knowest thou not that merit is always neglected?"

COUPLET.

He from whom fate, subsistence, fortunes spring,
Now makes a man of merit, now a king.

Maxim CI.

He may advise kings safely who has neither fear for his head nor cupidity.

DISTICHS.

Whether thou money at his feet dost spread,
Who truly worships God; or o'er his head
Wavest the Indian scymitar; no dread
Has he of mortal man: in this
True faith consists,—this orthodoxy is,

Maxim CII.

A king is for the coercion of oppressors, and the superintendent of police to repress murder, and the judge for hearing complaints against thieves. Two parties, whose aim is justice only, never refer matters to the judge.

STANZA.

Art thou assured that thou must justice do—
Then better do it gently, without strife.
Who pay not taxes willingly, will rue
The law's exactions, and the misproud crew
Of insolent officials. Stubbornness is rife
With a twin evil—shame and damage too.

Maxim CIII.

All men's teeth are blunted by sour things except the judge's, whose edge is taken off by sweets.

COUPLET.

The judge five cucumbers as a bribe will take,
And grant ten beds of melons for their sake.

Maxim CIV.

What can an old prostitute do but vow not to sin any more? or a superintendent of police discharged from office, except promise not to cease from injustice?

COUPLET.

He leads the hermit's life, who chooses it
In youth; for age cannot its corner quit.

Maxim CV.

They asked a philosopher, Why, when God Most High had created so many famous fruitful trees, the cypress alone was called free, which bore no fruit? and what was the meaning of this? He replied, "Every tree has its appointed time and season, so that, during the said season, it flourishes; and when that is past, it droops. But the cypress is not exposed to either of these vicissitudes, and is at all times fresh and green; and this is the condition of the free."

STANZA.

Place not thy heart on transitory things.
Long shall the Tigris on by Baghdād flow,
When all the glory of the Caliph kings
Has passed away. Be, if thou canst be so,
Like the date, generous. Canst thou nought bestow
From lack of means; at least resolve to be,
Like the green cypress, fetterless and free.

Maxim CVI.

Two persons die remorseful; he who possessed and enjoyed not, and he who knew but did not practise.

STANZA.

A miser may have merit; yet none see
His face, but strive his actions to abuse:
While twice a hundred failings there may be,
In those who do a liberal conduct use;
Yet will their generosity those faults excuse.

CONCLUSION OF THE BOOK.

The book of the Gulistān is ended by the assistance of God. Throughout the work I have forborne to borrow ornaments from the verses of preceding poets, as is customary with authors.

COUPLET.

Better patch up one's own old garment, than
Borrow the raiment of another man.

For the most part, Sâdī's discourse is commingled with pleasantry and cheerful wit; and this furnishes a pretext to the shortsighted for saying that it is not the part of wise men to rack the brain with absurdities, or expend the midnight oil unprofitably. It is, however, not concealed from the clear minds of the really enlightened, for whom this discourse is intended, that the pearls of salutary counsel are strung on the thread of my diction, and the bitter medicine of advice mixed up in it with the honey of mirthful humour; lest the mind of the reader should be disgusted, and he should thus remain excluded from the beneficial acceptance of my words.

DISTICHS.

I have fulfilled my mission, and have given
  Wholesome advice: my life's endeavour this.
What though men hear not. Messengers of Heaven
  Can but discharge their duty: and it is
  To tell their message—point the way to bliss.

Reader! for him who wrote this book, ask grace;
And let the scribe, too, in thy prayers find place:
Next for thyself whate'er thou wishest pray;
Lastly, a blessing for the owner say.
By aid of the all-gracious king,
This work here to an end we bring.

THE SUFIS

THE SUFIS is the pivotal work which heralded the revelation of the astonishing richness and variety of Sufi thought system and its contribution to human culture contained in Idries Shah's many books on the subject.
Today, studies in Sufism, notably through Shah's research and publication, are pursued in centres of higher learning throughout the world, in the fields of psychology, sociology, and many other areas of current human concern.

'Many forlorn puzzles in the world, which seemed to suggest that some great spiritual age somewhere in the Middle East had long since died and left indecipherable relics, suddenly come to organic life in this book'.

Ted Hughes: The Listener

'Sufism is . . . "the inner secret teaching that is concealed within every religion". The book has flashes of what (without intending to define the word) I can only call illumination'.

D. J. Enright: New Statesman

'Most comprehensively informative'.

New York Times Book Review

THE SUFIS
by Idries Shah
The Octagon Press

JORGE LUIS BORGES: SOURCES AND ILLUMINATION

Critics and general readers have for decades been excited, intrigued, baffled, entertained and enthusiastic about the work of the great Argentinian writer Borges. In his books and stories, ranging across the traditions of the East and the West, something elusive was constantly noted as appearing and vanishing: providing a sense of direction, only to disappear, as if some guiding principle was nudging the reader towards a perennial area of self-discovery.

Professor de Garayalde, intrigued by correspondences between references in Borges' work and current projections of ancient thought, decided to produce this first report linking the 'Sage of the West' with the thinkers of the Eastern tradition: about which Borges himself has said we must acquire what we can.

'There certainly is a fascination in the detective story, treasure hunt aspect of this book . . . . but it is the self-discovery and stimulus that Professor Giovanna de Garayalde found in her search that she is best able to communicate'.

Books and Bookmen

JORGE LUIS BORGES:
SOURCES & ILLUMINATION
by Professor Giovanna de Garayalde
The Octagon Press

TEACHINGS OF HAFIZ

Hafiz of Shiraz is unquestionably in the front rank of world classical poets. As a lyricist and Sufi master, his work is celebrated from India to Central Asia and the Near East as are Shakespeare, Dante or Milton: Goethe himself, among many other Westerners, was among the master's admirers.

As Professor Shafaq says:

"Hafiz attained perfect mystical consciousness: and his spiritual and mental power derived from this. The Path, projected by Sanai, Attar, Rumi and Sa'di each in his own way, is described by Hafiz with the very deepest feeling and highest expressive achievement."

History of Persian Literature, Tehran

This collection is by the eminent linguist and explorer Gertrude Bell who (as Dr. A.J. Arberry says) "early in her adventurous life conceived an enthusiasm for Hafiz which compelled her to write a volume of very fine translations".

TEACHINGS OF HAFIZ
Translated by Gertrude Bell: Introduction by Idries Shah.
Published for The Sufi Trust by The Octagon Press

LEARNING HOW TO LEARN

Condensed from over three million words, these conversations answer questions prompted by sixteen of Shah's books, his university lectures and radio and television programmes. He answers housewives and cabinet ministers, philosophy professors and assembly-line workers, on the subject of how traditional psychology can illuminate current human, social and spiritual problems. More than a hundred tales and extracts, ranging from the 8th Century Hasan of Basra to today's Ustad Khalilullah Kalili, are woven into Shah's narratives of how and why the Sufis learn, what they learn, and how spiritual understanding may be developed: as well as how it inevitably deteriorates in all societies.

'Learning How to Learn' is both the distillate of a million words and a guide to the whole body of the Shah materials . . . a book which surely marks a watershed in studies of the mind.'

—*'Psychology Today'–Choice of the Month*

'Bracing and often shocking. Shah's approach can best be described as a brisk and informed commonsense at its highest level.'

—*Books and Bookmen*

'Packed with important information'

—*New Society*

LEARNING HOW TO LEARN
by Idries Shah
The Octagon Press

TEACHINGS OF RUMI

THE MASNAVI

Jalaluddin Rumi's great work, *The Masnavi*, was 43 years in the writing. During the past seven hundred years, this book, called by the Iranians 'The Koran in Persian,' a tribute paid to no other book, has occupied a central place in Sufism.

'*The Masnavi* is full of profound mysteries, and a most important book in the study of Sufism – mysteries which must, for the most part, be left to the discernment of the reader.'

F. Hadland Davis

'To the Sufi, if not to anyone else, this book speaks from a different dimension, yet a dimension which is in a way within his deepest self.'

Idries Shah

'The greatest mystical poet of any age.'

Professor R. A. Nicolson

'It can well be argued that he is the supreme mystical poet of all mankind.'

Professor A. J. Arberry

TEACHINGS OF RUMI The Masnavi:
Abridged and translated by E. H. Whinfield.
with an Introduction by Idries Shah
Published for The Sufi Trust by The Octagon Press